Cracks in the Seam

(Volume II of the series *Reporting a War*)

By

Emery Buxton

ISBN: 978-1-917095-79-2

Table of Contents

Dedication

This volume is dedicated to Richard Hughes who has tirelessly read and critiqued all my novels.

Acknowledgment

"The author thanks the family members who gave advice during the initial drafting of the manuscript, the 'readers' who reviewed the first draft, and the editorial staff at AMZ Publishing Company for preparing the manuscript for publication. All those efforts are appreciated.

The 'history' contained in the writing is based on the lectures of M. Rasjidi and J.A. Williams in their Islamic History courses at McGill University in the 1958-1960 period while the author was a graduate student. The 'Carolina' setting of the two main characters is based on the author's own residence in the Charlotte area in the 1970's. However, the name of the university (Winston Meritt University—WMU) is fictitious, while the names of other institutions of higher education in the "Carolinas," such as Lenoir Rhyne and Davidson are real.

The cover depicting Ottoman and German forces at the Suez Canal is from a photograph preserved at the Museum of Military History in the United Kingdom and is used here with that institution's permission. The map is from the New Zealand government's collection of memorabilia of the New Zealand expeditionary force to the Middle East in World War I. "

About the Author

The author was a specialist in international affairs and served in the U.S. State Department and at two major North American universities, researching and writing articles and studies on Islamic culture and its manifestations historically and in the modern era. See *Sultans, Shamans and Saints: Islam and Muslims in Southeast* Asia (available from Amazon Books) Writing under the pseudonym of Emery Buxton he published a series of four novels on the Korean War titled *An Inconvenient War* (available from Amazon Books and on Kindle). He resides in the beautiful hill country of Southeast Ohio where the people are warm and hospitable.

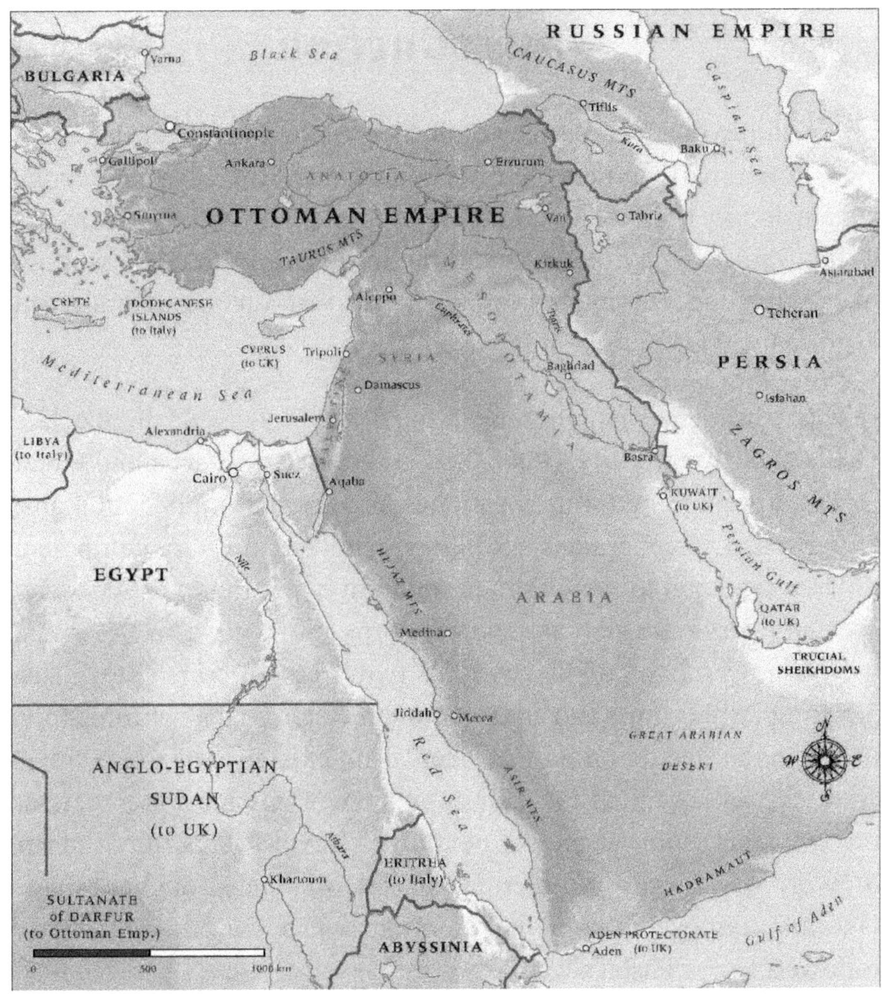

https://nzhistory.govt.nz/media/photo/map-ottoman-empire-1914

Introduction

This volume picks up where volume I ends on the eve of the Great War, now usually termed the First World War. It was not a foregone conclusion in 1914 that the Ottomans would side with Germany, as it did. Rather, many observers at the time forecast that it was more likely that the Ottomans would sit the war out as neutral. But historical events proved otherwise.

German influence in Ottoman affairs was noticeable in the late 1880s and, by the early 1900s, had an edge over France and Great Britain in providing military supplies and services to the Ottomans. In particular, the Germans sold armaments and military equipment in large amounts to the Ottomans and gave training to officers and specialty services, such as medical corps. Still, it was a fluke that the opening moves of the war led two German warships to flee pursuing Allied ships and enter Ottoman waters. That act forced the Ottomans to decide on how to handle the existence of those ships, while the Allies called for their expulsion. While most members of the Ottoman cabinet were for neutrality, Enver Pasha, the Minister of War, was solidly pro-German and deliberately sought to have Ottoman policy support the Germans. The cabinet reluctantly followed Enver Pasha's lead.

Despite losing the war eventually and even losing its existence as an empire, the German alliance was a sensible move by the Ottomans at the time. It had a mortal enemy in Russia on its northern flank and an expanding colonial power in Great Britain to its south. Commitment to Germany gave the Ottomans some hope of being on the winning side and, perhaps, of shoring up its tottering governmental infrastructure. Of course, it was not on the winning side, and a great unraveling happened in 1919 into the early 1920's by stripping away the Arab states and allowing only a rump "Turkey" to emerge. But that catastrophe was only latent in 1914, and the political moves of that year were made to forestall such developments. By the end of 1915, there was relief in Constantinople that the war had gone so well, for the Russians had not invaded, and the British thrust at Gallipoli had been repulsed. There was optimism that small gains in the East at Mosul could be rolled back, and there was hope that the Russian threat would likewise be turned back if it ever really occurred.

This novel covers the first two years of the war in the Middle East from the Ottoman side because it makes sense to do so. The key events were the Ottoman raids into Russian territory in 1914 and 1915, the Gallipoli campaign in 1915, and the anti-Armenian pogroms in 1915, all happening in Ottoman territory. These are all covered in this volume and illustrate how a news team of international correspondents might have handled the events.

Chapter One
Constantinople at the Onset of War

Background

In the first volume in 1913, Martin Mintz and Amelia Caruthers, both from the Carolinas in the United States, find employment with a news agency expedition designed to 'open up' the Middle East to modern news gathering and reporting. He is a political reporter; she is a photographer centering largely on portraits of prominent people and the activities of the social world through which the expedition travels. Their trip takes them from Cairo to Sudan and Aden in the British-held zone. Then, they move through an outer zone of Ottoman control at Yemen and Mecca, then to an inner zone of Ottoman control at Jerusalem, Damascus, and Aleppo. Finally, they visit the central Ottoman cities of Smyrna, Edirne, Constantinople, and Erzurum. Afterward, they visit Teheran in Persia. Their journey ends in Paris, where collections of their newspaper reports are collected, edited, and published.

Martin and Amelia like one another but agree not to be romantically involved while on the expedition, lest their passions upset the work of the team. They hold to that commitment for the most part while they content themselves with other temporary partners. While their newspaper reporting efforts run smoothly, all is not rosy for them. Marty and Amelia have some difficulties with other personalities in the same news agency. The leader and two other team members cause strife in the work of the expedition, and Martin and Amelia cause difficulties for the editors in their publishing ventures. An agency official, Boris Deckar, stands as their protector, assisting

4

them in overcoming the difficulties perpetrated by the alienated expedition leader and the disaffected team members. However, he does not assist them in their disputes with the publishers, and a new expedition is not formed, so their employment with the news agency is ended. They return to the Carolinas to wait for new opportunities.

The story continues in mid-1914, with Martin telling the story.

Graduate School Difficulties

In July and August, I was again in Istanbul, or Constantinople as it was called in 1914. This time I was a scholar rather than a newsman. So when the Great War started, I was already in one arena of that conflict, although I did not know it at the time. If I had ever thought my journalist days were over–which I did not think for a moment that they were–I was to be surprised at how easily I again became a member of the press.

I was in Constantinople because I was doing last-minute work on my dissertation for Winston-Meritt University. I was trying to please my graduate committee members, who found all sorts of things they wanted done before awarding the degree. None of the members of that august committee liked my first submission, which was based totally on my interviews during the trip I had taken throughout the Middle East in 1913.

"It stands by itself, and it should not. Why else do we have 'scholarly literature' if not to give context to the new learning as we discover it." These were the words of my committee chair, the head of the Sociology Department, who never read a footnote that he did not genuflect to first. The other two committee members sagely nodded assent and would have stroked their beards, except they were clean-shaven. They all urged me to spend the summer looking through the library stacks to find the treasures they insisted were there. The effort, they said, would give context to my study, which was so needed in their opinion.

It is in my nature to be accommodating, even when I know the other people do not have a clue what they are talking about. The suggestions they gave me, for the half an hour following their verdict, were all works I had used earlier in my studies and were but a prelude to what I was talking about in my dissertation. Eventually, at the end of a particularly rudimentary lecture on the virtues of a book I regarded as written by a cretin and could have been regarded as insightful only to idiots and morons, I abruptly changed the subject. It was the first words I had spoken during the session. "I get the point, and I will peruse the literature you suggest," Then I tried to guide them back onto an examination of my draft dissertation. I said. "What do you think about the five areas of examination I have identified? Do those hold water or not?"

The room was quiet for perhaps three seconds, during which time I concluded that none of them had read my draft dissertation. Professors are notoriously lazy and always talk around a point rather than answer a question head-on. They had only seized on the lack of footnotes as an obvious error and then read no more. The chair said, "Mr. Mintz, a dissertation should not be rushed. Rather it should be savored. We, your committee, have identified a serious flaw and want you to address it. None of us are prepared to move to the next phase until then. Do you have questions?" I knew by the answer that my supposition was right and that none of them had thought about my five points, let alone read them.

"No, I don't think so," I replied. "It was a most enlightening discussion today. One I won't forget for a while." I put my draft dissertation in the folder in which I brought it, rose, and walked from the room. I am unsure whether they caught the sarcasm in my final remarks.

The following noon, after sleeping on the train to Philly all night, I was at Princeton University, where I contacted the research librarian and was given a carrel and a user pass for the library. At my own expense, I was assigned a young man, about twenty years old, who had managed to first go on probation at the university for failing all his courses the previous semester and then getting himself expelled from the university for a semester until he had spent some time from his studies to reflect. I find that the draconian learning system used at most universities is filled with such high-sounding phrases as 'reflect' for what is a dubious punishment. He did not want to tell his parents he was no longer in school, so he spent his days in the library doing odd jobs. I was told he was an especially good researcher despite his quiet demeanor and great shyness.

I put Dana to work immediately, getting me some footnotes for my study, which he did with gusto and efficiency. In the three days I was there, he built forty-two multi-source footnotes that would certainly have my committee drooling when they next looked at my dissertation. I gave him a $100 tip. His only comment was, "It's nice to see something that is not the same old drivel. Thanks for letting me participate." I concluded that Dana had flunked out simply from boredom and had never been stimulated in ordinary college life. Notwithstanding, he certainly proved his worth to me.

Meanwhile, I went to work on the Arabic collection and located some matching material to what I had already used in my case study on Cairo. The business of building library collections is difficult, particularly in adding foreign newspapers, because they are in languages that the people who gather the materials cannot understand. When issues are missing, they do not know that to be true because of the mysterious fonts and spellings. I found only about half the numbers the card catalog said should be in the collections. I was admitted to the library section that deals with sorting 'serials, newspapers, and periodicals' and found perhaps a quarter more of the missing numbers. But I spent an entire morning on that task, which was less rewarding than one could imagine. Besides, I do not have time to do other people's work for them, which is what was happening with my sorting.

After my three days in Princeton, I knew I had to deal with a situation that probably could not be resolved in North America, So I went to New York City and booked passage on a ship to Liverpool, traveling steerage to save funds. I intended to travel by rail across England and the Continent to Constantinople. On reflection, I thought it was a long way to go to get the materials I needed for a dissertation, but I was determined to get the job done correctly, and my instinct told me that the trip was necessary after all.

When I was cleared dockside for boarding the ship, I pulled my passport from my inside jacket pocket and with it two letters. I remembered that in my hurry to leave home a few days earlier, the letters had arrived in the mail, and I had put them in my pocket, intending to read them later. Naturally, I had forgotten. So, after I got on the ship and found my bunk, I located a light and began reading the letters.

The first letter was from Amelia Caruthers, my fellow traveler the previous year on our press expedition through the Middle East. We were close friends and would be lovers if we ever addressed the issue head-on. But we both liked our causal relationship, and every time we came close to any kind of real intimacy, one of us always backed away. Since returning in December 1913, we had met once a month for lunch or dinner in either Hickory, Charlotte, Winston-Salem, or Fort Mill, depending on circumstances. Our meetings usually lasted for an hour and a half, and usually, there was a meal connected with the meeting. We talked about all sorts of things, but mostly about our previous trip through the Middle East and our remembrances of what occurred during those travels. To say that the trip had been enjoyable would be a vast understatement. The opportunity had enthralled us.

Both of us liked the experience and wanted something like that to happen again. We talked about the possibility of becoming newsmen again but never inquired of any newspapers or news agencies about employment. I guess we were not yet ready to do that: inertia or whatever. We also wrote to one another occasionally, and this letter was one of those times. It read

Dear Marty,

I was thinking earlier today about our visit to Edirne, near Constantinople, when we were trying to leave the city, and it came under attack by Bulgar raiders. We were pinned down for several days, with one whole day spent under a disabled vehicle, which was so uncomfortable that one wanted to 'give up' to straighten one's body out again. But no one would have taken our surrender, I am sure. They would have only shot us, so we endured the discomfort, even though, at times, it was more like agony. After we got out from under the car, we still found ourselves isolated in a barn, but there was not the terrible feeling of being cut off from everyone else. Eventually, the truce did come, and we were set free. I was amazed because, as we set out for the city later, it was as if the incident had never happened and that we had merely escaped some sort of warp in time that never really took place at all. Even afterward, when I told others about it, I sensed they did not see the gravity of the situation, and I wondered if they even believed me at all.

Sometimes, I think the entire year we spent there was much the same. It was not even reality but a passage to another dimension that we existed in for a year and then returned. Except for you, no one even remembers I was gone for that length of time, and most of my friends and family speak as if I were here the entire year. That is probably why we still meet every month. That is, we need to convince each other that the adventure we undertook was real and meaningful. What do you think?

The other thing I think about is the lack of lovemaking in my life. I have not gone to bed with any man since I returned, and I am in no hurry to do it either. I got to ruminating on this the other day when I was finishing off some film development from a rush job for a client. I narrowed down my sexual lethargy to some sort of inner longing for either you or Werner, as both of you are on my mind a lot. I remember Werner as a lover and you as a friend and mentor, although I must confess that, at times some sexual fantasies concerning you pass through my mind. But I suspect that it is Werner who excites me sexually, and I would like to see him come through the door and carry me away with him. Now, how's that for daydreaming?!

So, good friend, if you come across an opportunity for an adventure, grab it and get me included as fast as possible. If Werner is involved, I will wet my panties in ecstasy.

It is a couple of weeks until we meet again, but I was feeling more than a little offbeat today, so I thought I would unburden myself in a letter to you. I know you do not mind.

Your true girlfriend, Emmy

I was not so sure that the letter needed a response, as it was sent for understanding and not for advice or consolation. I refolded it and put it away in my suit pocket again.

The second letter was from my Aunt Bea, who was visiting France this year with my parents and sister. She wrote from there.

Dear Marty,

The entire family misses you, and a frequent complaint when we visit a museum or art gallery is: "If Marty was here, he could explain this to us," or, when Sunday afternoon arrives and friends are visiting, your Mom says, "It would be complete if Marty was only here with his latest girlfriend." Your father always grunts and says, "Indeed, I am unsure where he finds them. They are all treasures." Your sister simply sniffs at that remark, largely, I think, because she is jealous, although lately, she has brought two boys to the house as guests, both of whom seem interested in her.

We have not seen the Everetts here this season, as they went to Spain, of all places. I miss having Janet around because she is so nutty about you. She has sarcastic things to say to cover her real feelings of not being able to grab hold of you and make you her boyfriend, fiancé, and husband. She has real wit when she pours out her invective against you for ignoring her. She is a nice girl, so why not give her a tumble? With the wealth in that family, you would never have to work a day for the rest of your life. Something to think about.

It seems to me that there are more incidents involving European nations these days, although it may simply be my imagination. I fear that one of these incidents will stick in someone's craw, and a war will develop out of it that will bring the great one hundred years of peace to an end. Tell me I am a foolish old lady to think about such a catastrophe.

Kisses, your loving Aunt Bea.

This one did not need an immediate response either, although it did remind me that I had not written to Janet yet this summer, so I ought to do that and mail the letter when we get to Great Britain. I could reply to Aunt Bea at the same time. Letters would get to both fast if mailed on the European side of the Atlantic.

However, I did need some time to think through what Janet means to me. Is she merely a friend or something more? We have dated a lot since high school but never had a girlfriend and boyfriend relationship. We have kissed many times, sometimes with passion, but never caressed except to hug one another on meeting or leaving one another. I know that marriage to Janet would be pleasant enough as she is kind, funny, and attentive, all attributes I like. If I were an executive in the family's furniture business, she would be the perfect wife in the country club social atmosphere where we would certainly live. But I doubt that she would like to be a wife to a scholar or a newsman, which requires mixing with lots of other kinds of people and hearing different views. But how can I tell her that when I have not even told my parents about my aspirations to move my career in that direction when they assume that the furniture business will be my ordained future? I concluded that in my next letter to Janet, I would allude to another career path and see what her response would be.

It was equally important to do some thinking about Aunt Bea and what she meant to the family. She had been a popular woman when she was young, but she had the misfortune to lose her husband in a hotel fire while he was at a furniture convention. She had been married for five years at the time and was exceedingly close to her husband, even though they had no children. She never quite recovered, retreated from life for a few years, and only emerged when her older brother, my father, asked her to join his household to manage it because my mother was overwhelmed with raising her small family. Aunt Bea was a manager, treasurer, and counselor to all family members and was greatly respected by everyone, especially my father and mother. She never cleaned, seldom took care of the children, and was in no way a servant. She received a stipend from my father for her services but was always treated like a senior member of the family. We children saw her as an honored but very affectionate aunt, and we took all our problems to her for good counsel, which we usually followed scrupulously.

As I ruminated on this matter, I decided that as soon as I got settled in Constantinople, I would correspond both Janet and Aunt Bea and spend some time writing each of them a meaningful letter. Perhaps I could explain in each letter just how much I cared for each of them.

Traveling with Marta

A small, inadvertent, adventure occurred en route that slowed me but did not unduly interrupt my plans. In steerage, there is not much to do except sit or lie in a bunk and wait for time to pass. Occasionally, one could go for a short walk on the limited deck space available to steerage passengers. But there was no room to walk or play games, so, again, one stood and passed the time. As it was, in my compartment, there was a woman, perhaps twenty-six years of age, with two small children, four and six years old. She had immigrated to the United States from Austria with her husband when they were first married. He had gotten a job at a factory in New Jersey but had died the year before from a stroke. Her small jobs were not enough to meet expenses, so she was doing the 'reverse immigration quick step,' returning to her home in Austria, near Vienna. Her own family still lived there, and she expected they would take her in.

The woman had a pretty face, although her teeth needed tending as two were not quite in line with the others. She was relatively trim, although the effects of bearing two children had made her slightly pudgy in the abdomen. She was not well dressed, probably the result of being a widow on a small income with no spare money for keeping a stylish wardrobe.

As I said, she had two children; Gisele was the older, and Erich was the younger, who both wandered about our crowded compartment and made friends with everyone. I was friendly with them, showed them some of my books and photographs, and generally made conversation. When the mother, named Marta, came to collect the children, she usually spoke to me, and by the end of the sea voyage. she had told me all about her family, her husband, their life together, and her hopes for a new life in Austria. She spoke halting English, was very shy, naive about life in general, and knew little about traveling.

She had no clue how to get to the Continent from Liverpool, and so I took her and the children with me on the railroad, traveling second class and paying for the trip myself. My generosity set me behind a bit financially, but still, I was all right. In Calais, on my advice, she purchased second-class tickets through to Vienna, but on a slower train than the express that I intended to take. Since she was terrified of traveling alone, I agreed to stay with her as far as Vienna, so my trip was considerably delayed. But what does one do when confronted with such a situation? Mom and Dad had stressed to me that one should always help people in distress, regardless of what social class they come from. I acted on that teaching.

It took a full day to get to Vienna, so I passed it playing with the children, reading to them stories from children's magazines available at the news kiosks in the stations, and remembering some stories from my youth. The children were with me much of the time during daylight. Marta accepted my presence and welcomed my attention as a means of coping with life on the train. She was terrified about using the toilets at first, was shy and awkward in the dining car, and was only free of anxiety while I was in sight and in charge. She seemed to fear that I would desert at any moment, or so her demeanor and body language seemed to suggest.

That night, with the children laid out on the seats, I sat with Marta, who put her head on my shoulder and slept soundly while I slept fitfully, keeping an eye on the children. I got up twice to tend to them, especially to Erich, who had a call of nature midway through the night.

This sample of domesticity influenced me, and the notion grew in me that I had the opportunity to get off the train with Marta in Vienna and make a new life for myself. I could marry into a ready-made family if I wished. But the idea no sooner formed in my brain than it was dismissed as 'out of keeping' with who I am.

At Vienna, although Marta had supposedly sent a telegram ahead, no one met the train, so we had to figure out how to get her to the village of Pressbaum in the old Wienerwald area. She was out of money, so I took her there at my expense, missing my train connection, which was changed to the following day.

The family had not gotten the telegram and was not ready for a returning family member. The father and mother were less than pleased to see Marta and the children, whom they had not expected, as her letters had never been specific about returning home. In addition, despite Marta's explanations, they assumed I had come along to become part of the invasion of their domicile. But after several hours of explanation, the grandmother had warmed to the children, and the grandfather thought everything would be all right. I announced I was leaving and took them all to a nearby inn, where I bought a meal and drinks for the family, which suddenly ballooned to seven more people: Marta's sister, brother-in-law, and their children. This display of generosity on my part resolved the entire 'homecoming' issue, and I was a part of the family, at least temporarily.

As I prepared to leave for central Vienna to wait for the train the following day, Marta came to me and thanked me while I slipped a fifty Austrian Krone note into her hand, which I knew she would certainly need. She said I should stay the night so that she could give me a proper 'thank-you' and send-off. I could not think of any good reason not to do that as my train would not leave before early afternoon the following day. I accepted the invitation, thinking it would be an evening of drinking beer and schnapps, followed by sleeping alone on the floor before the fireplace. Before I knew what had happened, all the family members had disappeared, and Marta and I were alone in the back bedroom with a double bed and a feather tick.

I had not been with a woman since the ambassador's daughter in Teheran, whom I thought, at the time, as quite accomplished, but Marta proved herself equal to the occasion. She was enthusiastic, agile, and perpetually in motion. We only stopped our lovemaking when the door suddenly opened deep in the night, with both Gisele and Erich wanting to come into our bed because they feared their new surroundings. We snatched them off the cold floor and bundled them in between us. They shivered until our body heat, magnified under the feather tick, warmed them, and they fell off to sleep easily. I slept like a baby after that.

It was difficult to leave the following morning, with everyone trying to persuade me to stay. But I knew there was little professional interest in Pressbaum that was going to keep me occupied, and I doubted that Marta and I shared any kind of deep feeling for one another. The two kids had certainly wormed their way into my heart, but I knew I was no long-term competitor with their grandparents, who would spoil them rotten within a month. So I kissed everyone goodbye and sped away on the electric trolley to downtown Vienna.

I thought about the family in Pressbaum until the Bulgarian border, and then, my plans for finding Ottoman materials for my dissertation displaced all other thinking.

Learning Ottoman Turkish the Really Hard Way

In Turkey, the Orient Express stops at the Golden Horn, where passengers to trains on the European side must take a ferry across the Bosporus, where a great train station awaits. I was going no further, but instead, I went to the American embassy, where I found the consul was the same one that was there the previous year. He remembered who I was and suggested a tutor for my language lessons.

The tutor was an American expatriate married to a Turkic woman from Anatolia. They rented me a room, and I also paid board for two months. I was ready to relax from my long trip, but the lessons started immediately. As I unpacked my bags, the wife was there telling me the names of all the items and insisting that I repeat their names--correctly. For the rest of the afternoon and evening, either he or she was with me, badgering me over words and phrases I had already been introduced to or feeding me more information.

Fortunately, a great many Arabic expressions, words, and grammar have been taken into Turkish, which helped me, but, unfortunately, just as much had been taken from Persian, which was almost incomprehensible to me, so I had to learn everything taken from Persian from scratch. We counted, we told time, we numbered things, we used prepositions constantly, and, on the third day, we began to use tenses. At that point, I was ready to give up the learning experience as a hopeless cause, but I hung on during the next two days, and suddenly, my mind found itself in Turkish, and I began to think in that language.

But this change did not lessen the pace; for now, I had to think fast and use the correct language forms. Nearly everything I said was critiqued, and I had to correct myself repeatedly. At the end of the fourth week, I had a vocabulary of about 600 active words and another 400 passive words, while my speaking style was a little jerky but acceptable. The teaching had taken a toll on the expatriate and his wife, for they packed up and said they would be gone for three days. They left me in charge of a brusque, pudgy woman, about forty years of age, who wore glasses and drank voluminous amounts of tea. Again, she was with me all day long doing all the things my former 'jailers' had done, only she did it with a commanding and sarcastic tone.

When evening came, I was surprised because she invaded my bathroom when I was readying for bed and quizzed me on my knowledge of phrases used there. Then she took me to my bedside and told me the Muslim prayers to repeat and the formulas to use for all acts. She then crawled into bed with me and explained the entire sexual act in Turkish terms. It was all so clinical that I had trouble with an erection, which she then explained in detail what the ailment was called in Turkish. The sex was terrible, but the experience was surprisingly good because I had never known that repertoire in Arabic or French.

The three days with the woman were brutal because she was a constant critic, a sarcastic teacher, and a short-tempered vixen. She used swear words like a sergeant-major and blasphemy like a muleskinner. I felt humiliated by her unrelenting quizzing and vitriolic impatience. But she imparted new knowledge as well. She taught me proper conversation for dealing with officials, everyday folks, senior members of a family, children, servants, and even ladies of the evening. We role-played one entire afternoon, making sure that I treated each of the imaginary people in the tableau in the proper manner. On the third evening, she had me say my Muslim prayers and then kissed me on the cheek, said goodbye, and left. I found myself suddenly liberated and went to bed with great joy. There was no one around to cause me misery.

But the following morning, I was rousted out of bed by the husband and wife, who had returned, and we set to work on reading exercises. Now, Persian script, which is used in Ottoman Turkish, is roughly the same one used in Arabic, but there the similarities end. The words that emerge are entirely different. It is the same difference between someone using the Roman alphabet and trying to decipher something in English that has been written in French. But fortunately, I was into Turkish words, not Arabic ones, so they prevailed as I used the new alphabet. I found that the Turkish words emerged readily enough. Within two days, I was reading simple texts and, a week later, was into newspapers.

Our sessions then alternated between long conversations in the mornings and long reading exercises in the afternoon, with everything still in Turkish. Nothing ever grew easier, but the rate of learning certainly increased, and I had much more background to use to let me master the problems that confronted me.

Then, suddenly, my two months were up. The three of us had breakfast together, I settled my bill, and I was given blessings, hugs, and kisses and escorted through the front gate. The only surprising thing on the last day was the bill itself, which was twice as much as had been agreed to initially. This change was explained quickly as 'because of the facility of the student and the need to prepare advanced lessons.' I waved aside the explanation as unnecessary, paid the bill, and left a good-sized 'tip.' It came to within a dinar of what I had estimated.

I stood for a moment on the street in front of the house where I had been a 'prisoner' for two months and marveled at being free to do what I wanted. I then turned and walked into the city, where I found the editorial offices of Constantinople's leading newspaper. With my new language skills, I negotiated my way through the levels of authority and ended up in the chief editor's office. Having identified myself as a former correspondent with the *Tribune*, I was accorded some respect and asked what I required. "A three-month run of your newspaper, which I would like to read on-site," I explained it was for my dissertation.

The editor smiled, said he understood, and sent me with a junior editor to a storage facility where my escort identified the required series and left me to read them. It took two weeks to scan the papers, taking the references I needed. Then, I took another week to review a Turkish summary of provincial Arabic press articles for the same period as those in the Turkish run. After completing this task, I went to the chief editor and thanked him, who said it was a professional courtesy but that if I ever wrote again in the Ottoman world, he would expect a return on the favor. I assured him I would comply.

An Encounter with a Zionist

I was staying at this time at a pension, which included a very sparse room with a low single bed, a table, and a chair. There was a toilet and a washroom down the hall for common use. I was given a breakfast of either cheese and rolls or porridge, both of which were 'edible' but hardly constituted 'fine dining.' On the day following my last visit to the newspaper offices, I slept in and ate late. A man was eating at the common table, cracking a boiled egg, rather than eating porridge like I was given. I introduced myself, and he replied that he was 'Shimon' and was a kosher Jew. "That explains the eggs," I said.

He responded, "Yes, I realized that you noticed. Did you know I am supposed to look for cracks in the shells and, if I find them, realize that the eggs are not kosher?"

I answered, with a perfect smile, "When that occurs, you can give them to me."

"Not a chance in the world," he answered and dug into the first egg with gusto.

We talked a bit as we ate, and I learned that he was on a committee from a Zionist Congress in Basel, Switzerland, trying to persuade the Ottoman government to allow open Jewish immigration to Palestine.

"How's it going," I asked. "My experience has been that Ottoman officials will obfuscate and delay if they don't want to address the subject."

"Precisely, he said. "Our delegation was been here three weeks already. We have had four interviews, where we were told that higher officials needed to be involved. Yesterday, we sat in an anteroom all day but received no word about when our next meeting would occur. I suspect that same scene will be repeated today."

We chatted about the unusual pace of life in the Ottoman capital, and then I raised my problems of finding backup materials for the Zionist commune in Tel Aviv. He was surprised by my interest in it, and we talked for a few more minutes about what I had seen there and whether I had liked the experience or not. Then he pulled out his watch and said that he had to go to the waiting room. "If I am not there, the official will say we were not on hand when the meeting was scheduled. We must talk about your visit to Tel Aviv when next we see one another. Perhaps tomorrow if I can convince the host to give me boiled eggs again."

We met for breakfast the next day, and Shimon had several books and pamphlets with him. However, he also had a bowl of porridge and said, "I can't be kosher today unless I allow an increase in the cost of the room. I will not pay on principle. Besides, I doubt if there is anything in this porridge that contaminates it ritually. At least that is my justification."

One of the books was in German, called *Die Judenstaat (The Jewish State)*, by Theodor Herzl, which Shimon said was the chief political document of the Zionist movement. Shimon said he thought that Herzl was too full of nonsense about European achievements and how they might be a guide to the construction of a new Jewish state in Palestine. He also found Herzl's views about the inadequacy of Hebrew and Yiddish as possible modern languages to be culturally demeaning.

He then moved on to David Gruen, a Russian immigrant who settled in the Galilee area and made himself a name as leader of Zionist enterprises in that region. Gruen wrote no full books but was often quoted. Shimon showed me several newspaper articles that spoke to land settlement, Jewish historical rights in Palestine, and the need for international recognition of those rights. They contained numerous references to the 'transformation' of agriculture and, especially, societal reorganization. They fit well with the analysis outlined in my dissertation.

Finally, Shimon had some materials that emanated from the Tel Aviv settlement itself, written by one of the leaders of that specific commune, which well summarized what I had been told during my interviews there. In the eyes of my dissertation committee, written words had more value than spoken words, so I knew these documents would be useful, as well as the works of Herzl and Gruen. I took the materials and made notes for my dissertation and then returned the materials to Shimon the following morning.

Two days later, I went to breakfast and found a letter there from Shimon, saying he had completed his work in Constantinople and was on his way back to Basel. "The Ottoman official charged with delivering an answer to the delegation's request stated that one new commune could be created in the upcoming year. Further expansion would be reviewed by the provincial governors, but such a review would not take place for at least another year." The letter told of Shimon's disappointment with the outcome. He concluded the letter by saying, "One meets interesting people at strange times and in odd places, but amicable friendships are made, nonetheless. So it is with us, Marty. I look forward to meeting with you again, and I hope it will not be long before that happens. Shimon."

I spent nearly a week getting my dissertation in order with all the new notations and material, had it typed by a professional typist at an exorbitant rate, and mailed it by fast surface mail to Winston-Meritt University. It would be a long wait, I was sure, and the committee would find some new 'shortcoming' in the dissertation, for which I would be taken to task. In the meantime, I was free, but not really. My expenses in the past few months had eaten up all the advances I received on my publication in Paris at the end of the previous year. I wanted to replenish those funds and decided that I needed to contact the publishers of the *Tribune* in Paris to find out whether sales had been good enough to merit another advance.

The Crisis of the German Cruisers

On the way to the telegraph office, I stopped at a first-class hotel to get a copy of the *Tribune* since they are sold in such venues rather than in newspaper kiosks. I passed by the entrance to the dining room, where I saw Boris Deckar standing, apparently waiting to be seated. He had just lighted a cigarette, and I remembered that he was a chain smoker. He saw me and said, "As I live and breathe, the prodigal son returns!"

"Boris!" I answered as though I had just seen him. "Why are you in Constantinople? I thought your offices were in Bucharest."

"They are. But things are moving fast in the international world, and I am here taking care of some business. Two German battle cruisers are on the loose, and I need a correspondent who can cover the issue. They raided French port facilities in the Mediterranean and fought with several French naval ships to escape. They are headed here as they have no other options for escape in the western Mediterranean. You didn't happen to pick up Turkish since I last saw you?"

"As it happens, I did," I responded. "I did a two-month intensive language course and speak good Turkish now. Why do you need that?"

Boris looked surprised at my revelation, as if he could not believe his good luck. He explained, "Chances are that two German battle cruisers are coming here, and I need someone to talk with Ottoman officials about the case. Are you able to give me some time on this one?"

"Yeah," I answered, "I just finished a project and have nothing on my plate just now. How much time are we talking about?"

"A couple of weeks for this story, but I think I am going to need someone here for some time if war breaks out the way it is envisioned. The European countries have all begun mobilization and are ready to begin hostilities in a matter of days, if not hours."

Just then, the maitre de came to Boris and was ready to seat him. "Have you had lunch, Marty? Join me. We need to talk further."

So we ate lunch together, and at the end of it, I was again on the payroll of *Tribune*, this time with the Bucharest branch. My salary was that of a full correspondent, which meant that it was enough to live on. He told me to move to the hotel used by international correspondents, which was considerably nicer than the pension but, of course, "not as posh as the hotel in which we were having lunch. You are on the clock right now," said Boris. "You have my card, so you know where to file your stories. We have no one else in the Ottoman area just now. I do not think Emile does either, but I will check to make sure you can coordinate if that is the case."

"Finally," he said, "Try and get a hold of your female pal with the camera and convince her to come to Constantinople. I will hire her out here, but not in the States, as the contract is much more complicated there. Besides, I would also have to pay moving costs, which is a pain to be avoided. She will make it up in bonuses. Only one of you needs the language; I want her for her exquisite camera work."

Moving into the correspondent's hotel, by chance, I met Werner Aussenfeld, Amelia's one-time boyfriend and a German staff officer, who was in the lobby talking with a journalist. The two of them were talking in Turkish, so I waited until their conversation was complete and then lightly touched Werner to get his attention. "Excuse me, Major," I said in Turkish, "You may not remember me, but I am a good friend of Amelia Caruthers, with whom you were good friends last year in Smyrna and here in Constantinople." He looked at me quizzically, and then his face brightened as he recognized me.

"Herr Martin," he said, "Are you in touch with Amelia? She was such a wonderful woman, and I would give anything to be with her again. Is she, perhaps, with you? I know you both traveled so much together and even published books at that same time?"

"No, she is not with me, Herr Major. She is at her studio in Winston-Salem in America, so far as I know." I paused, not knowing how much more information I should give him.

"Too bad," he said, "I have never been so struck with a woman in my life as I was with Amelia. When I gave her up that night in your hotel, my heart nearly broke in two. Now, my wife has left me and gone back to Germany. I expect any day to get the divorce papers. Helga is a strong woman and does not back down easily, but she is also realistic and understands that her days as my wife are numbered."

Based on that statement, I decided he was quite serious about Amelia. I said, "I am about to send her a telegram asking her to join me here as a correspondent. I know her well enough to understand that if you are ready to receive her, she will return. She was absolutely in love with you when you left her in the hotel that night. Moreover, she did not cease loving you; only felt it was a sad situation that family life made it impossible to continue the affair. Shall I tell her that?"

"Do, Herr Martin. Please do!" He handed me his card, which listed him as a staff major in the German Army's mission to the Ottoman Empire.

A day later, I telephoned the major and told him that Amelia sends 'kisses' and would join him within a fortnight. Her telegram to me said, "I would have come anyway, Marty, to work with you again and have another adventure. You know, of course, that you and I are like 'peas in a pod,' and I would never miss a chance to be with you. But the presence of Werner there is 'icing on the cake.' I know you understand the difference between the two of you."

I went the following morning to the Foreign Ministry, where I had an appointment with a "high official in the ministry." When I called for the appointment, there was no hesitation, and I was put through to the appointments' secretary, who knew who I was and called me by name, "Effendi Martin from the *Tribune*." He said, "We are delighted that such a prominent journalist has joined the press corps here in Constantinople. I am sure we will have many productive contacts. Will your colleague with the cameras be joining us?"

"I am afraid not, as she is still in transit, and she will arrive only in a fortnight," I answered.

If I was pleased with the initial contact, I was even more pleased with the appointment itself. It was with the top government leader dominating foreign affairs, Enver Pasha, who had been the architect of the earlier German-Ottoman alliance. He stood as I entered the office and introduced himself, although I was aware of who he was. One of his minions stood alongside us and had three books open for signing. All three were French editions of my accounts of the Near and Middle East made the previous year. Enver said, "I know you will do me the favor of signing a personal copy of your books, but I must also ask for your indulgence in signing two more for my two colleagues who have other duties this morning. I knew he was referring to Talat Pasha and Cemal Pasha, the other two legs of the triumvirate that currently ruled the Ottoman Empire.

"Any message you want included with the signatures?" I asked. He gave them to me, and I entered them on the open title pages and then signed my name with a flourish. The books were blotted and handed to Enver, who kissed them and said, "Today, I will be the envy of my colleagues."

I was invited to sit with him and two aides at an oblong table in his office intended for such meetings. Enver asked, "I have heard that you speak French, but I find you are using Turkish fine. Which language do you prefer for today's session?"

I answered, "If you don't mind my occasional mistakes, I think I would like to use Turkish. I have just come out of an intensive language course and still think in Turkish. Why change now? I know I can do well enough."

He nodded, and we began. He said, "As you know, the German cruiser group–Gobben-Breslau–is outrunning a British task force and attempting to reach Ottoman waters before they are captured. The Ottoman government wishes the commander every success in attaining his goal. There are rules concerning entering the waters of a non-belligerent nation–which the Ottoman Empire is–and we intend to comply and enforce those rules. The cruiser group, if it requests to enter our waters, will be allowed to do so, just as a ship from any other nation, such as Great Britain or France, would be allowed to do. After entry, there is a set period the cruiser group may stay in Ottoman waters before being required to exit them, and there are rules for such an eventuality. The Ottoman government will observe international law on these points."

I asked, "Then the Ottoman government does not intend, at this juncture, to enter hostilities on the side of the German Empire, with whom you have a treaty of friendship."

"That is correct," he answered. "As the spokesman for the Ottoman government," Enver said, "I can only say that the Ottoman government is distressed at the breakdown of peace in Europe. It hopes that the nations that are now mobilizing will listen to reason and reverse the head-long dash to war. Such a war would do none of us any good and cause a great deal of suffering."

I asked, "About the treaty of friendship with the German Empire, is it still valid?"

"It is," he answered. "It says nothing at all about warfare or peace, and we regard it just as valid today as yesterday. I have heard nothing from the German embassy to conclude otherwise."

"And will the German mission remain, as well?" I asked.

"Certainly, it will. That was affirmed earlier today in a telephone conversation with the German embassy." Enver was enjoying himself with these unequivocal statements.

I asked two more short questions and then thanked Enver for his time and information. Afterward, I said, "Off the record, sir, "Does the presence of two German cruisers complicate your life?"

He laughed and said. "One could say that, Marty. But I have been in office long enough to know that within the week, enough other things will occur that this matter will be swallowed up, and what was once a problem will have a solution." He stood, and I did too, "On a personal note," he said, "You did fine with Turkish today. Continue to use it, and you will be its master." I was ushered to a neighboring room where there was a light buffet of hors d'ouvres, coffee, and tea, which I sampled and then left.

I knew that what I had was a special interview with the most powerful man in Constantinople now and that it was official policy on how the cruiser crisis was to be handled. I was anxious to get this out to the *Tribune* immediately. So, still in the Sublime Porte (Foreign Ministry building), I asked at reception whether there was a typist who could assist me. There was, and I spent the next half an hour dictating my 'special report' to the *Tribune*. I had no sooner finished dictating it than the typist pulled the copy from the machine and pulled away the carbon paper. There was the original and three copies. All four were stamped 'Official' with the Ottoman seal alongside it. A censor came, read the paper, and attached his signature as well. Then I was asked for the *Tribune*'s telegraphic address that I would normally use, and the report was sent immediately, with a receipt and one carbon copy returned to me. It was clear that I was being used that day to relay to the international community just what was going to happen when the German ships entered Ottoman waters. Talk about 'big-time stuff!'

At the hotel, there was an employee of the hotel who oversaw newsmen's requests, provided information, and handled mail, telephone, and cablegram contacts. All clients were required to contribute to his upkeep and, on occasion, to give him tips as well. My initial share was large, I thought, but it was explained to me that the *Tribune* was expected to use the man's services more than most other reporters. I did not complain but simply paid the bill, charging it to the *Tribune*, as I was expected to do. I did not work for a 'cheap' publisher.

This day, I returned to the hotel, and Mehmet, the 'reporter's friend,' as he was known, was waiting for me. He handed me three pieces of paper. The first was a cablegram from Boris, the second an appointment with General Liman von Sanders for that afternoon, and, finally, a note from the American embassy that I should contact the ambassador's secretary as soon as possible. As I accepted the three letters, the other reporters, about eight of them, were clapping. News had gotten out about my tete-a-tete with Enver Pasha. "Damn," said the reporter from the London *Guardian*, "I wish that plum had come my way. Good job, though, Marty!"

I sat down in the lobby and read the three papers. Boris's note was short and to the point. "Jehoshaphat," it read, "I didn't expect results like this so quickly! Good job. We are printing extra editions in Paris and Berlin. Keep up the good work."

The appointment slip with General Liman von Sanders said that French would be the language of conversation as it had been the last time I had met with the general. So, he remembers, I thought to myself. I reread the note from the American embassy and put it aside until the Liman von Sanders interview was passed. At this moment, the Germans were important, but the Americans were not.

At the German mission, I was met at the gate by Werner, who shook my hand sturdily in Germanic fashion and called me "*Liebe* Herr Mintz." I referred to him as "*Liebe* Major." He was wearing the aiguillette of a German staff officer. We quickly walked, without any conversation, to General Liman von Sander's office, where the general, with a colonel, also wearing an aiguillette, stood waiting for me. Both officers came to attention and clicked their heels as they shook hands with me. The general motioned for me to sit at a staff table, where Werner joined us. He had risen in importance since my earlier visit.

The general said, in French, "I understand that you have met with Monsieur Enver Pasha, who handles foreign affairs for the Ottoman Empire?" It was a question, but whether the general expected an answer was difficult to judge, so I chose to answer.

"Yes," I did. He chose to use the newspaper I represent to inform Great Britain but the French as well, I suspect, that the German naval ships were to be received here in Constantinople. It was intimated that any interference by an outside power would be regarded as a serious breach of international protocol."

My response was unexpected, so the general looked sharply at me, and then he smiled as the import of what I said had its effect. He said, "So, you see Monsieur Enver's remarks as highly favorable to the Germans and as a warning to the British?"

"I do," I quickly answered. "How else can such a statement be seen?"

"Perhaps as 'politically correct,' as 'stating the obvious,' he answered.

I again responded. "It occurs to me that Enver faced a hard choice. He could have refused entrance of the warships and curried favor with the British, cementing a neutral stance in the coming conflict. However, he chose to help the Germans in this instance by clearly stating that the ships would be allowed entry. He bought time for you to think of some way out of the problem of having to return the ships to hostile waters."

"But that time will come as well," said the general.

I am but a reporter, not a high-ranking adviser to governments, and even then, my country is not involved in this matter, so I decided to leave my suggestions out of the conversation. Had I been asked, I might have suggested the Black Sea, where the German cruisers could have played 'cat and mouse' with the Russian navy. So I answered, "Yes, that time will come."

It was apparent that this line of conversation was finished, and the general recognized it. He turned to a new subject. "Monsieur Enver Pasha believes the *Tribune* can be trusted to deliver national statements to the international community. I wonder, though, since it is published in Paris, the capital of a mortal enemy of Germany. How do you see the situation?"

I thought a second or two and then responded. "The *Tribune* has a lot of American money in it, and it aims to satisfy an English-literate readership. Its place of publication is not relevant just now, but

French preferences may erode that status if hostilities last. But now the *Tribune* is not taking sides, so any statements you and your German colleagues must make will be eagerly taken by the *Tribune*. Try it, and you will see. As for myself, I am dying to know what you have to say,"

The colonel's aide said something to the general in German, and the general responded in kind. Then the general turned to me again and said, "You are right. Let us try it." Then he reached for a written statement and read it in English,

> The German military mission in Constantinople, aware of the dangerous conditions existing in the international order, has been concerned about the safety of the two battle cruisers of the German Mediterranean Fleet. This office applauds the action of the Ottoman government in informing all the nations involved that its harbors are open to the German ships and guarantees safety for them while they are in Ottoman waters. This meets our expectations of the Ottoman government, and we are pleased that the German-Ottoman friendship treaty will remain in place to give context to continued German and Ottoman cooperation on matters of mutual concern.

The general passed the paper to me and asked, "Will this appear in a forthcoming issue?"

"I'm not the editor, so I do not have the final say, but I judge that the statement is important enough that the *Tribune* may even run a special edition to see that this statement is made public immediately."

I left, went to the hotel, and used a typewriter there to write the report. I then went to the censor's office, where I was sent to the head of the line, and the censor did not even pretend to read the text. He applied the censor's stamp, and minutes later, the press office had the missive sent to Boris. I waited for a reply and got what I hoped for. The message said, "Tell General Liman von Sanders that his statement will appear in the four-p.m. edition and will be distributed worldwide with the night edition. Everyone will see it tomorrow morning, bright and early."

I used a messenger to send the message to Werner, knowing he would inform the general.

It was rather late when I finished with the general's interview and its aftermath. Still, I had time to call the American embassy and contacted the ambassador's secretary, a woman. She said, "Thanks so very much, Martin. You will be pleased to know that we are putting together the Fall Bridge tournament schedule. We need to know the level of play that you and your wife compete at."

I was amazed at the question, as I thought that bridge would not get much attention at present, but it did at the American embassy. I said, "I'm sorry, Ma'am, but I am not married."

Not dissuaded, the secretary answered, "But you do play, don't you? We have two unattached women, one an advanced beginner and one at the upper intermediate level. Would either of them meet your requirements?"

"I'm sorry, Ma'am," I patiently replied, "But I am a foreign correspondent and, now that major international news is breaking, cannot commit myself to anything like a bridge tournament for the next several months, if at all after that."

"But you are an American, aren't you? Surely you will have enough time for some leisure each week with your fellow countrymen. Otherwise, how else will you get to know them?"

"I'm sorry, ma'am, but I am being paged here at the correspondent's hotel, so I must go. I am sorry I could not be of assistance." I hung up without waiting for a reply.

British Reaction to Adverse Journalism

The following morning, I was awakened early by a knock at the door. It was Mehmet, 'the reporter's friend, who said that the British ambassador had called and wanted to see me at nine a.m. It was quarter past seven just then, so I knew I had time for a wash, shave, and even breakfast. I was at the embassy five minutes early and was ushered into the ambassador's office at precisely nine a.m.

The ambassador was in shirtsleeves, but his coat was nearby, as if ready to be donned at some strategic moment. He did not greet me but simply said, "I was amazed at Enver Pasha's statement and your endorsement of it."

I, in turn, was surprised at the bluntness of the assertion. I had expected a more conciliatory tone to begin with. I was immediately on guard. "You are mistaken, Your Excellency," I said, "Certainly, the *Tribune* quoted Enver Pasha's statement fully, as it would any statement made by a public official in such dire times. However, there was no endorsement of that statement, actual or implied."

"Come now, you could have explored somewhat, such as asking why Ottoman ports would not be closed as is also consistent with international law."

I laughed lightly and said, "I guess because I chose another line of questioning, namely about the continued relationship with Germany in general, which I was interested in. As a reporter, I'm given a great deal of latitude in such matters."

He regarded my attempts to make light of his remark as a breach of manners and said so. "This is a serious matter," he said, " and I will not entertain a flippant attitude on your part."

I said, "Calm yourself, your excellency; you have no cause to speak to me that way. I am not in your employ, and I am not even a British subject. We do not want an international incident on our hands, do we? I understand your chagrin that a report that you do not like was issued from a territory where you have standing and that it affects you professionally. I am sorry about that, but I also have responsibilities, and had I done anything to prevent the publication of that statement, I would have been grossly guilty of not doing my job as a newsman."

He was not placated by my remarks but decided to 'have it out' with me about my favoritism towards the Germans and the Ottomans and about my deliberate slighting of Great Britain's interests. After nearly fifteen more minutes of strong accusations and my defenses, he said, "Tell me, Mr. Mintz, do you think your embassy will stand by and allow the 'Hun' and the 'Turk' to perpetrate their savagery on this world? I think not. I am writing a memo of protest to your ambassador about this matter and your unconscionable effrontery here today. Good day to you, sir! Please show yourself out!"

I left, just a trifle hot under the collar. But I was cool enough by the time I got back to the hotel and arrived just in time to take a call from the American ambassador's wife, who said, "My dear Martin, we have not met, but I understand that you have declined to take part in the Fall bridge tournament. Please let me persuade you otherwise. Our community depends on all members taking part, and I hope that you and your wife will reconsider. Tell me you will."

I responded, "Sorry, Ma'am, but as I told the ambassador's secretary, my correspondent's duties will have me busy for the next several months, so you will forgive me for not participating. Another time, perhaps. Again, thanks for calling. I appreciate it. Goodbye."

The reporter for the *Guardian* said, "How did it go at the Embassy? The ambassador has a reputation for 'reaming' reporters. He took me to task three months ago for some missing information in my reporting on the Dodecanese Islands. I can only imagine he must have been beside himself about your great sin in delivering information he didn't get first."

"He was everything you say he was," I answered. "He threatened to protest at my embassy."

"Sounds about right, but you'll weather this fine. I know the editors at the *Tribune* are much like those at the *Guardian*. They have no patience with officials who try to cow their reporters. But write up the gist of what he said to you and send it to your editors marked 'For the record.'" So I did just that and got a message back that said, "Message received and filed."

The Solution to the Cruiser Crisis

The following day, the German battle cruisers arrived and were halted at the entry to the Bosporus by the pilot ship, which delayed them only a moment while officials visited the 'Gobben.' Then the officials came back, and the pilot went over to the 'Gobben', and the two battle cruisers made their way slowly down the waterway, presumably to port facilities. The meeting was held considerably far out in the waterway, and even at my vantage point, the happenings on the ships were difficult to discern with any clarity.

I had with me a cameraman from the Ottoman newspaper that had allowed me to use their archives for my dissertation. I had received a call from the editor when my interview with Enver Pasha appeared in the *Tribune*, who wanted the return of the favor for the earlier access to the archives. "I want you to take my reporter with you when you get entre to special events, as you seem suddenly to be the darling of Enver Pasha," he said.

"I don't think that will work," I responded. "It would be viewed as attempting to choose among local newspapers, and Enver and his staff will want to make that choice themselves. But what might work is for you to assign me a cameraman, which I really need just now. If he happens to be a reporter, who is to be the wiser."

The editor was agreeable, and Mirac, who was a cameraman and aspired to become a reporter, was assigned to me. Ottoman authorities who gave me access to special events over the next week had no difficulty with Mirac as part of my legitimate entourage. I noticed in the *Herald* that Mirac was given second place on a by-line on key articles but full credit for the photos that appeared alongside. So Mirac was feeding his information to another, more experienced writer. I noted, with some satisfaction, that some of the commentary I made in the presence of Mirac was reflected in the newspaper articles.

I was rather disappointed with the access we had to the arrival of the 'Gobben' and 'Breslau' but could only hope that in the next few days, more opportunities would present themselves. At seven p.m. that evening, a courier came to my hotel with a note that the following morning, about eight a.m., there would be a ceremony at the dockyards and that I and my cameraman were encouraged to be there. The courier, who waited for my response, noted that his next stop was at the cameraman's home, so I responded to the sender of the note that I would attend.

After the courier was gone, I went in search of the *Guardian's* correspondent and found him in the bar, at a booth, working on a manuscript. He gave me a friendly greeting when I sat down opposite him. I ordered a beer from the ever-alert waiter and said, "What are you doing tomorrow first thing?"

"I have a meeting at the National Bank with the inspector general who is stating the national debt figures. They are expected to be down over last year. The meeting is at ten a.m. Why do you ask?

"Well," I said, "A courier just gave me a notice that a newsworthy event is to take place at the dockside, and I am specially invited. Undoubtedly, it is about the battle cruisers. Care to come as my guest? I have a cameraman and will share some photos. Interested?"

"Hell, yes, Marty, hell, yes!!" Then he paused and said, "But why me? There are others you could have asked."

"Undoubtedly, *the Times* is not invited as its editorial line is straight British Government, so I imagine its reporters are not welcome. But the English press should be represented, and I think no one will object to your presence, as it is not unfriendly to the current Ottoman government. But remember, you still have to get whatever you are filing past the censors."

'Oh God," he responded, "You would remind me of that."

The 'event' contained a surprise. With the briefest of explanations, the two battle cruisers were passed over as a 'gift' from the German government to the Ottoman government. Their complete crews and officers were included. The ceremony marked the transfer when the two ships were given new names. The 'Gobben' was named the 'Yavuz Sultan Selim', and the 'Breslau' was given the name of 'Medli.' It was announced that German admiral Wilhelm Souchon was made an admiral in the Ottoman navy and would retain command of the ships. The 'Yavuz Sultan Selim' had a complement of 43 officers and 1,010 crew members and was one of the most powerful cruisers built by the Imperial German Navy. The 'Medli' was a much smaller craft with a complement of 18 officers and 336 crew members.

A statement from the Ottoman War Ministry was distributed, which announced that the two ships needed to be refitted and repaired after action in the Mediterranean. After repairs, the ships would take their place as the backbone of the Imperial Ottoman Navy. No mention was made of international law on the subject, but it was implied that since the ships were no longer those of the German Navy but the property of the Ottoman Navy, they were no longer excluded from the Dardanelles region. In a three-way conversation afterward between the cameraman, the *Guardian* correspondent, and myself, there was agreement that the Germans and the Ottomans had side-stepped a serious international problem. "Damn clever," said the *Guardian* correspondent. I had to agree.

A few nights later, I was tired beyond belief because of the news rounds I was making and the heavy stress of filing several news stories every day. That night, I went to bed early, so I slept like a log. However, I did notice something disturbed me slightly in my sleep. When I awoke in the morning, there was Amelia nestled into me and holding onto one of my hands. I had not expected her for another day or two, so I was surprised but not unduly so. She had on her skivvies, as usual, whenever we slept together. It was like old times, and I did not move so as not to disturb her and to enjoy her presence a while longer. My breathing must have changed as she instantly awoke and said, "You haven't changed. You lay in the same position and rarely move when you are asleep. I missed that in the States, so it's nice to be back."

Chapter Two
The Naval Raid

The Arrival of Amelia and Her Welcome

The arrival of Amelia went differently than I expected. I thought there would be time to discuss our jobs and divide up our reporting, editing, and camera work. Instead, our jobs were described to us in some instructions given to Amelia by Boris when she was in Bucharest.

We spent most of the morning with one another. I had already planned for us to have three rooms–two rooms with beds and a large storage area that was half the size of a room. The storage room had no windows, which made it perfect for a developing lab; Amelia breathed a sigh of relief when she saw it. "It's perfect, "she said, immediately moving a mess of developing equipment into it.

As for the other bedrooms, we agreed to have the double beds taken out and two singles put in one room, while the other room became our office with a table for each of us. I found a used typewriter, and it was placed on a convenient table and designated for the use of both of us. By noon, everything was in its proper place.

We went to the dining room for lunch, but on the way, I stopped at the press center and introduced Amelia to Mehmet, who proved to be the shyest person ever in the presence of a woman. That was so unlike his usually sure and competent self. But he had three messages for her and one for me. Mine asked me to come to a reception at the home of Enver Pasha that evening "with your colleague, whom, I understand, has just arrived."

Amelia's messages were related to that reception. They were from three different wives of officials, who said they were happy that she had arrived; they looked forward to discussing her books with them at the reception and at other future times."

At lunch, Amelia told me of her meeting with Boris when she had stopped in Bucharest to sign her contract. "He said the war looked like it was not going to be over any time soon, as neither side seemed to have scored a 'knock-out punch' in the early campaigns. Diplomatic contacts might lead to an early armistice. He said that he was surprised at the great expression of nationalism on all sides and how much the populations were driven by a desire to win at all costs against their enemies. He even predicted that the Ottoman Empire would enter the fray on the side of Germany within six months, simply because the Germans wanted them to do that." Amelia said, "On the basis of our travels last year, I would never have predicted that."

But she saved the 'bombshell' announcement until the end. She was not hired as a photographer but as a correspondent-photographer and was not attached to me in any way. We were colleagues—nothing more—and we were each to pursue our own stories. If I wanted to use her photographic skills, I would have to discuss such arrangements with her. I was not overly surprised at her revelation of this clause in her contract but a little chagrined that Boris had not told me what he had in mind. I consoled myself that I already had a photographer from the Constantinople newspaper and was hopeful I could continue that arrangement.

"Marty," Amelia said, "I have a feeling you may not like it that I am now officially a correspondent since you have always had that function in our team. You may feel I am treading on your turf, and in a sense, I guess I am. But I did not intend it as any kind of slight against you or to make you my competitor. I hope you know me well enough to understand I have too much regard for you to do that."

She was quiet for a moment, and when I did not respond, she continued, "You are silent, which usually means you are unsure of how to answer lest you alienate me with your response. Please don't think ill of me, but let me explain so that you get my full justification. Please say something so that I may continue. Okay?"

I did not want to answer, but she had just called my bluff and was demanding that I interact with her, so I said, "Amelia, my love, I will try to keep an open mind as you tell me about the terms you have negotiated with Boris. You are right that giving you the 'correspondent's title' has hit a sour chord with me, even though I know full well I should not think ill of you. I will try to overcome my pique."

"That's better," she said, "I think we can get through this now and still be buddies."

"Let's hope so," I responded.

She immediately continued her justification. "You don't realize it, but it is upsetting to submit work to Paris and have the editors there treat me in an entirely different way than they treat you. They see me as a photographer, a technician, who they can ignore at will, dictate to, and deal with no consideration for my feelings. I don't think that's a nice way to treat fellow professionals, but they do it because there is a different view of me than you. It is based on my use of the camera to tell stories rather than words as you do."

"I was not at all aware that you were treated that way, and I certainly had no idea that you found their treatment of you demeaning," I said. "You hid it from me rather well."

"Or maybe you missed it all because you did not pay much attention and thought everything was all right," she said. "But you should have noticed something was not right when I swore and was upset when unwelcome news came from the editors."

She paused, and I was silent, but after a few seconds, I said, "I'm thinking here, Amelia, so give me a moment. I promise I am not trying to ignore you for effect." She nodded, and after a minute, I said, " I have run over in my mind several instances where this might have been true. I must say that I think the editors make more corrections on my copy than on yours, but you are right in that the editors respond more quickly to my submissions than to yours. I always thought that it was due to the technical nature of dealing with your work. As for how polite they are, I have no way of knowing. The editors are not always very polite to me, and it would take some convincing that you are treated more harshly or less respectfully than I am. But I will take your word that your charge is true for the sake of your argument here."

"Well," she concluded, "It has become a major complaint with me, and I decided to see if I could correct it while I had the opportunity. So I asked and demanded the change in title when we were talking terms. Boris was so concerned about getting another experienced person out here that he would have agreed to a lot more. Knowing that, I pushed for being independent as well, not really believing that would happen. It did, and I did not see any reason to retreat from it since you need to make concessions as well as I do. If you use another photographer, that is fine with me, although I will always be available to you. All you must do is ask, which, of course, is different than expecting it to happen. Your attitude will change as well, and our interaction as colleagues will be leveled a little more."

I said, "I guess that, after your explanation, your change in status is much more acceptable to me than it was to me when you originally described it to me. Thanks for your patience in explaining it to me. I get the point of it all and will try to be more aware of how things are managed in our office as they affect you. I will try to be less selfish, although that may be difficult for me, as I am not always aware that what I may be doing is selfish."

"Really?" she said with a smile on her face. If her sarcasm was back, I knew we were on good terms again and had escaped a potentially nasty breach in our relationship.

All twenty members of the Committee of Union and Progress government officers and their wives were present at the reception. Most of them, including the wives, had degrees from European universities, and nearly all spoke some European language fluently. They also dressed–at least for such social occasions in Western garb. While the women did not mix with men as much as European women might, they were by no means secluded. I found this surprising, considering that the veil was in common use at Constantinople and seclusion from men was common.

As we entered the home of Enver Pasha, he and his wife greeted us and immediately, Amelia was whisked away to the company of the women in a neighboring room. She said later that she had signed copies of her book 'forever', it seemed, and she had to answer the same set of questions repeatedly. "What was her favorite moment in her travels," "which was her favorite photograph," and "Why were there not more pictures of the central Ottoman lands, rather than so many photos of Arabs?"

There was a society reporter, a woman, who got in among the guests and, before she was identified, asked a series of very personal questions. The first was, "What is your relationship with the correspondent Mintz? It is rumored that you sometimes sleep together." The second question was, "Are you still romantically involved with a German liaison officer." She said she laughed both questions off, saying about sleeping with her colleague, "I hear he snores, so if I did stay with him, I would get no sleep." To the question about the liaison officer, she said that she replied, "A German officer, you say. Do you know which one? I would love to meet him?" Both answers elicited laughter from the other women. When the reporter's identity was discovered, she was hustled out of the room.

My own remembrance of the evening was being introduced to ministers I had never met. I enjoyed the session, as my Turkish was developing rapidly and was strong on correct grammar, so the officials that I conversed with found it a delight to speak with me. I was lauded on many occasions for my speaking ability, but I discovered afterward that I gained only limited insights into the government or its inner workings because of the conversations that I had. Obviously, I had violated the cardinal rule in reporting: do not let the conversation be about you yourself, but rather about the other person or the situation the other person knows something about.

At one point, Enver and another cabinet official drew me into a study, and we talked for a time about the 'great war' that had descended on the world. They wanted to know how other correspondents in Constantinople saw the neutral position of the

Ottoman Empire. I replied that the best way to find the answer to that question was to read the submissions of the correspondents themselves.

I said, "There are only a few foreigners here anymore, so the job would not be difficult. *The Times* editor left immediately after the cruiser incident. The *Berlin Tagesblatt* went on home leave several months ago and has not returned. That leaves *Il-Messaggero,* the Italian newspaper, and the *Guardian,* both of whom reflect the scene the way they think their editors want it interpreted. The Italian newspaper holds that the Ottoman Empire was on the verge of a breakup, which would further Italian interests. The *Guardian* regards the neutral stance of your government as a sign it does not want to alienate the British and certainly not fight them.

This opened a discussion that, in turn, led to several other ministers at the reception joining us. Enver Pasha said at one point that he had not given much thought to the issue of public response to his actions concerning the cruisers. He said he had wanted to favor the Germans all along because "they have provided us with invaluable military training and supported us diplomatically, while others proclaim us 'dead meat' and 'wait impatiently to divide the carcass.'

The Minister of the Navy, who was known to favor good ties with Britain because of the Ottoman Navy's heavy reliance on British shipyards to provide modern ships of war, took issue with Enver. "If I am not mistaken, dear colleague, the German Kaiser has, himself, sometimes said that if our nation fails, that he lays claim to most of Anatolia. So much for his deep concern for us." This was followed by a discussion of whether any foreign group could be trusted, as all European countries had laid claim to parts of the Ottoman territory at one time or the other.

Eventually, the subject came back to the starting point of how one could know what the Ottoman public was thinking. The conversation centered on what the Turkic sector of the population had in mind and, particularly, the sector found in Anatolia. It was revealing to me that these leaders saw the 'nation' in those terms when there were Greeks, Armenians, Kurds, Arabs, and numerous other people the government claimed to represent and protect. But if it were clear to me what the conversation revealed, I am not so sure that the ministers would have accepted my definition of it. They would have denied that they were acting only for Turks and would have claimed wider cultural representation.

Then, late in the session, a second point became clear. The leadership was not so much interested in what the population believed of its own volition but in how much of the population identified with the leadership and its position on matters. So Enver was less interested in whether the population wanted peace but whether the population was clearly enough identified with the Committee of Union and Progress's own pronouncements on what should be done about the war. It was clear that Enver wanted full support for Germany and its allies; it was much less clear what the other leaders wanted. It seemed to me that Enver was the only one clear in his position, while most others were ambivalent.

Amelia and I left the reception at different points in time and for different reasons. She went to the home of a minister and, with two other wives, had an 'overnight,' in which the group stayed up until dawn drinking wine and telling personal stories. She got in at six a.m., still a little tipsy, and went to bed to sleep off the worst of the alcoholic reaction. I got in at a respectable two a.m. after going to the home of Talal Pasha to see the artworks displayed in the first minister's palace. Only Talal and his wife were with me, and we enjoyed a conversation about our own families, but it did not last long. So, by the time Amelia got home, I was sober again, even if the hangover did last until noon.

There were some unwritten rules between Amelia and me about sharing the same bed. When we were seeing other people sexually, we absolutely did not seek one another's company. That is easily understood. But, the second taboo concerned alcohol–and I suppose drugs would be included–when we did not cohabit, largely because alcohol was likely to lead to a lessening of inhibitions, and we did not want accidental or unthinking sexual contact between the two of us. When Amelia got in that morning, she went to her own bed without comment, nor was any needed.

Amelia was immediately invited to go with three cabinet members' wives on a tour of interior Anatolia–Eskisehir, Konya, Mersin, Diyarbakir, and Ankara. The women's affiliate of the Committee of Union and Progress was the sponsor, and the group was to meet with the many women's clubs that existed. The meetings were to share information and plans about making the Ottoman nation as great as it had been in the past. Amelia was a featured speaker at many of the meetings, and also she autographed copies of her book. Boris was delighted with the news.

The League of Ottoman Journalists

I went in another direction. I discovered a small group of journalists in Constantinople who had formed a League of Ottoman Journalists, who tried to bring about cooperation on meaningful matters. One of these was to establish a network of journalists throughout the country that could be used at important moments to garner basic information about 'thinking' or 'opinion' in the nation.

I made an unobtrusive visit to the league offices, which was simply a 'cubbyhole' in a workingman's district of western Constantinople. I came unannounced and without telling anyone else of my mission, fearful of suspicions that anyone, especially officials, would have of me. Who knows, the league members might be secretive and not want their work noticed, particularly by the government.

There was no one there but an old man, who was a war veteran–he wore an army tunic and sported a kepi--with a missing leg, who occupied an open space near an apartment house further along the street. Obviously, he was the unofficial watchman of the district. After observing my perplexity, when I got no answer at the door to the 'office,' the man said, "Stranger, No one will be there for another hour or so. The newsmen have their paying jobs and come here afterward to talk about things. But one or more always come. If you are willing, I will have coffee and pastries brought from nearby, and you and I can play chess until they arrive."

I thought about that for a moment and decided that to come back was a bigger effort than merely staying. Who knows if I could find the place again? So I accepted the invitation, and the veteran sent one of the ragamuffins from the street to get the refreshments while he himself set up a well-worn but serviceable chessboard on an old vegetable crate. The pieces came from three different sets originally, and all were scratched and marked.

The coffee was good, the pastries heavenly, and the chess lively. I preferred the 'queen's gambit' approach, while the watchman employed the 'Sicilian defense.' We played fast and were just finishing the fourth game when one of the league members arrived. The score was 2-2 at that point. I gave a silver coin to the old veteran, thanking him for the entertainment. I also gave several copper coins to the ragamuffin who had gotten us the refreshments. He told me his sister had prepared the coffee and pastries, so I gave him some coins for that as well. Everyone was satisfied when I stepped over to the league offices. The veteran gave me a military salute and called me 'effendi.'(i.e., sir).

The league member I first spoke to said his name was Ayaz, and he was from Adana on the Mediterranean coast. He was almost dumbfounded that I had come to see him. He had difficulty believing that the league and its work interested me. He stuttered and stammered with nervousness and even sweated a little. He begged me to wait for his fellow members to arrive since he felt one of them might be more erudite and capable of talking to a foreign journalist with such good strong Turkish language skills. He offered me a soft drink that was warm and had an acidy taste to it, as if the seal were not tight and the drink inside was fermenting. Actually, I think, in retrospect, I was spoiled from the coffee I had earlier.

Three more league members eventually joined us, and little work got done that evening as they sat and discussed journalism, the state of the Ottoman Empire, and the emerging war. Midway into the session, the war veteran hobbled his way into the room on his crutch and found a place on a stack of old newspapers, which seemed to be his place during such discussions. No one objected.

All the league members were shy at first but warmed to the conversation and, as midnight approached, were almost erudite as they all expressed their views fully. A few of the neighborhood men sat just outside, but with the doors and windows open, they heard everything that was said. None of those outside felt comfortable enough to voice an opinion, and it was evident that they held the league members in high regard and never contradicted their views.

A constable came by once but, seeing nothing but people talking, moved on without comment.

When I left, I still had not said anything about my reasons for coming. There was universal agreement among the league members, however, that I must return and even join them in their endeavors if I was willing. I made an appointment for three evenings hence. I had trouble getting back to the central city, using a horse-drawn dray for an early part of the trip. Eventually, I found a terminal of the trolley line but had to wait for a tram on the abbreviated night-time schedule. It was five a.m. when I got home and, after six, before I got to bed. I sat and thought about Amelia on her trip to central Anatolia and wished she were there to discuss the evening with me. Reluctantly, I went to bed and slept till afternoon.

On the day of my second meeting with the 'league of journalists,' I visited the shipyards and saw the cruiser, Yavuz Sultan Salim, in great disarray. Its engine room had been gutted, and the boilers were either being repaired or replaced; I could not tell which, as I could only see the work from outside the ship. But the dockyard near it was filled with material taken from the ship so that work was possible. I was introduced to the admiral, who was a small man with a mustache and, seemingly, very gentle. However, I knew from press reports that on his trip through the Mediterranean to get to Constantinople, he was anything but mild and peaceful. He had shelled Algerian shipyards, engaged British ships in combat, and had given fright to Entente[1] ships in the area he traversed.

---

[1] During World War I Russia, England and France were known as the 'Entente Powers,' while those of Germany, Austria and Italy were labelled the 'Central Powers.'

When I was introduced, I asked whether he was acquainted with the American naval Captain Franz von Kipper, who had once visited my family in Hickory, North Carolina, and had just returned from a European tour with the Navy, where he met numerous European officers. The admiral said he had, indeed, had the pleasure. He asked me whether I knew Captain Austin King, who had once been a naval attaché who was assigned to his ship during German naval maneuvers. This led to a brief discussion about my own travels in Europe and his travels in the Orient. We had many acquaintances in common. We spoke French for our entire exchange. The admiral said nothing about the state of his ship or when repairs would be complete.

This time, my visit to the league was better timed, and I had a taxi on hand to get me back to the central city. However, I arrived a few minutes early and played two games of chess with the war veteran, who had heard I was coming and had the board already set up. He was teaching some children how to play the game, and they avidly watched our quick, sure moves when we played. We split a game apiece.

I took only two hours of the members' time that evening as they explained their organization, which was truly national in scope, with member reporters and editors from throughout the Ottoman Empire. Although they were concentrated in Anatolia, there were some from the northern Arab provinces, Mesopotamia, and the Caucasus areas under Ottoman control. There were seventy-five provincial members. There were no dues or membership fees, and all cooperation was voluntary. They were just completing an assessment of the state of newspaper work in the region and found it to be stronger than was initially believed. The number of reporters and editors was much more extensive than had been realized at the beginning of the endeavor.

They were now planning to see whether they could find a way of translating local views into an overall national viewpoint. I lauded the effort and said I would even help find some modest funding if the project began to bear fruit. For an hour, Ayaz, who was the thinker of the group, and I went over a plan for the first 'survey' to be conducted. It consisted of three questions: 1) Do people identify as Ottomans or as members of other cultural groups?; 2) Does the Ottoman Empire have a great past?; 3) Are you satisfied with the Ottoman policy regarding the war?" It was decided to have a discussion on the planned survey two nights hence.

At the next meeting, we decided to break the third question into three parts: 1) Do you agree with government action to allow the German cruisers to seek refuge in Ottoman waters? 2) Do you agree with the government's decision to accept the German cruisers when they were given as gifts? 3) Do you agree with the Ottoman policy of neutrality in the current war?"

All of us liked the three questions but still believed that the first two questions about Ottoman citizenship were important, so it was decided to go ahead with the project. Cevdet, who oversaw finances, said there was enough money to mail out the survey to the members but not enough to provide for 'return postage.' I did not want the momentum to be lost on this valuable survey, so I said that I had access to some funds to provide the 'return postage.' It proved to be less than I estimated, so I was surprised when the figure was given to me. Why else do I have an expense account?

It took ten days to get enough responses to consider counting and tabulating. We got a 95% response, which we considered good, which was better than the previous request for information from editors and reporters. Answers to the first question indicated that most members saw cultural allegiance as higher than Ottoman allegiance. On the second question, nearly everyone saw the Ottoman past as 'great,' indicating the schools were doing their job in socializing their pupils and students and that, perhaps, an Ottoman identity was emerging. The three questions about ships and neutrality had 80% ratings, and all respondents answered those questions the same way, that there was strong support for the Ottoman government's actions. We discussed the results for over two hours.

Then the question of whether we should try to publish the results or not was undertaken. I held back my opinion until there was near consensus that the results were important enough to merit publication. Then, there was a short discussion over whether the results should be published nationally, internationally, or locally. It was agreed that all participating members would get a copy to do with as they wished. But efforts should be made to get national and international publications. At that point, I said I could guarantee both but wanted the league itself to try to publish the results in the *Tribune* and in the *Herald*, the paper where I had my local arrangements. I said it was important that the league be recognized as the source of the material, not me. Everyone agreed.

The following day, Ayaz and I met in my hotel room and translated the article into English. Afterward, we sent it to Boris in Budapest with my explanation of its origins and meaning. At the same time, I handed the Turkish version to my cameraman, who knew, after a brief explanation, what to do with it. We waited an hour before a response came from Boris, who accepted it, said that he wanted international rights, and named a handsome figure. Ayaz's eyes bulged out of his head as he saw the figure and accepted it immediately. Shortly afterward, the cameraman returned and said the *Herald's* editor wanted national rights. Ayaz went to the offices of the *Herald* to negotiate that matter, as it involved the promise to the local editors. Eventually, the matter was settled with a modest fee coming from the *Herald*.

Amelia and the Rumor Mill

Amelia returned at this point and, initially, was full of stories about all the people she had met, all the places she had seen, and, importantly, the photos she had taken. She spent hours in her dark room and had drying photos in every corner of the apartment. Some had to be cleared away to even go to bed. As well she had made copious notes on interviews with over fifty provincial notables, both men and women. Those people saw the Great War that was unfolding as a potential threat to Ottoman security in that Russia was involved, and when Russia was involved, it meant military action against Ottoman territory. The interviews also spoke about a tightening of conscription laws, as more young men were being drafted, and the employment situation was good because war preparation called for more goods from factories and farms. Amelia filed ten reports immediately and several more later outlining those interviews. Boris sent his congratulations on her good work.

But there were some bumpy spots during the trip. Amelia spent at least an hour a day learning Turkish, but she felt that the CUP women with whom she was traveling were impatient with her progress. They grew tired of translating for her and insisted she use her weak Turkish. She said that she tried. She admitted that sometimes she tried to use language that was too complicated for her Turkish vocabulary, and this led to incomprehensible sentences and sentence structure. Her companions grew short-tempered with her for that failure, and while she tried to simplify her sentences, there were still too many instances when she failed. She was deeply disappointed in her own performance and, especially, with the impatience of her companions.

Near the end of the trip, the woman reporter who had invaded the reception earlier managed to get into the press sessions of the CUP meetings and concentrated her attacks on Amelia and her 'German lover.' Amelia's cute answers no longer sufficed, and her CUP companions wanted to know whether there was truth to the allegations. When they decided there were, they were condescending about the matter, insinuating that 'proper ladies' did not engage in such wicked behavior,' whether they were married or unmarried. At the end of the trip, only two women were still speaking to her.

I got wind of the matter before Amelia returned and was dismayed at the adverse feelings the matter caused. The first telephone call was from Enver Pasha himself, who said that his assessment of me was of the highest order and that he looked forward to a long and fruitful association. He continued, "However, my wife has informed me of the apparent improprieties of your fellow journalist, Amelia Caruthers, who enjoys flaunting to the press the sordid details of an affair she is having with a German army officer. Please do something about it, or the government will demand her recall."

I responded quickly, as I felt he was about to hang up after issuing the ultimatum, making the situation irretrievable. "I understand the position it puts you in since the interviews occurred at events hosted by the government. I apologize for my colleague, whose use of Turkish is minimal. What you may have mistaken for 'flaunting the details of her affair' may have simply been her attempts to defuse the situation with clever wording that would make light of the matter. Obviously, she has deepened the problem rather than resolved it. Enver, friend, I am distressed about the matter because I do not want you to think badly of us. I also know that Amelia is not a troublemaker nor someone who flaunts social customs. I know for a fact she is not in contact with the officer any more, not since she was here last year, so the matter is not likely to go further. I will meet with her and offer her some counsel about handling such sensitive matters. I am sure that will help."

There was a pause, and I was aware that Enver had not broken the connection. Obviously, he did not want a rupture in our relationship, so I said, "If I may change the subject, I wondered whether you had seen the article by the local group of journalists giving estimates of public opinion concerning the government's policy on the war?"

He responded with new interest. "Yes, I did, and I think you had something to do with it. The two set-up questions about cultural identification and Ottoman history were the most interesting questions. Who formulated them?"

"The group came to me when they needed an English translator, and I helped them at that point, but the original formulations were their own. It is a good group, and they may be on to how to measure public opinion. A grant to help them might be in order, but I'm sure you've already thought of that."

He responded quickly, "Precisely, such a group could use some assistance. I'll check to see that the grant is given quickly."

I closed the conversation, having deflected the reprimand that was delivered earlier. "And I'll take care of that other matter," I said and broke the connection.

Half a day later, Liman von Sanders, the commander of the German mission, called and had similar comments. "Herr Mintz, I have been impressed by you as a man of integrity, so I am puzzled why a reporter in your office has chosen to disrupt the marriage of one of my finest staff officers. Are you aware of this scandal?" He spoke French.

I replied in French, saying, "I am aware that there are rumors of an affair, but I thought they belonged to the previous year when Miss Amelia and Major Aussenfeld had been in contact with one another socially. I can speak with great certainty that since Miss Amelia had been assigned here this year only three weeks ago, there has been no contact between the two of them."

"That's what Aussenfeld says as well," the general said. "This is embarrassing, and I want it to go no further. The officers' wives are up in arms about the matter, feeling that a foreign hussy has invaded their domain and put a question mark over the honor of the entire assembly of military officers' wives here. Aussenfeld has assured me that he will not contact her in any way. Can you see that the same goes with the woman?"

"I will certainly speak to her about this matter, but remember, sir, I am only her colleague, not her husband, so my word only goes so far. However, knowing Amelia as I do, I think that if the major has agreed not to contact her, then she will not contact him, as a matter of course."

Having the assurances he had called about, the general switched to a new subject. "Maneuvers will be taking place shortly, and I am hopeful that our efforts this training season will show great improvements in the Ottoman army. I am issuing a list of journalists I would like to have present. I hope you will find time to attend."

"There is nothing I would like better," I replied.

The following day, Amelia came to me in tears, saying she was going to resign her assignment and go home. I held her and comforted her for quite a spell. She sobbed out the iniquities that had been heaped on her since her arrival and insisted she had done nothing but defend herself against the nasty charges continually repeated about her. "I'm sure these CUP wives will poison government officials against me here as well," she said.

When she had finished her crying, she asked what was to be done.

"The first thing is to get your story straight and then tell Boris about it. The government here is making noises about having you recalled, and while I do not think they will do that, you had better prepare Boris for the worst. He's got to know."

So we had a long talk and put together a report that took a lot of the passion out of the story as it had unfolded but still told about the seriousness of the event. She then called Boris and was on the line with him for an hour. Afterward, she sniffled for a while and then came to the office where I was working. "He wasn't happy and nearly took away part of my contract making me a reporter. I told him I would go home rather than stay simply as a photographer. He says I am not to have any contact with Werner, and, also, I am to be very, very discreet in any other affairs I have. He says I am to discuss my choice of assignments with you before I do them to make sure I am not getting into matters that will cause me further difficulties." She looked at me directly and said, "Are you going to get into deciding what I am going to do and what not?"

"Of course not," I responded. "I don't ever remember doing that earlier. Why would I do that now? But I will warn you if I think danger lurks. Okay?"

"Okay," she responded and went to her darkroom to commiserate with her developing equipment.

I took the call from Boris half an hour later, who said, "This is serious, Marty. I know you two are chums, but you must really look after her this time. I got a call from your buddy, Enver Pasha, and he says only your vouching for her has saved her from expulsion. If she so much as 'squeaks,' she's on the next train west."

I said, "Enver didn't tell me that, but I believe it. He has the ministers' wives to contend with and is unlikely to be very lenient when faced with that group of harpies. Let her lie low for a while. She is trying to learn Turkish, so I will have her spend most of the time studying. She also has a lot of photos from her trip that need processing. They'll be a string of reports on all that stuff, I am sure, so not much production time will be lost."

It was about this time that I got a new letter from Aunt Bea, with a postmark of Madrid, where I had expected the family to go now that France was in the early stages of the war. The opening sentence told me this was so.

Dear Marty:

As you can see by the postmark, we grew alarmed about the war and moved to Spain, where the danger was less. Your father was especially concerned that the French army would not hold, that the Germans would overrun all of France, and that the police would not function for a considerable period. It was inconvenient to move, and we lost our rent money, but we hope that by next year, the war will be past, and we can return to France because we were enjoying it so much there this time.

We are located near the Everetts, who send their regards, especially Janet, who says she will be writing to you shortly in any case. You must be corresponding regularly with her as she did not complain to me about that feature of your relationship, as she did last year. I am glad you are doing that, or otherwise, she becomes a pest, always wanting to know whether I have heard from you or not.

We have a small crisis in the family. Your sister has a beau whose family belongs to the Watch Tower Society. If you do not know who they are, let me tell you they are a bad bunch. They are against blood transfusions, which many other people are too, but the Watch Tower people see it as a great sin for which a soul can be punished. That is taking it too far, I think. Also, they believe that the Book of Revelations foretells the end of humankind, that Armageddon is going to be a real, not an imaginary, or symbolic event, and that all the great armies of the world will be involved. Sherman is the beau's name, who holds that the present war is the beginning of the end because the chief armies of the world are already involved, and the rest will follow.

Well, our family is mostly Protestant and, especially, Lutheran, so we do not hold with all of this, and your sister does not either, at least so far. But she is protective of her beau and allows him to say upsetting things when he comes to visit, so we are concerned that he will convert her over to becoming a member of the Society.

I would say you should write to her and tell her to be on her guard, but I remember that she never listens to you in any case and thinks you are a know-it-all. So do not say a word to her. Your father thinks she will get tired of it and break up with him, but your Mother is not so sure. Since he lives in Cincinnati, we will no longer see him once the summer season is over. I hope that will be the case.

Kisses, with love, your Aunt Bea

Enduring Army Maneuvers

Maneuvers are maneuvers, and I am at a loss to see what they accomplish other than to send units through pre-described drills that have no real meaning. It was explained to me by Werner himself that much of the measurement is against the performance of the last maneuvers, and in that respect, there had been considerable progress. The event took a week out of my schedule, with over three days at the maneuver site itself, near Ankara, inland from Constantinople. The conditions were rugged. It rained every day, so it was difficult to get through the mud and slop. There was not a dry place to even sleep. We bedded down in straw that was wet through by morning. The food was half-cooked and often inedible. There was a minimum of transportation, and most of the action took place using donkeys rather than motorized vehicles.

Strangely, the two armies seemed motivated by the adverse conditions, and they moved with a speed I found difficult to comprehend given the conditions. On two of the four nights in the field, I slept in forward areas with attacking forces because that was where we were when it was no longer enough light to carry our attack forward. I stayed near commanders most of the time, who were tolerant of me and answered my questions as to what was happening. It was an unreal experience, but I really did like it. It was announced on the finale day that the Blue Team had won over the Red Team, and then a short review of important actions was undertaken as a learning exercise.

I was asked to stay on an extra day for the review when all the other journalists left. I decided that nothing much was going to happen in Constantinople when the whole army command was in Ankara. So I bided my time and was rewarded with a seat in the railroad car carrying General Liman von Sanders and his staff. Mid-way in the journey, I was called into a meeting, where the general, attended only by Werner, asked me questions about what I had observed. He asked if I thought the Turkish troops were 'stalwart,' that is, 'would hold the line against very heavy odds.' I agreed that they would do that since their training emphasized it, and they had an instinct, as I had observed the year before, to not give ground easily.

When the interview was over, the general exited the compartment for a visit to the facilities, leaving me alone with Werner. When the general closed the door, Werner said, "In two weeks' time, the general is giving me leave. He says I cannot spend the time in Constantinople because of the rumor mills about me and Amelia. But he thinks that none of that would exist if I went to Hungary for recuperation, either Bucharest or Budapest. Which do you think would be more entertaining, sir?

Without missing a beat, I replied. "I think you would enjoy Bucharest ever so much more. In fact, I will make sure that you do." I replied. Then, I left the car and went to my assigned seat.

The Naval Raid

In November, I was by myself while Amelia was once again traveling, this time to Bucharest for consultations with Boris and to spend some leave time. Again, it was the Germans, this time the office of the admiral, who had a Turkish interpreter invite me to attend the sea exercises of the Ottoman fleet, which had recently been refitted. The boilers of the Soyuz Sultan Selim were now functioning properly. I was told that the exercises would take about a week, as there was considerable sailing involved since the fleet went to different points to test its armament and equipment. I was told to bring my cameraman, as there would be ample opportunities to take photos. I rued not having Amelia there but settled on the photographer from the *Herald*, who was only too glad to accompany me once again.

The press corps on the Soyuz was sparse, with only three of us and two cameramen. The three correspondents were assigned one wardroom, which ordinarily accommodated only two, so it was crowded, and I slept on the floor. We came on board at night, without lights, and went below in blackout conditions. It was apparent that combat conditions were being observed and would endure for the duration of the exercise.

Breakfast was dry toast and cheese with black coffee, but plenty of it. We went on deck and were given assigned places, which were sheltered, but were given helmets to be worn while the artillery was in action. We then went back to our quarters. I tried to visualize our location and concluded that we were in the Black Sea heading northeast, which, in my reckoning, would lead us into Russian territory within a day.

Somewhere after daylight, we were taken to an officer's mess and briefed. It was a difficult process as the briefer was a German naval commander who gave his talk in German. Then, a Turkish interpreter rendered that talk into Turkish. The interpreter seemed insecure and consequently stammered and hesitated, so I was not so sure of the accuracy of his translation. But it was close enough. It was a one-sided process, and no questions were taken, which I found quite in keeping with the military mindset.

The briefing informed us that Russian vessels had made naval demonstrations against Ottoman territories to the south, close to the Dardanelles passage, so a response was called for. The commander said what was portrayed as a simple testing of weapons on some deserted coast had now been changed, and a real Russian naval target was substituted for the deserted coast. Under such conditions, the press was warned to be watchful while on deck observing the proceedings. Drydocks, ordinance depots, and ships under repair would be targets. Undoubtedly, there would be return fire from patrol ships and land batteries. It was suggested that those press members who did not want to be exposed to such conditions should stay below in their quarters. Of the five of us, only my cameraman, another reporter, and I agreed to witness the military strike against the Russian port.

My cameraman had decided not to use large cameras, as they were too bulky to be practical. Instead, he, like Amelia, used a small Leica camera, saying it was easier to enlarge than to try to get regular-sized negatives. He was placed alongside me just outside the bridge, while the other reporter had the same position on the other side of the bridge.

We got to our posts just as we were about to enter the outer limits of the harbor and had two other ships ahead of us, a destroyer and a minesweeper, I surmised by the chart I had with me as reference. We went in fast, I thought, which meant that there were no mines or that we were ignoring them. Suddenly, the destroyer peeled off to the left, and I could see a set of storage buildings on a wharf extending out from shore. Undoubtedly, that was a target, and before the scene fell out of view, I could hear the pom-pom of guns searching out targets. Ahead of us, the minesweeper went left and signaled for the cruiser to go right, and I realized the sweeper had discovered a small field of mines. We swept by so fast I could not observe how that ship handled the mine threat, but later, I heard several of them explode but apparently some distance from the ship, so that we were not harmed.

Then before us was the great port of Sevastopol, or at least, the large sign on a warehouse stating that was the harbor's name. Then came the pom-pom sounds of the first shots of the cruiser, followed instantaneously by the great roar of the big guns. The Yavuz was an advanced German battle cruiser with superb guns. The exercise was meant to test for sustained fire as much as for accuracy, as the roars of the salvos repeated themselves consistently over a fifteen-minute period. My ears were stuffed with cotton, and my helmet was stuffed with cloth to deaden the sound, but it seemed to me to make little difference. The sound was deafening, but I kept my eyes on the probable targets and saw shell after shell destroy the whole infrastructure of the harbor in minutes. Then, as we turned to new targets, a Russian destroyer came into view, and I saw bursts of gunfire aimed at us. Two events occurred simultaneously: we were hit, and the entire bridge section of the Russian destroyer disappeared along with its forward guns. I could feel the hard jolt of the enemy salvo, but it was to the far side, well behind the bridge.

But the enemy shell had done damage, and one of Yavuz's great guns went silent. But the other great gun kept firing, and as we completed our turn and headed out of the harbor, I saw fire after fire on shore where the great gun had done damage. My cameraman, who had been snapping madly, said something to me and, understanding that I could not hear him, pointed to the camera, indicating he was out of a film. He had three exposed rolls of film already in his hand, indicating the number of photos he had taken. Now, that is coolness under fire.

Then the guns went silent as we joined up with the mine sweeper and the destroyer. Both showed damage, especially the destroyer, which had a huge hole midway on the hull but well above the waterline. The minesweeper was covered in bullet holes as if it were made of Swiss cheese. On board our cruiser, what had been a deserted deck suddenly came alive with running figures heading toward salvage and rescue stations since the fighting was finished. No one came for us newsmen, so we moved around, making sure we got in no one's way.

I found my way to the other side of the bridge and could see from there that an enemy shell had destroyed a part of the deck and the rear of the second of the two great guns. The heavily damaged loading mechanism was clearly in view. I found the other newsman who had been given a post on that side. He was withered up in a ball and had found shelter in a small cubbyhole where the bridge met the superstructure to the rear. He was still in shock. My cameraman and I pulled him out, got him to open his eyes, and tried to convince him that everything was now all right. He refused to pull his hands away from his ears, and each time the ship made a turn, he winced, expecting to hear the great guns again.

Then, the officer who had assigned us our stations appeared and took the shell-shocked reporter and my cameraman away to quarters. I was taken to the stateroom where the admiral himself was seated, relaxed, while officers were assembling for a battle post-mortem. I was offered a cup of coffee and given a seat alongside the admiral, who said, "Nothing like Hickory, North Carolina, is it? He spoke French." He smiled and continued, "We caught them off-guard as we hoped and showed them that we are a formidable force, but the damage we inflicted is easily enough repaired. But the purpose of the raid was not to destroy the enemy, merely to create conditions where the Ottomans realized that the Russians were not ten feet tall but could be managed in a real war. The Germans need the Ottomans in the war, which was my purpose today. We had the Breslau, sorry, the Medili, and another light cruiser out raiding as well, and they report similar results."

I nodded but did not say anything, but I was surprised when he said, "Enver Pasha tells me you are a good judge of Ottoman feeling and opinion. How do you think the government will react, and how do you see the impact of the raids on Ottoman public opinion?"

I gulped because I was giving an assessment to a high-ranking naval official of a major power, and I was not accustomed to doing that. But I am foolhardy in any case, so I proceeded. "There is no Ottoman public opinion," I said, "only that of cultural communities, Turks, Greeks and Armenians, Arabs, and Kurds. The Turks will love it as poking Russia in the nose, which they always like. The Greeks and Armenians will wail because they will be accused of aiding the Russians eventually, as they always are. The Arabs will not care a bit, as they are self-absorbed, and the Kurds are off in their own world, concerned about Persia. Since Turks dominate politics, the war will get their support, but others will be lukewarm at best, and some outright opposed. Concerning the government, only Enver Pasha and two of the ministers are heavily pro-German. The rest like the German alliance but do not want it to involve them in a war. But they have no choice now and will support the war effort once the decision is made.

The admiral was taken aback. Enver had told him that a raid would galvanize the support of the entire nation, and there would be a groundswell of support for entering the war on the side of Germany. But he recognized me as an authority on public opinion for some reason and said, "Then you think the Ottomans may not come into the war on Germany's side?

"No," I said. "I believe they will because the raid has, in effect, declared war on Russia, and Russia will not back away from such provocation. There will be letters back and forth, but the outcome is almost preordained. The stances will harden, and war will be declared on both sides. Even Great Britain's efforts to keep Turkey out of war will not turn the tide.

"But that is good enough for me and fulfills my mission," the admiral said.

"Fine," I said and then bravely gave a warning. "Remember, you now have a war to fight against the Russians, and being on the southern front will not be easy. The Russians know this territory a lot better than they know their European front, and they are ruthless. The Turks are good fighters, as they have shown in the past, but I am unsure whether their industrial capacity can match that of the Russians. Think of that a year from now, when munitions get short because the Dardanelles passage to the Mediterranean are blockaded, and the lack of manpower through conscription lowers economic productivity."

The admiral had a scowl on his face, but his impeccable manners kept his voice level and his annoyance at bay. He said, "My officers are here for their after-action reporting. Thank you for your very frank views." The escort officer was at my elbow and almost pulled me from the meeting. He had not understood the conversation but could tell by the admiral's facial expressions that my comments were riling the admiral. I felt pangs of guilt and wondered why I had been so forthright.

The reporter who had refused to go on deck during the raid and the one who had made himself small in the cubbyhole wanted me to share my information on the raid, but I openly refused, telling them they had the same opportunity I did and they did not take advantage of it. They did not like that response, so I claimed the lower bunk, saying it was someone else's turn to sleep on the floor. It was spiteful, I know, but it changed the subject and made the other two see me in a different light. They believed my obstinacy in staying on deck during the bombardment marked me as a better reporter than they were. Maybe. Maybe not. But let them believe what they like.

Upon leaving the Sovuz at its naval berth, I went directly to my office, where I typed the report I intended to send on to Boris. I prepared it in two parts. The first was a full description of the raid as I saw it. The second was my own analysis, much like I had outlined in my conversation with the admiral. I was full of skepticism about being able to file either report, so I went to the censor, full of dread that both of my stories would be killed. The censor looked up at me, smiled, and said, "Ah, Effendi Mintz, how nice to see you today. I understand you went on a sea voyage."

He carefully read each report twice as if to be sure he understood what I was saying. The reports were in English, and it could not have been easy for him. Then he turned to me and said. "The action you describe sounds so real, and I was almost there when I read it. Surely you were afraid?"

"Indeed, I was," I answered. "But one learns to put that emotion aside when one has a job to do."

He nodded in response and then said, "The second report is also interesting because I have not seen the Ottoman Empire in just that way, but I must admit that it is true. As for how the government will react, you have it right; they do not really want war but will agree to it. I do not suppose it is a very flattering to say that a government does not really know what it's about, but what you say is on target. I see no reason to change anything you have said. Besides, the Ministry of War has sent a note concerning you personally, saying your reports on the Black Sea raid are not to be censored unless gravely at issue with national interests." He scribbled his initials on the block designed for that purpose. "I'm glad you were not injured on that trip," he said.

I said "Thanks" and moved on as well.

Telegraph lines were busy, and it was two hours before I got a response to my filings from Boris.

The message said.

Dear Traveler, you've really done it this time! Front row in the opening battle of a new Ottoman-Russian War! The description and photos are riveting and well done. Give your photographer a bonus; you will certainly get one. The analysis is first-rate, and I think it will prove itself true in the next several weeks. Incidentally, your buddy and her buddy both felt left out, and they were scurrying to find transportation back to Constantinople. Long live true love. Kisses, Boris

The editor of the *Herald* was next on the list of places I had to visit that day. He did not keep me waiting but passed his duties off to a subordinate when I came into the office. "You have brought new meaning to the definition of a newsman," he said. "Mirac, our good photographer, swears by you and claims you are the best reporter ever. He says you are as brave as Iskandar (Alexander) and as wise as Ibn Rushd (Averroes). Before he told me that, I was unsure he knew any history at all."

"He's the reason I'm here today," I said. I have word from my superior that Mirac deserves a bonus. What do you think?"

"Yes," he responded, "But it must be in line with what we ourselves give as bonuses; otherwise, it will cause deep jealousy." So we negotiated for about fifteen minutes and arrived at a figure that was satisfactory to both of us. I paid with a cheque from an Ottoman bank.

Our conversation then turned to the 'league of journalists', and the editor told me that the group had received a grant from the government for operations for the next year, which was minimal but allowed them to rent slightly more space and to issue more surveys. The next survey was planned for about two weeks from then, and it would address feelings about entering the war on the German side. The editor predicted that the survey would show that neutrality was supported, while I said it would prevail only among the Turkic population. The editor said I was too pessimistic about Greeks and Armenians, but we agreed that the Arabs were impossible to decipher in any case.

When I got back to my hotel, Mehmet told me that Stanley, the *Guardian* representative, was packing up to catch a boat out to the south before Great Britain and the Ottomans declared war on one another. I hurriedly organized a farewell party for him and successfully got some of his press sources to come to see him off. He cautioned me about the Ottomans. "They are not well grounded in tolerance," he said, "and wartime makes them suspicious of those in their midst that are different. I think it will be the Armenians this time who will feel their wrath. I only hope they don't do something evil, like kill them en masse."

I answered, saying, "I agree that the Ottomans are subject to such fits of ruthlessness and need watching. I pray it is not as pronounced as you think. Thanks for the warning."

Chapter Three
The Sarikamish Campaign

Interlude

The *Guardian* correspondent was not long gone before his room was let to Kurt Langer from the *Berliner Tagesblatt*, who knew Turkish from his student days when he had spent a year in a German college located near the Hellespont. I was one of the first journalists he met, and he said he hoped we might be good friends and colleagues. He was good-looking with dark brown hair and a sandy beard and was of medium height. He spoke clearly and slowly so that he could always be understood. That was an important consideration since he did not know much English, and I knew little German, so we had to communicate through our knowledge of Turkish. He was polite to a fault, but it was tempered with a fine sense of humor. A day later, when he met Amelia, he said he was ready to fall in love and said he 'adored' her playful use of German. His ardor was cooled appreciably when he discovered that she had a German army officer as a boyfriend, but he often went out of his way to be with her.

As for Amelia, she changed only slightly after her ten days with Werner. One might have expected more, considering that the dreadful Anatolia trip was behind her, and she had a chance to recover from it. She had hardly been my colleague up to this point, so I insisted that she take more interest in the work of our press office. For a time, she became interested in my work with the 'League of Journalists' and went with me twice to talk with them. But they saw her as an oddity, and they did not accept much of what she said. Perhaps it was her poor use of Turkish, but it seemed to be more that she was a female and, hence, did not have the status to be taken seriously.

But there was one bright spot. She was very interested in the Armenians and Greeks, recalling some of the interviews we had in Smyrna as giving us hints about abuses that might come their way. She had a map installed in the office on which she put the places where both Greeks and Armenians existed. She started her own clipping file to locate materials, and she practiced her reading of Turkish, exploring local newspapers for such articles. She found a significant number, but they were repetitious in their content and direction. Still, she persisted.

I did write to Janet and to Aunt Bea but not to anyone else. There just was no time to write personal letters. I had just heard from Aunt Bea, so I did not expect to hear from her again for at least a month. However, Janet wrote and was subdued in her message to me. The war concerned her.

Dear Marty

We are leaving Europe a few days earlier this year. It is a sad place because the war is worse than people imagined it could be, and everyone is alarmed about the astronomical casualty rates. More men are lost in a single day than an entire war did before this. It is chilling, and most of us want to get home to be away from the constant reminders of it.

Constantinople is under attack, only blockaded, so I am thankful for that, as it means you are not in immediate danger. But Marty, you are an international correspondent. Will you please not reconsider the decision to be one and resign from that job? If you don't, I am sure that within several months, you will be on some battlefront where life and limb are at stake. I tremble when I think about it, and I want you to know what a loss it would be for all of us if something happened to you. Please do give the matter some immediate attention.

Daddy says that the war is going to change the furniture industry, that it will be mobilized to produce such things as desks, chairs, beds, and whatnot for military use, and that it will have to be mass-produced and made in a hurry. He believes that you, and others like you, should high-tail it to North Carolina and begin planning for the great increase in production and for the conversion of the plants to wartime products. It seems to me to be good advice for you because you know something about it and can be on the ground floor in the new expansion. Please consider what I am telling you. It is important this time.

I think a lot about our last date when you were home between assignments. You spent an entire day with me and gave me great attention. I was starved for you and would have even gone to bed with you if you had indicated you wanted to do it. But, as usual, you held back at the crucial moment, and we did not consummate our deep friendship. I wish you could make it over that hurdle, as I know we would be wonderfully happy as a couple. Even though that happened several months ago, it rolls around in my memories as though it was only yesterday. I hope you remember it too.

Loads of love, Janet

I barely knew how to handle the relationship with Janet, and I understood if I did nothing about it, that I would sooner or later marry her. Sometimes, I thought that would not be the worst thing in the world. At other times, I thought it would be a disaster. I compared her–one should not do that, but I did anyway–with

Amelia, who I like but have not found a way to deal with either. When I thought about which one I wanted, it was usually Amelia I chose, but Janice always was a close second for a multitude of reasons. I knew the matter needed some more thought.

Meanwhile, there was work to be done on the project, transforming the presence of two reporters into a news agency that relied on more than just our contributions. Part of the fee that I paid for services at the correspondent's assistance booth at the hotel included access to several news services that provided collections of items from local newspapers, government agencies, and other miscellaneous outlets. Amelia used this one extensively. One was a daily summary of events in the central Ottoman lands, issued from Adana, so it always came a day late, but it was invaluable for what was happening in most of Anatolia. There was also the daily summary of the Arabic press, which covered Syria and Palestine but had occasional items on areas south of Palestine. That summary came only once a week and was often late. Finally, there was a service that would deliver government agency releases, including the Sublime Porte, the foreign ministry, which I used often.

I hired a clerk to go through all the sources as they arrived, with a list of topics in which we had an interest. It amounted to between five and twenty pieces a day. Since most were in Turkish, I reviewed the collected items and decided if any were newsworthy. Amelia's Turkish was now good enough that she could do some follow-up stories on selections of interest. Mostly, she chose selections that dealt with minorities and women. I handled the remainder, usually those matters dealing with the government and with international affairs. Depending on the volume, I would spend anywhere from one to as many as five hours a day working on those articles, turning them into submissions for Bucharest. Amelia and I often spent our lunchtime going over the articles, so that we always knew what was going to be submitted that day and the importance of it.

I was disciplined in my approach to this chore, feeling that the sooner it was complete, the sooner I could get to other matters that interested me. I had to arrange interviews with people who were in the news. Amelia, on the other hand, saw this as an abhorrent chore and objected to doing it more than once a week, claiming that, since she had the photo collection to keep current, she had no further time for reading press summaries. So, at lunchtime, she often had nothing to report for several days and then would have three items to make up for her inattention. I adjusted my own work to fit with her, sending in more of my work on days when she was not reporting. Amelia said nothing about this and seemed not to care how her erratic schedule affected me. I found it annoying at times when I was forced to cover for her. I regarded her failure to submit anything after three days as taking advantage of my goodwill. I doubt whether it bothered her at all.

In my spare time, after completing my daily work and searching for interviews, I prepared for the next great crisis I believed would be coming our way. I determined it would be war in the Caucasus, in the old Azerbaijan area, which was now Russian but formerly had been under Ottoman control. I thought it highly unlikely that there would be a winter campaign, but I did not rule out an early spring offensive. But to be on the safe side, I ordered winter gear from Norway, which had extremely good equipment because of the natural conditions there, but also because Norwegian explorers had trekked to both the north and south poles. The gear was expensive, and Boris complained about it but paid for four sets, including snowshoes and small tents. The gear came in late November. Amelia and I spent weekends trekking in upland areas above the frost line after riding trains up to the locale. The equipment really worked, except it was cumbersome, and working in it was difficult. Writing was impossible. But with practice, moving could be done easily. Amelia was enthusiastic, as she was determined to go into the northern Armenian villages, which experienced long and deep winters. These adventures were about all we ever did together for the rest of the time she was with Werner.

I noticed it at the time but tried to block the implications from my mind when Amelia did not do her work as well as she had on our earlier expedition. Certainly, her reporting on her trip to Anatolia had been acceptable, especially with the photos and their descriptions. But her reporting since then was spotty, and she did not seem to ferret out stories well enough. There were dead-ends, inconclusive story lines and sloppy submissions. I attributed much of the failings to her new role, where she had to choose what she would write about and carry through some sort of a plan and itinerary to produce articles on a regular basis. She simply did not do it very well, and it was only my own efforts to fill in for her that the office maintained an even flow of news to Bucharest.

The Great Northern Trek

In early December, I received word from the Ottoman War Department that I and a cameraman were to be part of an expedition into the northern area. We were given a short departure date. The letter said to dress for cold weather. I asked Amelia whether she wanted to go on this trip, and she said she did. "I'm prepared, and why should you have all the fun anyway? You have gone on maneuvers and been on a sea raid. I've been left out both times and want things changed."

I wanted to defend myself against such unreasonable attacks since both events had occurred while she was not in Constantinople. I was unsure just what it was that needed changing. I had just included her in this adventure, which was the first one where she was available. Although her attitude annoyed me some, I decided not to say anything about her complaint.

We went on troop transports using horses and traveling at night, again for security purposes. We arrived after a week in the locale where the expedition was to take place. I featured maneuvers like what I had experienced two months earlier, and, at first, it seemed that history would repeat itself. But I was mistaken. The group from Constantinople was only a part of the force that had been assembled. The entire IX Corps, stationed in the region, was already in place, and it was apparent that a major effort was underway against the Russians.

We were assigned to a reconnaissance unit, which had a captain, a lieutenant, several sergeants, and about fifteen regular troopers assigned to it. The captain wondered aloud to me why we were assigned to him, saying, "We move fast, so you two had better be good hikers because we don't wait for laggards. Our mission is to get to the target first, encircle it, and set up a defensive perimeter. Are you up to it, or do you want to stay here?"

"We'll give it a try," I said. "We're both in good condition, and I think we can do it. If not, we'll find our own way back in a day or two."

"You'll have to," he answered. "I don't have anyone to spare to bring you back."

Other units had donkeys they were using as draft animals, but our commander said that donkeys "will only slow us down, we would have to feed them, and probably kill them when it gets too cold."

I asked what our target was, and he said, "I'm surprised no one has told you. It is no secret in the IXth Corps that we are heading for Sarikamish to give the Russians a bloody nose in the middle of winter. Let's hope they are happy and content in their winter quarters and not watching for us." I had a map with me and discovered that Sarikamish was in Russian territory on the Black Sea, just beyond the Ottoman border.

We were up at four a.m. when the temperature was slightly below freezing, packed up our gear, and went on the road. It was clear on the first day when we covered ten kilometers. We walked at a pace that was designed to move well but not be overtiring or inducing sweat. One man dropped out from a torn ligament in his leg when he slipped on sharp stones during a detour over rocks. We ate sparingly of the smoked meat, dried fruit, and candy bars we carried. In the evening, we made a fire and heated snow for water. People were quiet and went to bed shortly after seven p.m. The temperature had dropped several degrees by that point so that ice was forming in puddles on the road.

The next morning, we were up again at four a.m. in temperatures that had dropped ten degrees, and the weather did not show any signs of improving all morning. At noon we crossed our first mountain pass, which was not high but rather steep. The road deteriorated appreciably, and our pace dropped accordingly. The commander, however, kept an even pace, even while the speed dropped, since we took shorter steps on the incline. Late in the day, we crossed a second hill line, and then we camped in about six inches of snow.

The temperature dropped again. We were all winded from the experience, and it took time to recover. After eating, we put up our light tents and tried to sleep, which was not at all comfortable because of the wind that howled around us. Not everyone had tents, so our small tent was assigned two additional people, a sergeant and a small recruit who could not have been more than fifteen. With the heavy clothing, no one guessed Amelia was a woman. They thought she simply had a funny voice, although she spoke little. We carried a small canvas sheet with us for a windbreak when we squatted for a bowel movement. Amelia used that as well when she had to pee, so no one noticed that feature of her either.

There were three more days of this hiking along a passage that was never a road anymore, usually only a trail and sometimes little more than an animal trace. The commander always had a trailblazer in front to locate a suitable hiking trail. He changed the person doing it regularly, as the person was exposed to the wind at times and demanded great attention to determine where the trail took unusual turns. It snowed softly off and on, as it does in cold weather, and the temperature stayed around zero degrees Fahrenheit. I thought about the wisdom of getting the Norwegian equipment, especially the boots, for I never had cold feet on the trek to Sarakamish. Neither did Amelia complain. In fact, neither of us complained about anything, as it took all our energy just to continue the journey day after day.

Finally, we came out on a hill line covered with pine growth, from which we could see in the distance the Black Sea. It was near dusk, and the sea itself seemed dark and foreboding. For the first time, we did not build a fire lest any population below us would notice since burning pine logs would certainly have announced our presence. The commander said the main body would be coming up the next day, and Amelia and I could stay there and wait for it, as it might have a few more amenities that would make life easier for us. The lieutenant had broken his arm the day before, and he was going to wait and go back with medical evacuees. We declined and said we felt safer staying with the unit. The commander shrugged and said, "As you wish. I know you will keep up."

It took two days to move along the hill line to bypass the small city of Sarikamish. Then we cut across the small coastal plain and, avoiding any residential areas, arrived at our destination to the south of the city, with the river on our left. The snow was about a foot deep there, so we dug into it and formed small igloo dwellings. Ours, located in a gully, had a ceiling of two feet with packed snow. We could not have any fires, but the lack of wind and the insulation from the snow kept the temperature near twenty-five degrees. By the standards we had experienced on the journey so far, it was comfortable.

The following day, we had nothing to do but wait. We might have been discovered by a man with a sled operating a trap line along the far side of the river, but he paid attention to his work and was in a hurry to get out of the cold. He wasn't there very long.

Other units were scheduled to fill in alongside us so that, eventually, Ottoman forces would ring the city. But no other units came, and while we kept a good eye on the ridge line, we saw no movement which would suggest that anyone else followed our markers. When we looked with field glasses, we could barely see activity that indicated a building up of snow trenches along the top of the ridge line in the place where we had emerged from the forest beyond. The commander surmised that Ottoman forces were congregating there for an attack straight down the long hillside. He complained to his first sergeant, "Why go to the trouble of developing a plan to encircle a city if you don't intend to do it? I wonder who changed the general's mind on this? A headlong rush into the city is not likely to work, as the distance is too far, and the attacking force will be seen long before it gets there. Russian forces will be waiting for them. The best they could do is cover the distance at night and attack at the city edge early in the morning."

The commander proved to be a prophet because the next morning, about ten o'clock, we watched as the mass of men at the top began their descent, not in clean, sharp, organized units but in a pell-mell rush to the bottom. While we could not see it, the Russians undoubtedly did come out to meet them because the long line of Ottomans flattened as it reached level ground, and the Ottoman soldiers began to build snow trenches at the edge of the city. It was at least two miles from our vantage point to the battle site, so the sound was not very distinct, but when the wind shifted slightly, the sound was apparent.

The sergeant and some of the men were anxious for us to join the battle, but the commander said it was not yet time. "We are scheduled to be the last into battle, coming in from the opposite direction of the major attack to disrupt the defenders from behind. We can't even get close enough to the city unless our forces drive deeper into the city."

 We stopped watching and rested ourselves. It was another cold day, with the temperature not rising above zero, but we were sheltered and warm in the snow caves we had built.

That night, the commander held a council with his sergeants, and there was consensus that a crucial part of the battle would be fought the next day, so we would move that night up the frozen river into the city and attack from the rear. We went to sleep knowing we would be on the move the next day and that we would be involved in the fighting by ten o'clock the next morning. Amelia and I rarely spoke during our entire trip, but we whispered to one another that night. Neither of us was particularly scared about losing our lives, but rather enduring the huge physical effort all this movement was going to thrust on us.

At two o'clock the next morning, long before dawn, we headed up the river and arrived at the city center, without incident, at five a.m. We climbed out over the river embankments and found ourselves just to the rear of Russian lines, in an enclave of several buildings. Near to us were trenches and tenting, indicating the presence of a sizeable Russian force. We dug in as best we could, although we did little more than move snow around. We lay down and rested, and I even managed to sleep for half an hour. I was already tired from the exertion of the river march, and I could see that Amelia was as well.

As dawn came up around seven a.m., snow began to fall. It snowed all day, and conditions continued to deteriorate. The commander put us in attack formation with Amelia and me to the rear, where we would be out of the way of operations. At his command, we moved forward and surprised the trench of Russians ahead of us. It took us fifteen minutes to cross the triple trench line that had been established. We created havoc as we went. The riflemen fired point-blank into the trenches as we crossed them, and the Russian soldiers there were not ready to respond. By the time we were halfway across, the Ottoman pickets understood what was happening and gave support as we came through. We found ourselves behind our own lines a half hour after starting.

Meanwhile, Ottoman troops had been roused, and they threw themselves into the breach we had made. Because of the disorder caused by our passing, they managed to break the Russian line. By noon, however, the falling snow had nearly obliterated all traces of activity, and the movement of troops became problematic. At that time, the Ottoman general decided it was time to end the attack and ordered a retreat. The temperature never reached zero for the rest of the day.

Our unit, which had not seen much fighting except in the morning, was designated as part of the rear guard, and we stayed on the trench line while the units around us disappeared one by one until we were alone on the battlefield. Our number was down to fifteen, but there was only one wounded soldier. He was able to walk with some help, so we prepared to leave. The commander had been deep in a trench looking at a map, discussing with a sergeant the best way out of the area. He decided where we would go and, coming out of the trench, led us to the southwest rather than along our previous trail to the southeast. We found our way to the top of the first ridgeline, where the snow was even deeper than in the city, and realized there was no way to advance further. Fortunately, we were not followed.

We dug into the snow and let it blow over us. The wounded man died that night from loss of blood, and we buried him in a snowbank. At seven a.m., the snow abated but promised to dump more on us, so we stayed put. A Russian patrol came by once but did not see us, although we could have fought it off. By noon, the commander had five men out searching for the entry to a trail that he envisioned would take us south to the Ottoman territory. A scout found it at five p.m., but the effort had been exhausting enough that we stayed in place to rest until morning. By then, enough snow had fallen so that even moving several feet was difficult. The snowshoes Amelia and I carried as part of our equipment were confiscated by the commander to be used by scouts to mark the trial ahead and for lookouts on our flanks. We covered only three kilometers that day.

The long time on the trial began to have a heavy impact on all of us. Everyone was cold and in danger of frostbite; we had no hot food since leaving Ottoman territory over a week earlier, and we were demoralized. The commander decided not to move for a day while we constructed small shelters of fallen branches packed with leaves and snow. He started a fire in two of the shelters, and people removed their boots and worked their feet to bring back circulation. Other parts of the body that were cold were warmed as well. Some of the meat we had was cooked, although there was not a lot left, so the meal was skimpy. By five p.m., we were all in relatively good shape and slept well before setting out again.

We covered five kilometers that day and six the next, discovering twenty bodies of Ottoman soldiers who had fallen out of their units and, unable to care for themselves, died of frostbite. All of us were disheartened by that. Then, we lost track of the days. All we knew was that the snow was never-ending and never seemed to get any warmer. We moved like zombies and ate the last particles of food we had with us. We drank snow water after that.

Then, one day, we came down a long pine-covered hill and saw a railroad train operating in the distance. We knew then that we had survived. Two hours later, a horse patrol came upon us, received the commander's information as to who we were, and left to inform the authorities. Two sleighs were sent out to take us to warm barracks, where there was hot food, baths, and beds. Amelia and I ate and then, stripping down, climbed into bed together and warmed each other till we fell asleep. We awoke in the middle of the night, took baths, and returned to nestle against one another again. By morning, we were warm again. Hallelujah.

The following morning, I saw the commander, and he said that the raid had been a total disaster, with over a third of the Corps lost in battle and to the terrible cold of the trip. The general was expected to be relieved of command. "It's not surprising," the commander said. "Think of us. We left with thirty-two people, and only fourteen of us returned. That is terrible. We were supposed to surprise them but could not. No wonder generals are losing their jobs; at least those that survived are. Well, I'm a captain, but tomorrow I'll be a major or a lieutenant colonel, and I will be happy enough because I prospered at others' expense." Before I left him, he said, "I wondered about you and that frail cameraman of yours and didn't think either of you would last the first day. I am amazed at the resiliency of both of you."

We took military transportation back from the front to Constantinople and wrote our reports as we traveled so that when we got back to our hotel, all we had to do was type them up and send them. But we both dreaded the censor and decided to do all that the following day. Amelia did call Werner to tell him she was all right, which put a smile on her face for the rest of the evening. But we were both in bed by eight p.m., as if we were still on the trail. However, Amelia went to her own bed this time, and that decision on her part–I am sorry to say-- disappointed me.

My report was on the movement of our reconnaissance unit, its action under fire, and finally, its retreat to Ottoman lines. It had some photos of the difficult terrain, the endless hills, and the flat plain that Sarikamish occupied. Amelia concentrated on the hardships of traveling, particularly the toll that the cold weather took on humans as they endured the journey. She had photos of early frostbite, of the broken arm of the lieutenant, and the bloody tendon of the early dropout. The most graphic, she showed the snow mounds of the Ottoman dropouts in the retreat. Neither of us mentioned casualties.

The censor was the same one as I had after the naval raid. He nodded and said, "Good morning Effendi. You've been traveling again and you've taken your colleague with you. Let's see what you have." He read slowly and looked intently at the pictures. He signed my copy without comment and then read Amelia's report. He looked at the photos twice and said, "Could these be Russian bodies rather than Ottoman bodies?"

Amelia understood the question and answered. "I am unsure, sir, they could have been from either side. We could simply label them as "frozen bodies of the fallen." The censor liked that, made the change to the script, and signed the form.

Twenty minutes after sending the reports, Boris responded. "Thank God both of you are all right. I have been worried about you, especially after the reports came in about the depth of the disaster. Your reports make more sense out of this action than any I have seen so far. You must be exhausted, so get some rest. Kisses, Boris."

Rest, Relaxation, and Reorganization

The routine of office of agency work reasserted itself after we returned from Sarikamish, or, at least, it did for me. Amelia did not readjust very quickly, and her transition back to the normal workload took over ten days. Even then, her work was sporadic. She spent more time with her camera and developing film, as well as reorganizing the photos that she had already collected. Alongside this, she spent much more time with Werner in clandestine meetings and was absent for several days at a time to be with him.

After her vacation with Werner in Bucharest, Amelia took it for granted that they had 'permission' to continue to meet if they kept the matter secret. When I raised the issue with her, saying that there had been a ruckus earlier about the affair with Werner, she said,

"That was because it was in the open; it is now totally hidden from the public. It will remain hidden unless you decide to make it public again. I am sure you would not do that to a colleague. Would you?" she demanded, which came across not as a question to be answered but as a demand or warning, that she would not tolerate.

I answered, saying, "Of course not, Amelia. But if someone publicly charges that an affair exists, I may have no choice but to confirm it. Please don't put me in that position."

"Posh," she exclaimed, "You are such a worry wort! It's not your life, so leave it alone! As for my work, you have nothing to complain about. I'm busy with the 'minority investigation.' If Boris insists on a detailed explanation of what I am doing, tell him that. If someone else makes the charge, then deny it. Actually, you do not have to deny or confirm anything. I don't work for you, in any case. Stop acting like I do."

Werner was still an aide to General von Sanders, so it is difficult to understand how he managed to find time for the number of midday meetings the two lovers arranged. It was all obvious to me, and it was beyond what could be expected of a woman with a professional career. I was almost certain the general would call me to complain again. The call never came, but I knew, intuitively, that the general did not like what was happening and was about to solve the problem his own way. 'Reassignment' was the most likely solution, so I calculated that within a month's time, Werner would find himself reassigned to Baghdad or Jerusalem.

Obviously, the relationship between Amelia and me suffered. We were not as friendly, even at lunches and during the few dinners we shared. She was building a private life centering on Werner and was willing to let our own relationship lapse if it got in the way. I once raised Protocol Number Two with her, which we had agreed to shortly before she met Werner. In that protocol, we agreed that if one of us became involved with a lover, both of us had a responsibility to continue our own relationship with kindness and goodwill.

She looked at me after I raised the issue and said, "My god, Marty, that was in another world and has little to do with the adult world we exist in today. Face reality." Then, to change the subject, and obviously embarrass me, she asked, "Have you gotten a letter from Janet lately, and are you any closer to deciding whether you are going to marry her or not? You should, you know, you both have one-track minds." I let the remark go without comment. The meal was over, so we left the restaurant and went our separate ways.

In early February, I got a call from Boris, who said that it was time for me to get out of Constantinople and spend a few days in Bucharest talking about the project and the changes in organization that were occurring throughout the *Tribune* system. I tried to beg off, saying I had too many irons in the fire and that some crucial ones needed my attention just then. He was unsympathetic, answering that he had not seen much reporting from Amelia in the past two weeks. Why couldn't she look after some of these matters?

In any case, he said, "The subject is not up for debate. There are important matters that need to be addressed, so catch the train tomorrow morning and get here as soon as you can. Turn everything over to Amelia, as she needs the responsibility." He did not spend any time after that on 'small talk,' but did tell me that I needed a clean suit and some dress shirts, as the first part of the stay would be business. The last part would be given over to relaxation. "You need it, Marty. All work and no play make Jack a dull boy." He ended the call.

Amelia was going out with Werner that evening and did not like it when I found her primping after I finished the call with Boris. When I explained, she sighed deeply and said, "Can't this wait until morning, Marty? I must get ready to see Werner. He's found an exquisite restaurant, and we want to do a little celebrating."

"Sorry, Sis," I said, "But Boris wants me on the first train out. It leaves at six a.m. You know that work comes before your personal life, so drop what you are doing, and let's go over what needs to be covered. It will not take long, and then it will be out of the way. I am going to have to work half the night just to clean up what needs to be done tomorrow."

She scarcely paid attention to my instructions in the half hour it took to explain what jobs needed her attention in the next several days. She said, "Yeah, yeah, I get it," or "Oh, really, why does that need to be done? It could wait until you return." The second time she said, "It could wait," I said, "Hey, Sis, I don't remember giving you static when you took off to meet Werner in Bucharest when I covered all your stories for you. How about returning the favor, whether you want to be cooperative or not?"

She grunted and said, "Okay, I suppose so, but it's all so inconvenient. Boris always does things at the last minute and wants instant compliance. Why don't you stand up to him, Marty? One would think you are afraid of him."

That riled me a little, and we had a tense conversation for a few minutes, but I finally got her on topic again and finished the instructions I had for her. But the time it took away from her primping was crucial for her, so she was late getting ready. Werner was a little early but clearly did not like that he had to wait. He sat in the office in Amelia's chair and swiveled in impatience. When

Amelia came out of the bedroom, he said in German, "Finally ready," and she replied, "Talk to him about it, not me." They left without any further conversation.

I did not see Amelia in the morning when I left at four a.m., as she was not back by then. That was not surprising, as usually she came back about seven or eight a.m.

I slept most of the trip to Bucharest, perhaps because the train was slow and there were several intermediate stops. The train arrived in the late afternoon, where I was met at the station by one of Boris's aides. He took me to the correspondent's hotel, which was a step or two in quality above the one we occupied in Constantinople. After checking in, the aide took me to the hotel restaurant, where two correspondents were waiting for us. Both were veteran reporters for East European affairs and immediately said the Ottomans were 'shitheads,' and that "it must be hard working among such 'fuckers.'"

I laughed and said, "Hell, guys, you know how it is. We can get used to hell if we're there long enough." They laughed as well, and one asked, "What was it like to go on a raid into a Russian harbor without any real protection? My God, they left you naked."

"Frankly, I didn't notice that was the case until the raid was over." That opened the conversation, which lasted over an hour, while we ate and then adjourned to the bar for a beer. They talked about their close calls as well, especially in the preceding Balkan Wars two years earlier. They had early morning assignments, so we parted. Surprisingly, after all the sleep I had on the train, I was still tired, so I excused myself and went to bed. I did try to contact Amelia to see how she was doing, but there was no answer, so I decided to try again in the morning.

I was up at seven a.m. and was at breakfast at about seven forty-five when Frank, the aide, arrived. He said we had an eight-a.m. meeting with Boris, and Boris had asked that we arrive on time. So we hurried to the *Tribune* printing plant and went into the publisher's offices, which were well furnished, with oil paintings on the walls. We went directly past the receptionist, through the staff office of Boris, and quickly into his office. It was exactly eight o'clock when the door closed behind me, and I stood before Boris's desk. He was standing, reading a typed paper, with his suit coat on a chair nearby and his sleeves rolled up. He had a cigarette in his hand, as usual, although I noticed he did not twitch as much. The doctor had given him some medicine to take care of that affliction.

"Thanks for being so punctual, Marty," he said with a slight smile. "It's nice to see you again." Then he went to the door, called a secretary, and said to her, "This is ready to go. Get it to the editor's office, would you? Thanks." He returned and sat at his desk, motioning me to take a chair in front of his desk.

"Yesterday at eight a.m., a team of two employees from this office knocked on the door of your team office in Constantinople, expecting to find Amelia Caruthers there. No answer, so they returned at nine, ten, and eleven o'clock, but still no answer. At noon, as they were about to knock again, Amelia arrived in an evening gown and with a bad hangover."

I knew then that this meeting was not going to be pleasant, and I knew, by reference to a 'team office,' that it was not simply Amelia's conduct that was at issue. I was due for a rough time as well. But I do not like to do the accuser's work for him, so I remained quiet to discover what was going to be said next. I did not have to wait long.

Boris said, "When the team identified itself, Amelia said, "O, shit, I'm in trouble now. How about you people disappear until five o'clock when I will have slept a little and be able to deal with you." The team left and informed me of what happened. "Tell me, Marty, what do you think about what happened?"

I hate being put on the spot, and my tendency is to say as little as possible. "I'm surprised that happened." I bit my tongue lest I say more.

Marty continued, "About the time you were rolling into the Bucharest train station, I called Amelia and read her the evaluation I had for her. You might like to see it before we go further." He passed over a carbon copy of her evaluation. It started with the statement that Amelia had failed repeatedly to fulfill the duties of a reporter-photographer, had systematically alienated others, including potential sources of information, had concentrated on personal matters to the great detriment of her work, and had taken advantage of the goodwill of others to do what little satisfactory work she had done. The recommendation was that she be dismissed as a reporter. Her work as a photographer had been satisfactory but was by no means as advanced as might be expected given the opportunities she had. The Sarikamish trip was mentioned as a specific case where she had failed badly. If it was decided to keep her as a reporter, it should only be on probationary status.

After reading it, I passed it back. I said nothing. He finally asked, "Your reaction?"

"I guess I understand your reasoning," I replied. "From my perspective, she has done some things right and is growing in her role. On the Sarikamish Campaign, for example, she showed considerable endurance, dedication, and commitment."

"Well, of course, she did," said Boris with some annoyance. "She bravely volunteered, not realizing what she was getting into, and then had to perform miracles to get out of a situation that she didn't want to be. And at the end, you wrote most of her report. She provided you with a set of mundane photographs that you could have taken with a hand-held camera yourself."

Boris paused again as if to allow me to speak. I did not. So he said, "After I read the evaluation to her, I asked her why she had not been at the office in the morning when she was expected to be. She answered with considerable impatience: 'Obviously, I wasn't expecting an invasion force. My social engagement ran later than I thought it would, and I did not think it would really matter. One does not always get it right. Marty would not care, why should you?'"

Again, I did not respond, and Boris said, "Is that true, Marty, that you wouldn't have cared?"

I said, "No, that is not correct, for I do care. She is rarely late for work because of her social engagements. She sees me as the watchman, and once I was gone, she thought she was scot-free. This is not my fault. I do not want either you or Amelia thinking that I am the guilty party. I meet my obligations and expect her to meet hers. Almost always, she does."

"You're right, Marty," Boris said, "This is not your problem, but hers, even if at times you seem to enable her."

I did not like the aspersion of guilt that he gave me anyway, so I said, "Well, Boris, I did not hire her as a reporter, nor was I asked whether I thought she could do the job. If asked, I would have voiced reservations. Since then, I have worked with her without complaint and tried my best to develop her; what more would you like?"

There was a short silence, and then he said. "Right again, Marty. Well, in any case, I told her she was suspended until her case was reviewed when a final decision would be made. We have almost done that. Let me ask you, Marty, whether you know of anything that would be important enough to keep her?"

Without hesitation, I said. "The Ottoman Empire is likely to implode from the pressures this war will put on its social structure. Great Britain will peel away the Arabs with modest difficulty, but it will be the Greeks and Armenians who will have the most difficulty. They will bear the brunt of Turkish animosity and bad feeling that has been there for decades. There are reports that Armenians are not answering their draft notices. To her credit, Amelia recognizes this and has amassed a collection of several hundred newspaper and magazine clippings concerning incidents of this type. It would be worth three months, I think, on a temporary contract, to get some initial results. If it's valuable, the temporary contract could be extended. Otherwise, she would be finished."

Boris listened, rubbed his hands over his face, and said, "So you did come up with something to save her after all. I knew you would. But I will admit it is worth considering. I will say 'yes' if you agree to let her do her own work and you remove yourself to your own quarters away from her. She is poison, Marty, and I do not want you covering for her anymore. Do you agree?"

That was a hard proposition to agree to. She was more than a friend to me, and I did not want to part with her despite her obsession with Werner in recent days. But I knew in that instant that, unless I agreed to his caveat, then she would not get the temporary contract and that my own future with the *Tribune* would be in jeopardy as well. So I said, "Yes, I agree. But chances are that she will not take the temporary contract."

But I was wrong. Boris called while I sat in the office and told her that she was no longer employed with the *Tribune* as a reporter and photographer. But she would be offered a temporary contract for working as a reporter on the 'Greek-Armenian' project and as a collection archivist for photographs for three months beginning immediately. She was still allowed local expenses, but her hotel room would be smaller. She was to no longer report to me but to the new office manager, and her hours would be regulated.

After the conversation was complete, Marty gave me the phone and left the room. I wondered how Amelia would react to me, and I was ready to deal with her persona as the independent woman who wanted to tell the world to 'go to hell.' However, she said, "I really messed up, didn't I, Marty? I'm so sorry to put you in such a bad spot. You've saved me several times and really helped me, so I know you did the best you could. The temporary contract was your idea, wasn't it?"

I said it was, and she said. "I would like simply to go home, but I can't do that and show up with my tail between my legs. Besides, I dread going back to becoming a still photographer in Winston-Salem. Three months will give me a chance to set some things right. Boris has made it clear that he wants you and me to cut the cord, and I understand completely, although it will be hard to do. I should say goodbye to Werner as well because he is far too serious, and I have no great yen to live in Germany as a *Hausfrau*." She broke the connection, and I felt as depressed as I had ever felt.

Boris disappeared at lunchtime, and the aide took me to the cafeteria to eat. Afterward, there was an hour-and-a-half briefing for me when the new organization for the *Tribune* was described. The *Berliner Tagesblatt* and the Bucharest edition of the *Tribune* were creating an agency to gather news in the East, with local offices initially in

Vienna, Budapest, Warsaw, Bucharest, and Constantinople. At each office, there would be an office director, his translator and aide, an assistant for reporters, a photo archivist, and a document archivist, with these expenses shared equally among the two newspapers. Reporters would be assigned to these places as needed by the two newspapers, and the newspapers were responsible for their expenses. Our team was already in place in Constantinople, and when I returned, I would be part of that organization, nominally reporting to the office manager. Reporters would receive their assignments from a senior reporter with due recognition of the strength of the reporters themselves.

I asked lots of questions and, as the day wore on, was convinced that I would not like the new arrangement very much. I couldn't put my finger on the problem exactly, but ultimately decided that I wanted to be free to make my decisions as I saw fit. Now, I would be part of an organization where I would be much more accountable than I had ever been.

At four o'clock, I was ushered again into Marty's office, who had several editors with him, only one of whom I recognized by voice. But they all knew me. Boris said, "Marty's been through a rough day, people, so let's cheer him a little." He turned to me and handed me a paper. It read, "This certifies that your work is of outstanding value to this organization, and it is with great pleasure that you are promoted to senior correspondent, with all the privileges and remuneration such position entitles you."

I guess I looked puzzled because everyone laughed. But someone thrust a glass of champagne in my hand, and another person yelled, "Toast." We drank. Then it hit me that I was going to have as much freedom as I ever had and would not have to put up with the problems of the office. Later, when I realized that my salary had nearly doubled, I realized it was a promotion worth having.

The following day, I took my bonus cheques and back pay and went to Greece. I spent four days in Athens and later visited the island of Pylos, where the houses are built up hillsides, because the islands are so narrow. I had formed a liaison with a schoolteacher from Florida, whom I met at the Acropolis in Athens, and we lived together for the next five days on Pylos. Obviously, I did not want to go back to Constantinople at the end of the vacation, and neither did the woman want to go back to Florida. But my job beckoned, and she thought she owed it to her husband, which was the first time I heard that she had a husband. But then, neither of us knew the last names of each other.

Chapter Four

Traveling Around the Empire

A Baffling Homecoming

Things changed in Constantinople when I returned from consultation and leave. For once, I felt rested, and I enjoyed the trip back, first by boat to the mainland and then by train to the city itself. I wired ahead that I was coming, and I was met at the train station by a car and driver. Tribune operations had upgraded considerably and even had a leased car for routine business.

The driver did not know who I was and assumed I was a visitor to the office, so when he discovered that I knew Turkish, he tried to point out sites of interest. Constantinople is a beautiful city, especially in the sector where the palaces and museums are located. Topkapi Palace alone is worth ten days in Berlin or Paris. The views along the Bosporus are stunning–in another way–than the rivers and bridges of Paris. Of course, I knew everything from my visits and stays in the city. I almost corrected the driver on some of his observations, which he had entirely wrong, but I held my tongue as I always do when someone makes a mistake like that.

My make-shift office, carved out of Amelia and my living quarters, had been left behind, and the new operations had office space some distance away near a much better hotel. The office was in a multi-office complex, but our suite was located off the main entrance, with lettering larger than the other tenants. The office was manned by a manager, an interpreter-aide, two typists, the driver, of course, and several functionaries whose duties I could only guess. All were

Slavic except the interpreter-aide, a female, who was a Turk who had spent considerable time in Europe. The manager was European, I would guess either Polish or Czech, with the name John Bylice. He had an office, as did his interpreter assistant, while the typists operated in a partially closed-off area exclusive to them.

There was a roomy area marked 'reporters' with five small desks in it. There were three typewriters, all vintages with European keys. The typists in the other room had new machines, so I immediately noted the difference. I also noted that there were no machines with Turkish keys, but, if there were, they were located somewhere else.

There were no reporters in the office at the time, which I found odd. Kurt Langer, the *Tagesblatt* reporter, certainly should have been there, and Boris had told me that three or four others were due to join us 'momentarily.'

There were windows. The rooms were bright and airy, and the office had a 'buzz' about it that indicated good things were happening. People seemed relaxed and were working on tasks that were causing them no difficulties. I sensed busyness, but I reminded myself that busyness is not necessarily purpose. The interpreter aide greeted me by name but did not introduce herself, which I thought was not right, but I was willing to overlook the gaffe in the interest of office harmony. She took me to the reporter's room, where she suggested I wait until the manager was ready to see me, which, she said, would not be very long as he was just finishing some important matters that could not wait.

She turned to go, but I stopped her by saying. "This is strange that there are no office supplies on the desks here. How do people work?

Where are the ink pots, paper, and pencils? How do people get any work done without office supplies?"

She turned, facing me, and looked at me with considerable surprise as if to say, 'Why are you interested in such trivia at a time like this?' "I'll have a pad and some pencils brought to you immediately." Pointedly, she had avoided the gist of my question.

She turned again to exit the room, but I interrupted her again. I asked her where the photo archives were located. She paused, frowned slightly, and said it would be better to raise that matter with the manager, who preferred to answer questions of the organization himself. She then left. A male functionary, who did not introduce himself, brought me a paper pad and two sharpened pencils, as well as a fresh cup of tea and a scone. I wondered, 'where the hell did they get the scone?' I had never seen another one in the city since I had been there. But it tasted good.

As I jotted down some thoughts on my new paper pad, I wondered why the reporters' working area looked like it had never been used. It could only be that way if, indeed, none of the reporters had been there. The office had been open for at least two weeks. Why would that be true?

The manager kept me waiting twenty-eight minutes, which I knew he would. He was not doing some 'important' tasks but letting me 'cool my heels' to show that he could do so. He could not let it be half an hour because I might fuss at that. He wanted to tame me, not anger me. Sometimes there is a fine line. But I knew what his game was, so I sat back and waited, looking out of the window at the passing scene, which had a view of a street and the enormous amount of traffic that was on it. I noticed that the number of horse-driven vehicles had risen, which indicated that the war was sending petroleum prices up, and people were adjusting accordingly. I was in a reverie about other changes that would soon occur when one of the typists came to tell me, "Mr. Bylice, will see you now." She addressed me in English. Again, she did not introduce herself. I was beginning to get the picture that I was regarded as a simple visitor, not an integral part of the office.

I walked into the office, and Bylice came out from behind a large desk, which was loaded with all sorts of paper piles. I could not imagine that the office had generated so much work in the short time it had been open. Bylice was of medium build with a good physique as if he either did running or worked out in a gym. He had curly black hair, worn medium length. He wore a suit that was cut in European fashion and wore exquisite Italian boots. His handshake was everything that popular magazines would have recommended: firm grip, meaningful shake, and quick withdrawal.

In a well-modulated voice, he greeted me in English, saying. "My congratulations, Marty–I am sure you will allow me to call you that– on your promotion to senior correspondent. You will give real status to our developing newsroom."

I had been away from the Ottoman world for two weeks and was thinking in English and knew that I needed to begin thinking in Turkish again. In fact, I had begun talking Turkish at the railroad station. So I responded in Turkish, saying, "You will excuse me, Jon, but I prefer Turkish because I must use it every day. Do you mind.?"

His face reddened a bit, and he said in poor Turkish, "Sorry, Turkish is not a real working language for me yet. Would German do instead?"

Having leveled the playing field, I answered with a smile. "Well then, if that is the case, we can use English. I am happy to be home again and am sorry I was not here to welcome you to Constantinople when you first arrived."

He had trouble readjusting after my language ploy, so I pressed my advantage. "I was told that we were to have several new reporters when I arrived back and ....also, that there was an aide for the reporters. I did not see anyone of that nature when I arrived. What's happening that everyone is gone?"

He tried to catch up with my conversation shifts, and it was apparent that his plan of 'taming' me at the first meeting was flying away quickly. "We have only two other reporters–Langer for the *Berliner Tagesblatt*, who is out on assignment just now, and a young Greek journalist who covers local affairs. He has the morning off for a dental appointment. As for the reporter's assistant, she is busy with a task for me just now. When she is available, I will have her introduced."

I answered, "Well if she's a reporter's aide and is not busy with some other reporter's request just now, let's have her meet me in the next hour or so, as I have some things I would like some help with. Okay?"

He opened his mouth as if to say something, but I gave him no opportunity. "Do you mind if I sit while we talk?" I sat in the chair that was there for guests and said "good" when I was seated. John remained standing. I opened my briefcase and proffered him about ten pages of handwritten copy. "Could you have a secretary type this for me? It's a thought piece that I promised Boris, and it needs to go out today." Then, as he took the papers and stood there wondering what to do, I said: "I asked your aide where the photo archives are located, and she avoided the question–which incidentally I did not like, nor did she ever identify herself–and said you would tell me. Can you?" I stopped talking.

Jon, or John, as he called himself, was momentarily speechless and merely stood clutching the papers I had given him. So then I remembered that there might be messages for me, so I said, "Also, are there any messages for me? Could you have them brought to me right away?"

He suddenly moved as if he had finally decided how to manage the whirlwind that had entered his office. He walked out the door and disappeared for five minutes. At first, I just sat there, but then I looked at the papers on his desk, which was near where I was sitting. They were in German and, from the little I could ascertain from the title page of one pile, dealt with Czech attitudes towards the war. How did this relate to our work? I was puzzled.

When Jon returned, his aide preceded him. She said, in English, "I apologize if you thought I was reluctant to answer your question, Mr. Mintz. I did not realize that you needed the information so urgently. My English name is Cynthia Cevdet." She stopped talking.

I said, in Turkish, "Good to meet you, Cynthia. So, where are the photo archives? Or is that a secret?"

She blushed and said, "It's no secret, Mr. Mintz, and I am sorry if you thought I implied that. It's on the floor above us while we hunt for an appropriate place, as it is warm there, and photos cannot tolerate the summer when it comes."

"Thank you, Cynthia," I said, "Will I find Amelia Caruthers there?"

"I'm afraid not, Martin," interjected Jon. "She works from her hotel room and only comes in when I want to check on her work." His poor Turkish was good enough to understand my conversation with his aide. He handed me a handful of letters and messages.

"But part of her contract calls for her to develop the photo archives section. When does she do that?" My remarks were addressed directly to Jon.

"I decided that work could be done just as easily by someone else, so that part of her contract has never been activated."

I had no way of knowing Amelia's feelings on the matter, but the picture that was emerging of Amelia's role in this project sounded as if she was being isolated from it completely. But I needed to talk with her first to ascertain whether that was true and whether she approved of the apparent isolation."

"Okay," I answered, "You are aware, of course, that Amelia's contract was carefully worked out between Boris and me when I was in Bucharest, and it was done with due consideration of her talents and experience? Is Boris in accord with your decision not to use her in the photo archives?"

"Not to put too fine a point on it," Jon responded, "Staff assignments are mine to make, so any previous arrangements are subject to my judgment. I think Boris would concur with my interpretation."

"Okay," I responded. "Will you please get the contact information for her? I need to talk with her about several matters."

"She is at the press hotel. I am sure you remember the number." Jon's answer was very cool as if he felt it wrong of me to want a simple address. Then I realized he felt I was directing him to do mundane tasks he regarded as beneath his dignity and that the near refusal to give me any information at all was his way of telling me that. I did not take the bait. Instead, I replied as if I thought his answer was everything I thought it should be.

"Yes, I do," I answered. "That is a big help." I thumbed through my letters and messages. There were about ten envelopes, with only two of them personal—one from Aunt Bea and one from Janet Everett. Among the telephone messages were requests from the offices of Enver Pasha, General Liman von Sanders, and Admiral Souchon to call as soon as I arrived back in the city. I held them up for Jon to see and said, "Here are three extraordinarily important messages that should have been given to me the minute I walked in the door. Jon, I understand that you want to run an efficient office, but this is a news agency. Let's see whether it can be run like one. Please assign someone, preferably your aide, who is listed as a translator, to make some appointments with these people. Major news articles could materialize from those interviews."

Then I stood up as if getting ready to leave. "Jon, when do the reporters meet next for assignments?"

He said, "There is not a set time. I meet with them individually and make their assignments when they come to the office."

"Well, as a senior reporter in a newsroom, it's my job to be part of that discussion," I replied with a serious voice as if insisting on my prerogatives. "That's the way newsrooms are run, and I am loath to depart from tradition." I had had enough of this office for now, and I did not want to proceed further lest I lose my temper over the lack of concern with the newspaper business. I decided to leave.

I said, "Now, I need to get to my hotel. Jon, can you have someone take me there or at least direct me to where it is?" I moved past the manager and the aide and exited the large room where no one was working. It was apparent that they were all trying to listen at the door to the drama that had just unfolded.

However, the driver was there in a trice and had my luggage with him. "This way, Effendi," he said in Turkish. I followed him. Everyone in the office was standing there looking at me as though a ghost had suddenly appeared in their midst, and they had no idea how they were supposed to react.

My hotel accommodation consisted of a suite with a bedroom, a large sitting room, and a bathroom, all nicely decorated. All my clothes and other belongings had been transferred there, and even the typewriter was in the sitting area. The hotel staff members were all very pleasant, and I was handed a small packet of correspondence. I thumbed through it quickly and found nothing of immediate import. So I used the facilities and then laid down for a quick nap, thought a few minutes about the teacher from Florida with whom I had spent five wonderful days, and fell asleep, which lasted two hours. When I awoke, the phone was nearly jumping off the hook.

It was Boris. "God damn it, Marty. You have John all upset, and I have been on the phone since you left, calming him and trying to make some sense out of his complaints and ranting. I'm at a loss. Tell me what the problem is?"

"Sure, Boris," I said. "I had a fine time in the Greek Isles. Thanks for asking. Your demand that I take a vacation worked wonders on my disposition, even if Jon doesn't think so. But then he tried to tame me too quickly and put me in my place. When I entered the office, his aide refused to tell me where Amelia was, and John decided to keep me cooling my heels for half an hour. So, I know when I am being manipulated and strike back. You know that."

Boris answered, "Did he really keep you waiting half an hour."

"More like twenty-eight minutes, which is close and shows the same intent. I could not see whether the important matters he was occupied with and whether they were real, but I suspect it was all a ruse to justify his desire to make me wait and be compliant. But he does have other work that is certainly interfering. On his desk, he had several manuscripts dealing with the Czechs and the war. My guess is that the typists, all central European, were working on that rather than anything dealing with news gathering in the Ottoman Empire."

Boris was not in a good mood. I could tell because he does not ordinarily curse or swear. "Dammit, you are imagining things. He's hired to run a newspaper office, not do odd jobs for central Europeans or for you either."

I interrupted before he could go further. "Moreover, I don't think there has been a reporter in the office, as the space set aside was vacant and did not show any signs of use. You've seen their work areas. They are always so cluttered and messy with half-eaten food that one nearly vomits. There were no office supplies, and I had to ask for a paper pad and pencils, so one pad and two pencils were finally brought to me. There is no sign of anyone else, and when I asked, I was told the others were on assignment or at the dentist. I'll bet you, Boris, that when I go to the old hotel, I will find the *Tagesblatt* reporter still there."

"Shit, Marty," uttered Boris. "You are about the worst human being I have ever met. You are obviously making this up as you go. If you weren't such a good reporter, I'd fire your ass right now! Straighten up and get along with other people!"

Being called 'hard to get along with' is a term that has sometimes been applied to me, but I don't let it bother me too much since I'm usually on the right track when I have arguments that lead to the use of that epithet. I knew Boris would not exactly thank me later but that he would see justice in my remarks. So I plowed on. "Well, Boris, this office did not give me my mail until after I was in the manager's office when I specifically asked for it. Guess what I found there? Three telephone calls from the three most important officials in the city–the German admiral, the German general, and the Ottoman Minister of War. They should have been called to my attention the minute I stepped into the office, or better still, have been gotten to me when I was in the Greek Isles. All three wanted to see me immediately. The office staff has no idea how to run a news office."

"Jesus, Marty, now we're into your appointments," said Boris defensively. I suppose you are saving the treatment of your protégé until last."

"Actually, I wasn't going to say anything about it," I said, pleased that the subject had been raised, "but now that you've inquired about her, I have a question. "How come she's not allowed to come to the office, and the part of her contract giving her charge of the photo archives has been scrapped? I know you were aggravated with her, but I didn't think you would isolate her and not let her do the things she came to the project originally to do. That's really shitty."

"I'm sure that's not true, Marty," Boris answered, "Why would I make a contract and not fulfill it?" You know I do not operate that way. You owe me an apology."

"I'll apologize after you check out what I have said."

Boris ignored my last remark but said, "Oh, hell," Boris said, "I've had enough of all this. You have ruined a perfectly good day when I was going to get a lot of things done. Now you have said your piece, so let me do some checking with Jon. All this is your 'touchiness' and 'inability to get along with others.' You are too much of a cross to bear at times." He was no longer swearing, so I suspected that he was believing what I was telling him. He said, "Stay away from the office today, and I'll call you this evening after I've talked with him again. Anything more?"

"No," I said, "enough is enough. I'm sorry your day is ruined, but you called me."

He answered with a slight chuckle, "I did call you, didn't I." Then he said something I clearly did not expect. "Amelia will not be ostracized; I can assure you." He broke the connection.

I went to my mail and spent the afternoon reviewing it all. First, there were the letters from home. Aunt Bea had little to say of importance, but it was nice to be brought up to date on family happenings. However, she was still very much exercised about my sister and her beau. She said:

> Last week, when he came to see your sister, he brought two members with him from his congregation, and they brought their Bibles and their tracts. When they were introduced to the family in the living room, they went into their spiel about Armageddon, the final days, and all sorts of other matters that they took out of context from the Good Book. All of us family members were at first too polite to say much, but when they got to the issue of blood transfusions, your father said that they should stop talking as he had heard enough. He told them that the family is Lutheran and views religion according to the teachings of Martin Luther, not the Watch Tower.

> He said, as well, that it had been interesting to hear the views of the Society but that it was not very polite of 'you people' to invade our home and make us listen to something that was abhorrent to us. "Please do not do it anymore! Now, if you want to stay while we have some popcorn, you are welcome to do that. Otherwise, we will say goodnight."

> They left, but your sister stayed. She was furious, saying that her dad had been rude and that her beau might break with her for such behavior. She said that when that happened, she might

as well go to a nunnery, as it was apparent that she was going to be an old maid. The beau came by the next night and said that your sister should leave home as she was with a very dogmatic family that would cause her to be sentenced to perdition. But you know your sister. She got her dander up on that and told him to leave and not come back. She cried for a whole day, but afterward said her romance with the 'fanatic' had really been a wake-up call. I nearly shouted 'Hallelujah' and 'Amen.'

The letter from Janet Everett continued the theme she had introduced in the last letter about leaving my profession and coming back to the Carolinas to be with her. The key portion of her letter said:

Marty, I have talked this matter over with others at the country club, at the church, and among our friends, and they all agree that you are being unduly resistant to common sense and that a war zone is not the right place to be right now. They have all seen horrible pictures of the fighting in Flanders that is terribly upsetting, and all of us do not want you to be caught up in it. If you have a choice, why are you so stubborn about it? Come home where you will be safe.

I still miss you like crazy, you know, and long for you to be with me. If you were here, we could work out the differences between us. I know that I could persuade you to see me as your life's partner instead of that girl from Fort Mill, who is obviously not a very moral person, if she carries on with a German soldier. Don't carry a torch for her, but come home and make a life with me.

There were three other letters that were interesting. One, from the (London) *Times*, which was postmarked late June, asked whether I was interested in a correspondent's position in the Middle East and cited my knowledge of Arabic as the reason for the request. It was too out of date to be worthy of an answer. Another, dated more recently, was from the *New York Times*, which wanted to know whether I was interested in coming into their stable of correspondents working on international affairs, particularly the Near and Middle East. The third letter was from Emile Boudoin, my former boss in Cairo, who inquired about my health and said that, if I weren't already employed, he would be interested in talking with me about work on his team of reporters from the *Tribune.* I put that aside to answer when I had more time. The remainder of the messages were chaff to be disposed of at will. I was tempted to throw them out but then remembered it better to burn such missives in troubled times.

It was ten p.m. when Boris called again. He said, "The reporter from the *Berliner Tagesblatt* has been hammering the editorial staff in Berlin about the overgrown 'monstrosity,' he called it, that constituted the manager and his office staff. The reporter said he was only waiting for you to return before he asked for recall, hoping you might force some change. His complaints match yours. The *Tagesblatt* says that unless the change is immediate and meaningful, it will withdraw from the joint office concept. Don't you gloat, you son-of-a-bitch!"

He continued without waiting for an answer. "I talked with Jon about the 'Czech job' that was taking priority, and he explained it was leftover work from a previous job this unit had done in Brno. We hired the outfit with the understanding editing and typing of that manuscript would be completed as time permits, but we had no idea it was so large and invasive. We are working out compensation arrangements. However, the work is finished, and full attention will be given to the needs of our project. There will be no other priorities at all. Again, I do not want to hear, "I told you so!"

I had no intention of saying anything like that, even though I certainly thought it.

Boris continued, "I also talked with him about the treatment you got when you came in. He responded that he did, indeed, try to intimidate you since I had said 'he is a handful' and 'needs a lot of attention.' Given that description, he thought it best to get the upper hand immediately.

"He said he now fully understands what I meant and that he also understands that there was nothing that you said or did that was not correct or justified. He confessed that you were the consummate professional who had expectations and who had not received them in his newsroom. He assured me he would mend fences and work for a cooperative working relationship.

"He said that his aide was at the point of turning in her resignation because she had not met even your minimum expectations, and she regretted that deeply. He said that he must do the same sort of thing with the *Tagesblatt* reporter, who also is a 'handful.' The manager said he just was not accustomed yet to newsmen of this caliber but that he would adjust." As for the future, he would like to have a meeting between him, you, and the *Tageblatt* reporter at noon tomorrow to lay out press expectations and the organization of the office to meet those expectations. You can be there, of course?"

"Yes, of course," I replied, "So long as it's not held in his office. Let's have it in the reporters' space. That gives us the advantage."

"I hadn't thought of that," Boris said. "You are right on the location of the meeting. Let's do that and find out how serious Jon is about cooperation."

Boris cleared his throat and paused. "Excuse me," he said. I knew the next item was one with which he was uncomfortable. "There's one other item," he finally said. "You were right about Amelia. She was ostracized on the notion that she was a 'troublemaker,' which was probably my label of her. Jon took the term too literally and kept her away from everyone. What do you want to be done about that, Marty? I suppose you will ask for her reinstatement?"

"No," I answered. "You fired her for cause, and the cause was right. She has a chance at redemption, so let's move her over to the new project office and see if she can earn her way back to responsibility. I am unsure about that, but it may be possible. She can be irresponsible and a real pain at times, but at other times, she is 'tough as nails' and does incredible work." Then I added, "I love the woman like a sister, as you know, Boris, but I am not blind to her faults."

After the phone call was over, I went over to the old hotel and found that my key still worked to let me into the room I once occupied. It was dark, and a voice came out of the dark that said, "Is that you, Marty?" I answered that it was, and she said, "Well, get into bed. I haven't had a good night since you left." I stripped down to my underwear, slipped in beside her, and felt her nestle into me. We fell asleep without any other comment.

Attempts at Reconciliation

"It's been like living in prison," Amelia said at breakfast, which was simply some cornflakes she had located in some out-of-the-way food stall. They were not even fresh. "I am required to be here between the hours of eight a.m. and six p.m. six days a week. I go only to the office to report what I have been doing on the Greek-Armenian project when Jon gives me instructions on what to do next.

"He has no idea what he is dealing with, yet he writes down long lists and expects me to address each one the next time. Mostly, he wants my information files organized by area and how they might be related. The events surrounding the people are not of any interest to him. He chided me once for saying there was no evidence of beatings by Turks among some Greeks in Ionia when I have at least ten photos clearly showing that to be true."

"What about your work on photo archives?" I asked.

"All my photographic equipment was taken from me, but the cameras were left here. All my photos were boxed up and removed."

"Well, how about tagging along with me today so we can see if things can't change for you? I'm sorry this has happened."

"No, Marty, I think I brought it on myself, and now I am paying the piper," she responded.

"Amelia, what is happening to you is wrong, and I will not abide it. You will not be treated this way anymore, I assure you. Boris is sorry it happened as well."

Then suddenly, she broke down, crying. "O Marty, that's not the worst of it. Werner has called it quits with me and was reconciled with his wife. She came down from Germany to be with him, and she brought the children, whom he adores. What chance do I have against that? The great celebration that aggravated Boris so much was Werner's great farewell to me. Werner only told me the following week. I am so ashamed and alone."

I tried to comfort her, but she drew away and went off by herself to regain her composure. When she returned, she said, "To think I thought of breaking it off with him. I guess one should not want something like that because it is a very painful thing."

The meeting that afternoon did not start on time. Instead, copies of the contract between the two newspapers were distributed, with copies in both English and German. We agreed to take half an hour to review them. The contract resolved most of our issues, and it was apparent that Jon had never read the document or understood its importance. Otherwise, he would not have created the office that he had.

It was language that proved to be the big stumbling block at the beginning of the session. Kurt Langer and I wanted the session held in Turkish, as we could communicate with one another best that way. The other newsman, Michael, the young Greek man from Smyrna, wanted that as well. I wanted Amelia included, who knew English, German, and passable Turkish so that she would have been at some disadvantage with simple Turkish. Jon insisted on either English or German, which he said were the languages of the project. I said the contract did not specifically state that but that it could be implied by the contract's existence in two languages. So we went with German and English and a person could speak in either. A translator would render everything in Turkish as well.

Jon assumed he would be the presiding chair, but Kurt pointed to a clause on such meetings that said the senior reporter would have that role. So I assumed the role, much to Jon's discomfort. I called for an agenda, and our points were quickly put together by Amelia. There were four points: support for reporters and the reporting process; functions supporting reporting such as file archives and photo archives; the relationship of the manager and reporters; and space allotments.

The meeting lasted two and a half hours and was contentious. Kurt felt especially aggrieved by Jon's past behavior and castigated him repeatedly. I thought at times Kurt might have been excessive in his remarks, but I remembered I had not been there, so I figured Jon had it coming. So, I never came to Jon's defense. Amelia spoke only once, heatedly at that, saying that Jon's interference in her reporting by trying to determine what she would write could never be permitted again. Twice, the Greek reporter spoke up to support points made by Kurt.

It was Amelia who helped resolve most issues by pointing out in the contract when certain matters under discussion were already covered by that document. The most important of these split the time of the aide-translator so that the reporters received as much time from her as Jon did, which displeased Jon, who said he had more important demands than those of the reporters. The same was true for space allotments, where Kurt demanded that the manager have no special favors and that his office be no better than that of the two senior reporters. It meant that Jon would have to surrender his. He was livid.

It reached a point where Jon said he had little left of his role, only managing the staff and finances and doing the bidding of the reporters. He said he had a good notion to resign. Kurt dared him to do that, citing a cablegram he had from Berlin, saying that if he (Kurt) were unhappy with the outcome of the meeting, the Berlin firm would withdraw from the agreement. I came to Kurt's defense immediately and said that if Jon wanted to resign, he was welcome to do that, but that Kurt's mandate was clear and that I supported it. Michael and Amelia supported it as well. Jon backed down, saying he needed time to consider such a weighty decision.

The final debate was over the aide translator and who would have the first call on her. Jon wanted that first call, but Kurt wanted the reporters to have priority. I dissented for the only time, saying that the matter should be left to the aide translator herself to work out the matter, realizing the demands from several directions on her. The even-handedness of the aide herself in providing translations for the meeting was viewed with favor by everyone, so even Kurt supported my final motion on the matter.

After the meeting, I met with Jon at my desk, and we discussed the dismantling of his office and that of the aide translator for reconfiguration into a semi-open space equivalent to that of the reporting area. Jon did not see that it was necessary to do that, despite our earlier discussion, and said it was the final straw that meant his resignation. He was heated and drew the attention of those around us, so I decided that this was not the place for such a conversation. I invited him to go to an outdoor restaurant nearby, where we could talk without the entire staff listening to our conversation. He agreed.

At the café, he was no longer as livid as he had been in the office, so I tried a new tact with him, leaving the contentious subjects behind. I said, "New relationships are difficult, and those that experience immediate difficulties are hard to repair. Still, you and I must work on accommodation and learn to be civil with one another. That will help us work out some understanding of how to manage problems without the difficulties we are experiencing now. Let's see whether we can work out a simple guideline to get us through the first month, shall we? Are you agreeable?

He replied, "Of course. What you have just said makes a great deal of sense."

"Good," I responded. "First of all, get rid of your threat to resign every time something does not go your way. Someone is going to take you seriously, and you are going to be out of a job. As you are aware, both Kurt and I have great influence on our publishers and a serious request for your removal will have you gone by the end of the day. That is the equivalent of your threat to resign, and Kurt has threatened to use it today. So my proposal is that neither one ever be used as a bargaining chip in our discussions."

"He said, "I did not know what I was getting into when I agreed to be the director for this office, and if I had known, I would never have accepted. I suppose my threats to resign reflect my frustration of not really being 'in charge.' Who could blame me?

"Understood," I said, "But a threat is good only once. Repeat it, and it is no longer a threat but an admission that you have no power to force a decision. You are going to have to find another way to get what you want done. Try persuasion or even, heaven forbid, manipulation. But, of course, for those tactics to work, one needs to have personal relationships, and you have yet to develop them to any degree."

"But developing such relationships is a long and difficult task," he said. "I am not sure that I can develop them with any of the reporters. Somehow, we all got off on the wrong foot, and repairing such hard feelings is very difficult to overcome."

"Yes, it is," I said, "But if it is important, you will find some way of doing it. You need to broaden your range of personal skills. There is no reason you cannot do it, but it will take perseverance. I will try to start you off by trying to establish a good relationship between the two of us. I will always be civil in conversations. I will often seek your advice on important matters that confront me where I need advice, expecting you to listen and give good counsel. I will not talk behind your back, and I will always speak of you in positive terms with others in the office. I will not let past difficulties be a permanent impediment, and when we have differences, I will try to resolve them and avoid recrimination."

"That sounds like a peace proposal," he said, "Is it?"

"I suppose it is," I said. "But I don't intend to let you have your way on important matters or to be a straw man you can run over at will."

"I like what you said about avoiding threats and about developing personal relationships. I have always wanted those things, but the conditions I faced seemed to exclude those things. I will willingly accept your peace proposal and see whether I can extend it to the entire reporter's corps. Will you help me with that?"

"No," I said. "Such a proposal must come from one side or the other. It will have no great validity coming from me. Do it yourself. I can only tell you that I will not get in your way. A smooth functioning office is to my benefit, so I wish you success. But I leave you to fight your own battles. Kurt does not look like a pushover, so his case demands some skill. As well, Amelia is sore as the dickens right now and probably will not want a reconciliation; you may have to wait a while there."

We turned to the other matters we were expected to coordinate and, with the air cleared between us, went through the list very quickly.

When I went to my working space again, supplies had miraculously appeared, and my mail was there, as well as a draft of my think paper for Boris. Since the last item was not for publication, I had it sent off by telegraph as an internal memo and labeled as such. I also wrote up the proceedings of the meeting and sent that off to Boris as well. Amelia was in the photo lab, trying to make sense of the scheme that the woman who had overseen the collection had devised.

I was about to leave when the aide translator came to me and asked if she could speak to me. I said she could and offered her a chair. She then said, "I know you were deeply disappointed in me yesterday when I first met you and was so undisciplined and crass in the way I welcomed you to the project. I had listened too much to Mr. Jon, who told me not to get into any conversation with you or to reveal anything about the project lest it lead to negative results. All of us were fearful of you; I know I certainly was. So, I did not act as I should have. As a result, I did not even identify myself or welcome you. I am deeply sorry about that. I saw afterward in Mr. Jon's office how professional you were about all matters and realized that your statements and complaints were entirely correct. I was deeply ashamed of any obstacles I put in your way."

I did not interrupt because it is good to allow a person who has erred to make a statement of contrition without interruption. Apologizing is a difficult matter, and one should not be stifled. When she was finished, I said. "That must have been difficult to tell me. I appreciate it. But you are right; I was unhappy with your conduct yesterday. However, I was satisfied with the translation you did today, and I noted that you made very few mistakes, which is remarkable when dealing with multiple languages as you did. So what is past is past. I bear you no blame. Let us turn a new page on our relationship, which, I am sure, will be a happy one." I stood up, effectively dismissing her, and she left.

In the taxi on the way back to the hotel, Amelia asked. "What happens to me now? Do I stay at my hotel or come to the office to work?"

I replied, "The office. Your remaining office things will be picked up tomorrow. I am also certain that you will come to the same hotel as mine, but Boris has decreed that we must not combine our rooms as we did before."

"I know," she replied, "Still, it will be nice to know we're in the same hotel and that we can sleep together at least occasionally. I know we cannot make a habit of it. Too many people don't understand our relationship."

"Or they misunderstand it," I concluded.

That conversation led directly to her break-up with Werner. She cried a little, and we talked about it off and on for most of the evening. She said that it had been on her mind ever since they had reconciled in Bucharest that the fit with Werner was not good. He made continual comparisons of her with Helga, his wife, and lamented often that his children were not with him. He seldom talked about the future with Amelia, and she felt Werner was convincing himself that reconciliation with Helga was the right thing to do.

On the other hand, Amelia said, "Living with Werner was a dream. I found him devoted to me most of the time, and he was a splendid lover. I felt in those moments that I had found my 'one and only.' So it was a shock when he suddenly called our affair to an end. He did it just as dramatically as he had on the previous occasion. He asked me to meet him at the central train station, and when he arrived, he was with his family. He left them momentarily and came across the concourse to me and said that he was taking his family on a short vacation to Smyrna. On his return, he would be going back to live with his family on the German military base. He kissed me on the cheek and rejoined his family. None of them looked my way but went to the gate for the train they were taking."

We talked about the matter until deep in the night. That is what friends are for.

The Press Office, as we called it, changed immediately after the meeting. The following day the working effects of Kurt, Michael, and Amelia were moved into the office. I had already taken a desk with a window view. Kurt took the other, and Michael took a far corner. Amelia's materials were taken to the spacious upstairs room that had room for the photo archives and the reporter's archives. In the office itself, the typists were introduced to the reporters and told that their typing services were available. Kurt and Michael passed over several reports immediately. The aide-translator, Cynthia Cevdet, came by and got 'jobs' from the reporters and then cleared the priority list with me, but the list was so easy to assemble anyone could have done it. I let Cynthia assign the priorities.

That afternoon, Kurt received a message from Berlin, and simultaneously, I received one from Boris. They both stated that the decisions made by our committee the day before had been reviewed and unanimously confirmed, except for one item. That item was that a private office for Jon was allowed, although, if space were available, the senior member of the reporter's group could have one as well. This latter allowance was discouraged in parenthesis, which said (this is not a newsroom's usual custom and, hence, is not encouraged). When Jon asked me about it later in the day, I said I would stay where I was.

That decision was disliked by Kurt, who added to the grievance he already felt for Jon and never forgave him. The two were hardly ever civil to one another, and a good day at the office was when Kurt was on assignment, so they would not meet. Concerning my relations with Jon, we were civil, which was easy enough since I was on assignment for much of the next three months while he was still with us. I did bring some items by for his advice, but not many, and he sometimes raised issues with me about the reporters, and I gave him advice.

He ran a good shop, and the staff did what they were supposed to do, with few problems. Even those few problems were dealt with dispatch. The greatest change came in his attitude towards Amelia, who he discovered to have wonderful abilities to organize and serve others.

The German-Czech woman who had tried to put together the photo archives had not done well at it. She was terrified her job was gone when Amelia arrived. But Amelia integrated her into the photo archives operation and helped her set up the reporter's archives as well. The two of them spoke German with one another, and soon, the girl regarded Amelia as a great authority. She was particularly pleased when Amelia showed her how to develop negatives in the newly established developing room. Jon was pleased with the entire setup and the way that Amelia dealt with the German-Czech woman, but so, too, was Cynthia Cevdet, who sometimes brought instructions from Jon. However, Cynthia's role there faded within weeks because Jon sought direct contact with Amelia.

I liked the new set-up as I could write up my reports, and then, they would be typed and gotten ready for the censor, with my doing almost nothing but a little proofreading. Cynthia soon had good relations with the censors, and little was turned back to us, largely because of Cynthia's good humor and fine rapport with the censors. Of course, the censors were kindly disposed to us, in any case, because of Enver Pasha's favoritism toward me.

The biggest development over this period, when Jon was still with us, dealt with the professional relationship that grew between Michael and Amelia. She showed her files to him one day, and they decided, then and there, that they ought to cooperate. One week later, they began a series on "peoples of the Ottoman Empire" that appeared in Michael's newspaper, in the *Tribune*, and in the *Tagesblatt*. It proved popular and resulted in two short trips by Amelia and three longer ones by Michael to collect new photos and more information on contemporary conditions among these people. The series ran three days a week for a month. This had the effect of removing Amelia from Boris's 'bad' list and even gaining a slight toehold on the 'good' list.

Most of this I only heard about or witnessed in the few days I spent in Constantinople.

Three Crucial Interviews

My three interviews proved momentous. The first visit to the admiral was a request from him to review naval facilities and put out some 'news,' which would show a positive view of the navy to the Ottoman and German public and put a scare into their enemies, particularly the British. The admiral wanted 'power' emphasized as well as the great abilities of his naval force, both in ships and personnel. I do not suppose the admiral saw me as anything but a functionary of the propaganda department to whom he could deliver such ultimata. I was happy to have access, so I did not in any way disillusion him about the glory that was going to accrue to him because of my adulation and praise in print. I intended to write as I always have, with a discerning eye and a penchant for knowing when people are telling the truth, when they are lying, and the probable meaning of what I witness.

General Liman von Sanders made the same request. The only difference was that von Sanders was not as pompous and domineering in the interview and spoke to me as if I were a real human being rather than the robot the admiral regarded me. Nonetheless, he, too, thought I was there to do his bidding. Again, I did not disillusion him or insert any reality into what he was ordering me to do. The access to military facilities and the military mindset was well worth the short period of silence on my part that I had to endure while the general pontificated.

My third meeting, with Enver Pasha, trumped the other two and asked for the same thing for national defense in general. When I told him of the other two requests, he said, "What a wonderful opportunity to roll all three requests into one." He ordered an aide to make the necessary contacts with the admiral and the general after our own meeting. He laid on three tours throughout the empire, visiting battle fronts, defense facilities, armaments plants, naval, air, and military facilities, and other sites he would name en route. On these trips, he would sometimes accompany me. At other times, other naval, military, or civilian officials would have the job. I was to bring my cameraman with me, so I made the usual arrangements with the editor of the *Herald*. Amelia was disappointed that I did not consider her, but I told her that the contract with Boris that she signed did not include such assignments.

The meeting with Enver Pasha was the most pleasant of the three. Although Enver Pasha was known as 'difficult,' 'stubborn,' and 'insistent on getting his own way,' I seldom saw those attributes. First, he was a government official in a system where he had gained his office through election, so he was aware that other people have viewpoints and should be respected for the most part. Second, he recognized me as a person outside his jurisdiction of authority with whom he wanted cooperation. He realized he would only get such cooperation by treating me as an equal. He had already reaped great gains from some of my previous reports and saw no reason to doubt that I would deliver again if treated right.

He did know that there were limits to what I would do and what I would accept, but he hoped such obstacles could be gotten around or avoided altogether. If he did not get what he wanted, he knew he could drop me from the favors he gave me, and there was no one to whom I could complain, nor would anyone really care.

Accordingly, our conversation was friendly. He outlined the trip, told me my expenses would be covered, that filing my reports would be facilitated, and that the two of us could chat several times during the trips. He never even mentioned what he wanted from me as an outcome or product; he was wiser than that and willing to see what my reactions would be without direction.

I had one day to prepare for the trip, so I had to consult with Jon about the matter. He was so cowed at that point by the results of the organization meeting that he hardly listened to what I had to say. When I said that Amelia could cover for me, he said that arrangement made a great deal of sense. As it was, Kurt was invited as well, so Amelia covered for him, too. I was tempted to call Boris and tell him that Amelia was not as inconsequential as people had made her out to be, but I decided to leave the matter alone at present.

The First Peregrination

The first tour was to a munition plant, then to the Black Sea Fleet, the northern front with the Russians, and the border with Persia. It was expected to last a month, and railways would be the major means of travel, where available, and riding horses otherwise. There was a special train for that purpose, and it had sleepers and a dining car on it. There were twenty-five people listed, with fifteen officials and ten people associated with the press. As I have already said, Kurt was listed, but so, also, was the reporter-cameraman I used from the *Herald* with a fellow reporter. The other press people were from prominent newspapers, mostly in the capital. At first, there was little mixing, but by the third day, any restraints that existed began to break down and by the time we reached the Russian front, there was almost free association throughout the entire group. Well, Enver and his two aides were sometimes aloof when they dealt with government matters telegraphed to them. But they even mixed with the rest of the group when they had the opportunity.

Kurt was with us for only three days and had come along only to report on the Black Sea fleet and the role of the German mariners in the effort, particularly that of Admiral Souchon. He left immediately after that part of the tour was finished. Enver Pasha was not happy with that 'desertion.' In one of the few negative remarks he made about other participants, he said, "Langer said he would participate. I am surprised he thought he could renege without some dire emergency. Obviously, he will not be given another opportunity for some time."

But even during the examination of the Black Sea Fleet, Kurt surprised me. He indicated a strong respect for officials and military people, which I understand is so strong among Germans. It was more than respect, as he was almost fawning towards the German spokesmen during interviews. He simpered when the admiral addressed us. Given the bombastic, combative creature I had seen during our organizational meeting, Kurt seemed like an entirely different person. And, of course, his early departure was a mystery to me since such invitations are difficult to come by.

Our tour started at the munitions plant that was located some distance inland on the Dűcze River in the direction of Ankara. It was a sprawling factory, several discrete plants connected with one another, where the powder was processed in one plant and the shell casings in another and then assembled in the third. We wore face masks much of the time and donned long-sleeve shirts in the shell factory because of hot metal shavings. Of course, the most entertaining feature was the testing area, where samples of specific production numbers were evaluated and always passed the qualifications. Of course, there were constant small explosions, so we were advised to wear earplugs. I asked how long this plant had been in production and was told that it had been built in the 1870s and that the French had helped establish it. It had recently undergone renovation with German specialists employed in that effort.

The Black Sea Fleet visit took two days, as it was held in two different harbors, one for the ships themselves and the other where the naval headquarters was located. When we arrived at the first harbor, we saw six newly painted destroyers and two cruisers at anchor, which looked like they had been recently overhauled. Three hours later, we witnessed two weathered destroyers come into the harbor and go directly through their docking routines. The briefing officer explained this group had been out on patrol for the past week and was due for a minor 'refitting.' Two other destroyers would be sent out to their places within a few hours' time. Within the hour, two of the newly painted ships left for that duty. The briefer also said that there had yet been no major engagements between Russian and Ottoman ships since the war began, except for the raid I had taken part in earlier in the year.

On the second day, we spent a good deal of time at naval headquarters looking at charts showing areas of responsibilities and first-response stations. While the uniforms at the port were well laundered and pressed, they paled in comparison to the uniforms at headquarters, which were bleached white and marked with epaulets, insignias, aiguillettes, and other colorful paraphernalia. I once visited an American naval base in Maryland, where I noticed a similar obsession with stark white uniforms in an admiral's headquarters. It is a worldwide naval tradition.

The briefings were done well and imparted large amounts of information, more than I thought was necessary. Some of it was beyond what the public needed to know and might even give knowledge to the enemy. However, that factor did not seem to bother the naval authorities. One came away impressed with the demonstration of power the naval bases provided, just as the admiral wanted. Afterward, in an off-the-record chat with the admiral, I asked why he had broken off the engagement at Sevastopol when his ship was hit. "You had enough guns that you could have torn up the harbor significantly worse than you did, so why let a hit, as serious as it was, stop you from doing it."

He gave a restrained answer. "You are right, of course, if that had been the aim of the raid, but the destruction was not the purpose, but rather the element of surprise to show the Russians that they had much to fear from us if we decided to attack. That had already been accomplished." I was not totally satisfied with the answer but did not challenge it. Nor do I think the admiral would have countenanced any sort of negative response to his statement because he lives in a world where no one questions his statements.

We moved on to Erzurum, the headquarters of the Northern Command, which had charge of the land war against the Russians. I had visited it in 1913 before the war began and remembered it as a great establishment with fine facilities and a great sense of tradition. However, I expected to see a beaten army because of the unsuccessful raid against Sarikamish that I had witnessed a few months earlier. But that was not true at all, probably because the commanding general realized that he had no option but to put that terrible ordeal behind him and rebuild his forces. With the help of conscription, he was receiving large numbers of new recruits to replace the substantial losses suffered on the Sarikamish raid.

In fact, the entire northern army seemed to have been transformed into a giant training camp. This was particularly true of the IXth Corps, which had lost half of its fighting units during the expedition, large numbers falling because of the extremely cold weather. When I found the reconnaissance company that I had been attached to, the personnel were entirely different, as everyone who survived had been redistributed to form a new cadre around which recruits were added and training from the 'ground up' took place.

In a briefing by the commander of the Fourth Army, he stated that the training effort was only possible because the Russians had decided not to launch any offensive against the Ottomans, being heavily committed to fighting on the European front against the Germans and Austrians. He said further that the lull in fighting was being used to hurry training because it was unknown how long that pause in fighting might last. When allowed, I asked, "Surely there is heavy patrol action by both sides, which must lead to battles and casualties."

The commander answered, "That is sometimes the case, but both sides seem to be intent on keeping such contacts from happening too often, and even when they occur, there is a tendency on both sides to pull back as quickly as possible."

I followed up with, "Do you feature a time when you are strong enough to change that approach over to a more stalwart reaction to Russian patrols."

He smiled and said, "Hopefully, but it will not be soon, as our training is still in its elementary phases. Our fear is that the Russians will decide to become aggressive long before we are ready to manage that level of action. But, in any case, we will not retreat from such threats if they materialize."

In an informal conversation with the commander later in the day, I asked about the state of his officer ranks. I said, "My impression in Constantinople is that the military academy has done a great service over the years in providing the army with a sufficient corps of professional officers who seem capable of running this war. But what about company-grade officers? Can you find enough of them at present?"

He answered, "I'm glad you did not ask that question in the formal briefing because it would have spoiled the smooth picture of training I was trying to present. Frankly, we are short of company-grade officers. Training the large numbers this expanded army needs is a challenge that is not being met with any degree of confidence. We must take university graduates when we find them, but they are not very suitable officers. They regard serving with uneducated enlistment men as a challenge they would rather not confront. A considerable number have been found with pre-university education and in specialized jobs in general society, but many of those obtain deferments because of the crucial work they do. Moreover, they often regard military service as beneath their dignity, which is not easily overcome. Unfortunately, unlike European and American armies, there are almost no paths to officer ranks from the enlisted ranks, so we don't often promote sergeants to lieutenants, but we do have many of them taking the place of junior officers without open recognition of the practice."

I found the visit a 'mixed bag.' There was no doubt that the Northern army was overcoming its deficiencies, but it was equally true that there were severe challenges that might not be overcome at all. After four days, we moved on to the border with Persia. We stopped at several population centers of Armenians and Kurds. In general conversations during the evenings, Enver Pasha expressed considerable alarm over the autonomist tendencies of both groups and their inclination to see Russia and Great Britain as allies. He was most worried about the Armenians because of their behavior even before the war began in seeking protection from the Russians. There were rumors that Armenians were entering Soviet militias in significant numbers, and of course, we were all aware that there had been incidents where Armenians refused to accept conscription into the Ottoman Army.

The Kurds were different and remained antagonistic towards the Russians. Because of the location of the British-controlled Abadan oil refinery in Persia, they accepted British advances to assist them in holding the Ottomans out of the immediate area. That bothered Enver Pasha less than the Armenian 'threat.'

Among the correspondents, the most interested in these 'minority problems' were the two representatives from the *Herald,* and they took an interest in all activities at the villages we visited. They sought out cases where Ottoman authorities, security forces, or the military exhibited behavior that could be construed as prejudicial to the Armenians or Kurds. Enver Pasha's viewpoint on such cases clearly sided with the Ottoman forces, saying that when the facts were all in, it always was the minority group that was in the wrong, usually because they violated Ottoman law or challenged Ottoman authority. The reporters from the *Herald* felt that Ottoman forces were too often heavy-handed and could easily have been more sensitive in handling disputes. I convinced the reporter from the *Herald* to copy Amelia with his reports on any matters concerning minorities, which he was only too happy to do, seeing cooperation coming from her side in the future.

In one village, a serious case was presented to our group by an Armenian village elder. Before a group of about seventy-five local people, he told how an Ottoman militia group, composed mostly of Turks, had 'invaded' the village one evening, seeking an Armenian outlaw. They had searched the village at considerable inconvenience to the villagers and then took fifteen young men for questioning. They never returned the young men, and their shallow graves were discovered three weeks later. The speaker spoke directly to Enver Pasha, "What does the illustrious Minister of War intend to do about such vigilantism?"

Enver Pasha barely hesitated in providing an answer. "Absolutely nothing, my dear elder, other than to check to see whether a report was filed by the militia group. The group was acting under legal authority, and it behaved as it should have in searching for an outlaw. Most certainly, the men should not have been killed after interrogation, but the conditions under which they perished are not entirely known. I am sure that the action report will assure us that the actions of the militia were suitable to the occasion."

The elder said not one further word but merely walked from the group and disappeared. The assembly broke up without any signs of protest over Enver Pasha's callous remarks. The following day, he had a militia action report sent to the village, which did seem to have existed in the files of the regional Ottoman authorities. When the reports from the trip were reported in the press a week later, the *Herald* featured the incident on page one, with an op-ed article on the interior of the edition, both of which were critical of the Ottoman behavior. One other news outlet published the story, but from Enver

Pasha's viewpoint, and it was a minor item on an interior page. I presented the story to Amelia and George, who discussed the matter for some time and decided to hold the trip for other stories of a similar nature to make a more substantial article out of it with some corroborating evidence.

Other visits to the minority groups were civil but never approached any level of friendship or even understanding. We returned to Constantinople a little disappointed by the last part of it but enthusiastic about the results of the earlier part of the effort. Enver Pasha voiced this sentiment on our last evening on the train as we were moving towards the city. He seemed upbeat by what he had found, even accounting for the minority reaction to the Ottoman rule.

Chapter Five
The Suez Canal Campaign

We had three days in Constantinople before departing again, this time for the southern route as far as Jerusalem. While we were in Constantinople, of course, I filed all my stories, although several of them had not yet been cleared by the censor before I left, so I had to leave them to Cynthia.

Amelia and I had ample time to talk during that time, and we slept together all three nights, again with our skivvies on. She told me that the tension between Jon and Kurt was still as taut as ever and that neither seemed to want peace. She and the other office members were getting weary of the continued animosity. She could not remember a day when the antagonists had not quarreled, often in the presence of others as if to bring the entire staff into the squabble at hand. The issue was severe enough that Amelia said she had raised the issue with Boris, who said that he would discuss the situation with *Tagesblatt* officials and see whether one or other of the two might be transferred.

"Are you talking with Boris regularly?" I asked.

"Only once so far and a couple of notes at the end of messages, but our relationship seems to be warming," she responded.

The trip south took the Hijaz railway as far as Damascus. Our expedition was smaller, only twenty rather than twenty-five people. There were few officials with us now, and mostly, it was regional newspaper reporters and a few representatives from Constantinople, such as the *Herald*. There were no cameramen as the invitation to the trip specifically noted that they were not to accompany us on this trip. That disappointed me because I was accustomed to talking with Mirac, the *Herald's* cameraman who had assisted me on the trip to the North.

The countryside and the cities were a little different than when Amelia and I came through in 1913, over two years earlier. Our expedition spent most of the time southwest of Damascus at army headquarters, where we observed that serious training was being undertaken rather than basic training that marked so many of the garrisons with the large influx of draftees. However, the pace was not as frenetic as at Erzurum. But then, the army here had not yet been in action, so its strength, while untested, was more stable.

The briefings we received indicated that there was still an urgency with war. The British and French navies had control of the Mediterranean now that the Austrian, German, and Ottoman ships had left it. An Entente embargo had been placed on all Ottman ports along the Levant, which severely depressed the economy and made the prospect of war seem imminent. There was fear that the British or French might undertake a campaign to separate the Levant from Anatolia. An oft-repeated rumor was that a French strike would be aimed directly at Damascus while a similar strike by the British would be aimed at Jerusalem. I spent a few days trying to find corroborating evidence for such military action by the British and French and found nothing but rumor, based on speculation, based on predilections. There was not a shred of evidence indicating that such invasions were in anyone's action plan.

Reports had been received from Yemen, far to the south, which remained in Ottoman hands and had driven back attempts by Anglo-

Indian troops from Aden to take over the area. The rugged terrain seemed to have been the deciding factor in halting that invasion. To the east, Basra had been taken over by the British, and outposts along the Persian Gulf were turning their allegiance to Britain as well. It was felt that there would be a British attempt to move north towards Baghdad and other cities in the Tigris-Euphrates Valley.

In his own briefing to our group, the local commander of the Ottoman forces held that there was not an immediate danger to the Levant area because the British had still not built up enough forces to undertake a major land campaign to take Jerusalem or Damascus. Over the long run, this was the major threat. The short-range threat was British efforts to win tribal leaders, such as Sharif Husayn, over to their side and decrease Ottoman power in the area. It was good to hear an assessment that seemed to undercut the primary contentions of the rumor-mongers.

At Jerusalem, we discovered that the city had its own defense zone, and it was much less prepared for war than had been true at Damascus. The commander in Jerusalem cited a lack of manpower, ammunition, supplies, and willpower. He said that the political situation, where so many different communities and factions vied for influence, made a common effort difficult to attain. The mayor was much more despondent than he had been when Amelia and I had met him two years earlier.

The comradery among the members of our expedition was much more muted than on the trip to the north. In part, this was caused by the more pessimistic attitudes of officials we encountered, but in part, it was due to the impact of the British blockade, which depressed the economy heavily. Enver Pasha was not exactly 'out of sorts,' but he was not as enthusiastic as he had been on the earlier trip. He did not enjoy the evening sessions with the press members as he did earlier, and the sessions withered as he spent less time with them. Near the end of the trip, he ceased attending them altogether.

He did occasionally still talk with me one-on-one, but the subjects were mundane, except for one telling discussion. On that occasion, we talked about the empire in general, and he said, "I am more and more discouraged about its unity. The Turks are the backbone as they always have been, but the Greeks, who once identified closely with the empire's fate, are lost to us. The Slavic peoples have left, and the Arabs show little faith in us, themselves, or anyone else. I do not know what will happen to them. Even the Armenians and the Kurds want little to do with the empire any longer. It is time to reconsider our nation and build a place for the Turks and rid ourselves of these other, petulant people."

I knew he was depressed by lessened prospects of a successful war, so I did not question him further. Later, I recognized that the moment may have been the time of his 'great epiphany' when he left the Ottoman state behind and identified himself with 'Turkish nationalism.' I never met him thereafter when he recanted what he had said on that occasion.

One morning, unexpectedly, Enver Pasha called us together and announced that other events demanded his attention, and the expedition was, therefore, ending. Expedition members would be leaving that afternoon for transportation back to Constantinople. Enver left the meeting at that point very abruptly, it seemed to all of us.

We spent the morning packing, although that did not take us very long as we were all traveling 'light.' with very little baggage. I spent the morning pulling together the news stories I had been working on, although I judged it would make little difference if anyone ever read what I was reporting; it was not very interesting reading. A bus arrived about noontime to transport us to the train station, and I was momentarily held back when a strap on my suitcase broke, which took me out of line until I could jerry-rig a new fastener. It appeared that I likely would be the last person to board the vehicle. I didn't like that very much as it meant all the good seats would be taken and I might even have to stand during the trip.

As I was ruminating on my 'poor luck,' there was suddenly a person alongside me whom I recognized as one of Enver Pasha's aides, who 'saluted' me with a wave of his hand and said, "Effendi, how fortunate that I found you before you boarded the bus. I was afraid of the commotion it might cause. Effendi Marty, the minister, has sent me to take you to Major Cetin Yilmaz, who is about to depart for Beersheba and wants to meet you before he leaves. We can catch up with your fellow travelers before the train departs later this afternoon. The minister feels that your insights and vision would be of considerable use to the major and does not want to forego the opportunity to bring the two of you together."

I turned to the aide and said, "Whatever the minister wants, I am only too happy to oblige." The aide had two Ottoman army enlisted men with him, and one of them picked up my luggage and led the way to an army vehicle standing nearby, where he deposited the luggage in a rear compartment. The aide and I stepped into the rear seat of the vehicle, and the two enlisted men joined the driver in the front seat. As we drove, the aide passed me a pair of goggles as the dust from the dirt road started to hit one's eyes. The goggles helped. We traveled only a short distance until we came to an army compound. We entered through an elaborate front gate where a sentry spoke briefly to the driver and then let us pass into the compound. We went to a three-story building made of quarried stone and were deposited at the front door.

Inside, it was cool and quiet. We went into a reception area where several women office workers in army uniforms were undertaking office routines. This was the first time I had seen women in army uniforms, and I realized that the Ottoman army was drawing on women as well as men for its wartime manpower needs. The major domo of the office was a male with sergeant's chevrons, and he stood and directed us immediately into an office that had Major Yilmaz's name on the nameplate.

The Major stood behind his desk and reached across it to shake my hand, and gave me a greeting in Turkish. I noticed immediately that the aide had departed, and my luggage was alongside me in the office. The major said, "Good to meet you. Minister Enver believes you can assist me and solve a difficult problem for me."

Without a clue as to what the major was referring to, I responded, "I am only too happy to assist where I can. Can you tell me about your difficulty?"

"Certainly," the major responded, "I command a unit with the short title "Photographic Archives." Our task is to record the work of the Ottoman army in its mission. Right now, the Ottoman Army is about to begin a campaign to put pressure on the British dominance of Egypt, where the Suez Canal, the British training facilities, and French auxiliaries are all a threat to the Central Powers' position in the Eastern Mediterranean. We have been assigned as the unit to accompany the combat units and record their progress. Our photographic record will be useful to Army planners and policymakers as they assess the strengths and weaknesses of our army's progress toward success in this theater of operation."

I knew nothing about a campaign against Egypt but reckoned it was reasonable that the Ottomans would want to undertake one. Without any hesitation, I responded," That sounds like a formidable project. How can I fit in?"

"I have good cameramen, all trained in Germany, as I was for over six months," came the response. "I think we will get good footage of the campaign, including combat situations. So, photographically, we are in good shape. Rather, it is the accompanying verbal record that accompanies the film where we lack expertise."

"And you want me to provide such a record? I asked. "That is a tall order. After all, I usually write in English, although occasionally I do provide Turkish news copy for a newspaper in Constantinople."

Captain Yilmaz responded immediately," Fortunately, I have translators, both enlisted and officer, who have considerable experience in translating from one language to another, but it is the initial record that I need. It takes a special talent to provide commentary for camera footage where the observer is not always present. The Minister of War assures me that you have that ability and that you have demonstrated it at Sarakamish and on the naval raid at Sevastopol. Is that correct?"

I involuntarily scratched my head and replied with a wry look, communicating that I was not as sure of my abilities in such situations as the major thought I was. I responded, "In a sense, major, I can do that with a little practice, but I would need to be at the battle site itself in order to experience the progress of the action and the general flow of the battle itself. Even then, it is difficult to gauge whether the action that is being filmed is significant or not. It is a chancy business, at best, and I have not had any great experience in doing it. I am much more limited than you might think."

The captain sat down in his chair behind the desk and motioned for me to sit in the visitor's chair on the opposite side. He said, "My translators and I have read through the news reports you filed during the first expedition through the country that you only recently completed. All three of us liked what we saw. You are, above all else, clear. One understands from your reports what you are talking about in the report, and the description that follows is lucid and gives considerable insight into the action you are describing. You are aware of government sensitivities on certain matters, yet still manage to address most matters in a manner that leads to understanding by the reader. You do not speak "down" to readers. You do not overpower your readers with complex words and sentences, and you always strive for an understanding of the subject being addressed. Aside from the Minister of War's assessment of your strengths, our own investigation concludes you could do the work without a doubt in our minds."

I was perplexed. I was being asked to do something that I was not specifically trained to do. My immediate assessment was that I had about a 50-50 chance of succeeding. This was somewhat better odds than at Sarkamish, which I rated only at 30-70 against, and at Sevastopol, where there were slightly better odds at 25-75 against. So, there was no reason to decline the invitation. Having decided to eventually accept the offer, I decided to exact some concessions before I openly agreed. "Would I necessarily need to remain with the camera crew, or would I be free to examine the site of action freely without restriction, of course, keeping in mind that I could not interfere with combat operations."

The major was ready with a reply, which indicated that he had assessed ahead of time that I would be willing to accept the position. "You need to keep in mind what the camera crew has access to and what they are filming, but you yourself certainly would need broader context. You must be free to move about and take in the flow of battle and the general movement of forces in the cauldron.[2] You will need that freedom to provide good context in your commentary on the film. The film crew will be using small trucks to transport their equipment, but you could have the use of a camel to move about. I understand you are proficient in their use. Is that so?"

"It is," I responded. "I like that arrangement, although I wouldn't be so foolish as to ride my mount into a battle in which motorized vehicles were the chief mode of transportation. That could be disastrous for me." I forced a sort of grimace to give an indication to the major that such an action would be foolhardy.

I decided to ask for more concessions. "And my own reporting. Do I continue to be a correspondent for the *Tribune*? Can I file reports as I do now?"

Major Yilmaz was unperturbed by the question. "Of course, you may file your own reports on the battle, although this is a secret operation, and there will be no reporting until the battle is over. Then, the normal censorship process will be in effect, and you may file reports at that time. I can assure you that this office will put no impediments in your way on that matter. It may be that your own

---

[2] Cauldron. Military jargon for the arena in which a battle takes place.

reporting will be enhanced by seeing all our film footage. We have no objections to that either."

"Will I be in your employ or a volunteer?"

Without batting an eyelash, the major replied, "A volunteer. You are worth more to us in the long run not to have you as one of us but rather as a correspondent for a noted international news agency. We do not want to jeopardize that status."

"How long after the event must I remain in the area assisting you? There are limits on my time. I hope you understand that?"

"A week to ten days, I think. Like you, we have other things to attend to. We do a job and then move on. Like you, there are demands on us, and we cannot afford long periods to finish projects. We wrap up projects quickly."

I paused and then asked the final question. "Will you accept as final any descriptions I provide, or will you edit to suit your needs?"

The captain laughed a bit and then said, "You will provide us with a draft in English and Turkish. We will change it into our rendition of Turkish and German. I can assure you that the substance of what you say will not be much changed, but that it will be edited and sometimes shortened, probably several times, so that some parts of your description will see considerable amending while other sections will remain much as you originally submit them."

Later that day, as I was being outfitted for combat clothing suitable for desert use on camels, which was mostly a Turkish EM uniform with a desert veil, the assistant commander of the unit came to me. We met briefly after my meeting with Major Yilmaz. He said, "A complication has arisen, and we are short of an officer to handle our film development and initial storage. The woman officer who does this has departed for maternity leave two days ago and will be absent for at least a month or more. It has been suggested by German headquarters in Constantinople that you have in your offices a woman who could fill in during this period. The woman is agreeable but requests your approval for the arrangements. She says the home office in Bucharest has approved the request."

"Wonderful," I replied. "Having Amelia here would be welcome indeed! When can she arrive? "

"Within two days,' said the captain. "She is anxious to join us and will be on the train tomorrow morning."

My training session at Beersheba lasted five days. Two days were spent reviewing existing films. The first set involved the army maneuvers that were undertaken when I first arrived in Constantinople. While I did not understand much what was happening at the time, I found that I had absorbed a lot of the meaning of the maneuvers and could provide good text for the descriptive narrative that accompanied the film. It was decided to write a new description for the original photo record that pleased everyone involved in our exercise. We repeated the exercise the following day using archival footage for the Sarikamish campaign. Even though I was not in any way near where the film was taken in that battle, I was able to comment on the battle itself and figure out, by context, just what was going on in the footage that had been gathered. I rewrote the description for that campaign as well and agreed with the "recording team" that my new description should replace the original recording.

For two days, we worked on planning the upcoming battle and anticipating what sorts of filming could be done. The 'recording team' of which I was a member was only one of several teams that participated in this planning exercise. Amelia's team was included, and I discovered that she was as accepted in her new position as I was in mine. We both made substantial contributions to the location of cameras during the anticipated action.

The attack plan, in its broad outlines, anticipated a force of three Ottoman infantry divisions accompanied by a screening force of local Arab bedouins crossing the open desert and attacking Commonwealth forces[3] guarding the Suez Canal. After crossing the Canal, Port Said would be brought under control, and an infantry force would drive South to take Port Suez. Then the entire area would be fortified against enemy counterattack. The committee saw its work in three phases: crossing the desert, crossing the Canal at Port Said, and driving South to Port Suez. Using maps purchased in Egypt before the war occurred, the camera spots were located along the obvious routes that could be taken. There was a total of 20 such locations, but it was recognized that the later phases of the campaign could not be predicted with any great accuracy, and changes would have to be made at that time.

On the last day of the session, a general review of all planning was made, and some slight changes were made to previous arrangements. The meeting broke up in mid-afternoon after it was concluded that equipment would be sent to the first filming sites the

---

[3] Commonwealth forces were those affiliated with Great Britain who recognized the British monarch as ruler. In this case it was troops from Australia, New Zealand and India.

following morning and that by evening, actual filming would be undertaken.

For the first time, Amelia and I had a few minutes to ourselves and had an early supper together. She said that the request for her services had come via the German Army Command and was undoubtedly the suggestion of Werner Aussenfeld, although the message itself was signed with the signature of a senior officer in the headquarters. She said she had not heard from Werner about this matter or any other and that she was giving me this statement so that there was no suspicion that she was in contact with him again. Twice burnt by him was enough, she said. She noted that Boris, in Bucharest, had only reluctantly agreed to the arrangement, saying that "having Marty gone is enough of a loss, despite his assurances that news will not stop flowing. I rely on your local news to meet my needs while he is gone. Who will do that?"

"I assured him that Cynthia could do that, as could the Greek reporter who had joined us."

Amelia then launched into a scenario whereby she would travel with the filming team into Anatolia after the Suez campaign was complete, where she could get some footage of Armenians who were being persecuted according to rumors in Constantinople. "If this exercise takes a month, then that leaves about another month before the women lieutenant rejoins this unit, and I am sent back to Constantinople. That is enough time to gather something worthwhile."

I was skeptical of her plans but did not say so, believing that there was a 25% chance that her trip to Anatolia would happen and that she would get some film of actual discrimination against Armenians. That is somewhat 'long odds.'

Moving across the Sinai was the tricky part of the expedition, as roughly 17,000 troops and support facilities were involved, and they had to carry their supplies and armaments with them. The distance was great enough that it had to be done in secret so that the British and Commonwealth forces located in Egypt could not be quickly mobilized and brought to the Suez area, where they could attack before the Ottoman-German force established itself. Especially, pontoons made in Germany and shipped to south Palestine via the long, ponderous land route provided a 'secret weapon' that could not come to the attention of the British forces until the attack itself. Precautions were taken. First, the route was moved from the coast, where ships could report any movements. So, the line of attack was across the Sinai desert inland from the coastline. Second, air reconnaissance had to be prevented for the same reason, so constant German air patrols had to be flown to intercept and turn back any enemy aircraft that could report the caravans and what they were transporting, as well as the size and route of the expedition itself.

During this phase, I traveled via camel along the route and visited each of the sites that recorded the advance of the invasion force. The photographers reported that days had been clear and that good shots were made of the Ottoman soldiery, which seemed unbothered by the heat and dryness of the desert. The pictures of the pontoons being transported by camels were stunning.

I had good luck after consulting with the first camera crew, as I fell in with an 'engineer' platoon of ten men, headed by a sergeant, which was bringing water up to a rest station halfway up the peninsula, and combat units could take a break. The platoon was leading a column of forty donkeys, each loaded with small barrels of water. They were on foot, keeping the animals in line and proceeding at an average speed over rough terrain. I dismounted and walked with them for a time, asking questions as we went. The sergeant was bored and welcomed someone to talk with, so we had a conversation. He said the efforts to keep the mission a secret would not be successful. "The space out here is too open so that one could see for considerable distances a force of any size. The Ottoman columns stirred up dust as well, which would only lead to the curiosity of the few travelers across this wasteland. The British undoubtedly monitored the area, and they would discover the expedition in short order. By the time the columns reach Suez, they will be ready for us."

A small boy, perhaps six years of age, ran up to us and said something, but he was indistinct in his speech, and I could not understand what he wanted. He kept pointing towards my camel. The sergeant said, "This is Ces, our good luck charm and guardian angel. He joined us last year and has been with us ever since, eating in the mess area and sleeping in the kitchen on a small bed we made for him. He wants to ride your camel."

I said, "I don't mind, but the camel might. Let's put the boy in the saddle and see. I lifted him up, and the camel did not seem to mind the new weight on him. We walked on while the boy pretended he was directing the camel, but the camel kept to his steady pace and stayed near me. I turned back to the sergeant, who seemed eager to give me more of his commentary on the present excursion.

He said, "The Germans oversee this expedition, and details are important to them. Ottomans would have brought up water if the individual units had planned it, but with the Germans, it is a planning feature of the entire army to make sure that adequate facilities are available for our use. Fewer things are left to chance, and the welfare of the men in the ranks is a primary consideration. I don't know whether that affects the fighting power of the infantry or not, but I think it does. There is less to grouse about, and it will show when we go into battle a few days from now. Remember my words and see whether I'm not right."

He had other things to say as well, but I decided I needed to be on my way. When I tried to take the boy from the camel, he resisted, and the sergeant said, "He wants to ride a while, so why not take him to the rest stop where you will stop in any case? He has friends there and wants to see what they are doing. We'll find him when we get there."

I mounted the camel and moved on. The boy was jubilant as the camel set off at a brisk pace. The boy talked a blue streak, and although I could not understand a word of what he said, there was no doubt that he was happy with his camel ride. Two hours later, we were at the rest stop, and the boy dismounted and ran to meet other enlisted men, who seemed happy to have found him. After all, he was their good luck charm.

There was a squad of camel riders, all dressed in desert robes with Ottoman insignia. I identified it as a reconnaissance unit that was screening the front of the advancing infantry columns. I spoke to the sergeant in charge, who wanted to know who I was and what I was doing. When I mentioned the photo unit I was working with, he said, "Good that we have run into you. Your map of possible camera sites needs some adjustments. We went through the area this morning and think that there are some better possibilities. If you have a map with you, we can go over them while we take our break. We have been out since yesterday afternoon and need a little rest until we relieve the squad that replaced us."

I retrieved my map, and we relocated six camera sites. I would have to move across the front of the advancing infantry columns to locate some of them, but I estimated I had time to do that and still have time for a short break before I started. The sergeant was tired, and I knew he wanted to find a place to sleep until the unit returned to duty in front of the columns. Before he departed, however, he said, "It is likely that the 'Tommies'[4] know we are coming and have reconnaissance forces ahead of us marking our position and speed. They do not want to engage us in battle. They just want to know which probable direction we are taking so that eventually, they can establish a fortified area where they will make a stand. As you examine places for your camera crews, keep that in mind. Do not get into the area they are patrolling, as you are likely to be taken captive."

As it turned out, I discovered that the Ottoman infantry columns were to bivouac at the rest stop for the evening to have a full meal and a night's rest before moving on the following morning. After I had eaten, I found the headquarters of the advancing force and identified myself. I was sure I would be rebuffed but was welcomed instead. It seems that Enver Pasha had informed them that I might show up sometime during the advance. There was a lieutenant colonel in Operations who spoke flawless English who was delighted I had found him and took time to explain the progress of the advancing columns and probable next moves.

---

[4] Tommy. Casual term used by all sides in the war to refer to British troops.

Like the others I had talked to during the day, he, too, told me that there was no doubt that the British had discovered our existence and were trying to lure us into a zone where they had fortifications where they could erode our forces and perhaps deter us from advancing further. He said the reconnaissance patrols were seeking to find safe routes ahead of us, or at least to discover routes that would not lead to cul-de-sacs and disaster. He was confident that we would be successful. However, he cautioned that when we came closer to the Red Sea and the Canal, we would split our forces into five prongs and search for an open path to the waterways where we could attempt a cross-channel attack using the pontoons that the columns were bringing with them.

The colonel explained that the German strategy was to hunt for weak spots in British defenses and then exploit them with 'points of pressure' where concentrated infantry and artillery attacks could force the enemy line to give way and open the way for other Ottoman units to follow. This differed substantially from the general Ottoman strategy, which emphasized strong frontal attacks along a broad front. The colonel emphasized that the German approach had been rehearsed in training for the past several months and was familiar to the Ottoman officers leading the attack.

He studied the situation map I had and suggested spots for placing the camera sites and located three spots he thought would be suitable for viewing the upcoming battles. Those observation spots would probably be used by Ottoman headquarters units as well. "Be sure to identify yourself, or you might be shot as an interloper!" he warned.

Late the following day, our columns reached the fortifications of the British forward defense line. It was a trench line over a mile long with a series of machine gun emplacements along it. Indian Sepoy[5] troops manned it and easily turned back the first attempts of the Ottomans to penetrate the line. Attempts to move around the ends of the line found inhospitable terrain and were harassed by pockets of Sepoys who held up the advancing force and then retreated after eroding the enemy. The advance barely moved the rest of the day. But the following morning, an early assault carried the Ottoman columns past the front lines of the Sepoys. The columns rearranged themselves and drove headlong to the waterway, succeeding in reaching the shoreline in four out of the five zones.

Fighting at the waterway went badly for the Ottomans. The entire area was saturated with Sepoy troops, who prevented further Ottoman gains. Several attempts were made to bring pontoons up to ferry troops across the waterway to the Suez Canal itself, but most were destroyed before they reached the waterway. The few that were launched were immediately fired on and sunk. By late afternoon, it was apparent that the Ottoman drive was going no further.

The observation spot I used was occupied by the same headquarters unit that I had visited the previous day, and the colonel I had spoken with searched me out and willingly told me of the dilemmas of the Ottoman position. "The Ottoman commanders want to dig in, build fortifications, and besiege the Canal. They argue that the mere presence of Ottoman forces would close the operation of the Canal and achieve the goal of making the Canal useless to British shipping.

---

[5] Sepoy troops. A mixture of Hindu and Muslim troops from the north Indian states who were the backbone of the British army in maintaining order in the Indian states, especially in putting down the renegade tribesman of the frontier areas. The Sepoys were formidable soldiers, and they were being trained at this time for future use on the European battlefields.

The German commanders felt that such a presence at the Canal would be unsustainable. The Ottomans would have to mount a gigantic effort to supply the enterprise and to reinforce the force over a supply line that would be open to British interdiction, particularly by air. The German view was that it would be prudent to withdraw without losing more soldiers and building up strength for another attack later when the Sepoys had moved on to France, and a better opportunity would be available for a new Ottoman attack.

"Which do you favor, Sir?" I asked the colonel.

He replied without hesitation, "Staying and hanging on. Our history tells us we can do that."

"Which way will the matter go? I asked.

"We will retreat and follow the German advice on the matter. They are the more advanced nation, and it would be foolish not to take their advice. They know what they are doing?"

The following morning, the Ottomans tried to clear enemy forces from the eastern side of the Canal, but they proved unable to do so, and the German commander in the region decided to retreat. It took over a week to extricate the Ottoman infantry and move them back into southern Palestine, even though the British and Indian forces did not pursue them. The losses of the Ottomans were over 3,000, while the Anglo-Indian forces were less than 100.

Like Sarikamish before it, the Ottomans proved capable of moving forces across considerable distance to strike an unprepared enemy. However, problems of leadership showed that tactics at the fighting site itself were a failure, and despite Ottoman bravery and verve, they could not fashion victory once their presence was detected.

They had to ignominiously retreat with a long list of casualties, which no army could really afford.

I rode the entire way back on the camel assigned to me and then spent eighteen days reviewing the film and bringing together a storyline for the film that was produced from the various filming sites. The team of which I was a member was concerned that we did not label the expedition as a failure or a victory despite its unwelcome outcome. We pictured it as an expedition, emphasizing the considerable planning that went into it, the movement of a sizeable force over a considerable distance, the significant fighting that took place, and the orderly retreat when the battle did not favor the Ottoman forces. At the conclusion of our effort, Major Yilmaz himself pronounced it a significant accomplishment and lauded the entire unit for its bravery, its ability to perform well in adverse conditions, and its ability to complete its tasks according to schedule.

Before I departed for Constantinople, word came from the office of the Chief of Staff of the German unit in the area that the film was well done and gave proof that the Ottoman soldiery had experienced a setback but not a defeat. I felt that such a statement was slightly amiss as it might lead the Ottoman soldier to believe that setbacks were acceptable if the spirit of the army stayed intact.

My attempts to file reports from the field were another issue, and I was not as successful as I might have been. Not having Enver Pasha nearby to clear the way worked to my disadvantage. Clearances with the censor took some time. Initially, there was a refusal to approve my reports on the basis that the campaign was a clandestine operation, but that interpretation was rescinded after several days. Then, certain matters were to remain unmentioned, such as the route across the desert, because it might be used in a future operation. I amended my report to a general reference to a 'desert crossing.' Likewise, the pontoons and their origins were not to be mentioned, so that story had to be omitted. Finally, the names of the German officers involved were taboo until it was discovered that the local Turkish press was anxious to list the names of the Turkish leaders involved. Then, the principal German officers were mentioned as well. All in all, it took nearly a week to get the required clearances.

During the time I was in the Southern Palestine war zone, I met several Ottoman officers and had some lengthy conversations with several of them. From a distance, I had seen several German officers but never came close to engaging one in conversation. On the day our report was finished, I finally had my chance. An Ottoman lieutenant with an aiguilette came to my work site and asked to see me. I agreed, and the lieutenant came to my workstation, where I was tidying up the desk in preparation for leaving. He clicked his heels in the German fashion but did not salute, saying, "I am Lieutenant Aslan, attached to the Chief of Staff's Office, and the Chief himself, Colonel von Kressenstein, requests that you visit him as soon as possible for a brief meeting. If it is convenient Effendi, I have a car that can get us there quickly."

I was slightly surprised, but not unduly so, since I knew that Enver Pasha was not averse to advertising my presence, and I thought he had merely suggested to the colonel that I was someone worth talking with.

"Of course, Lieutenant, we can go immediately," I responded, "I look forward to meeting Colonel von Kressenstein." It was only a brief drive, and the lieutenant had nothing more to say, so I stayed quiet as well. At headquarters, we passed through an outside anteroom where several officers were waiting and then into the outer office of the Chief of Staff with six people at telephones doing various office tasks. The Lieutenant stopped in front of the desk of the 'Adjutant' and reported my presence. The German major listened to the report and, with a smile in my direction, said, in heavy-accented English, "Der kerr-nell will see you at wonst. Pleass come wid me." I followed him into the office of the colonel, who was sitting at a desk reading a book. As I was announced, he inserted a marker in his book, closed it, and took off his reading glasses, which he put on top of the book. He smiled and said, in French, "I have been informed that you gave Ces, the waif of the engineering platoon, a ride on your camel. What a kind thing to do. He always pesters me to get me to give him rides on my horse. Did the camel complain? They don't like unfamiliar people riding them."

I answered without hesitation, "Like you, I expected the camel to complain, but he did not. Perhaps he sensed it was a child who was loaded onto him. The boy rode with me about ten miles to the rest area. However, Ces has a particular language that I am not familiar with, so we did not have much of a conversation." I replied in French.

The colonel said, "It's Urdu, I am told. Ces has his origins with the Sepoy units in Egypt, and somehow, he found his way to us. He is a good luck charm, so we're not likely to send him back. Tell me, as a knowledgeable correspondent who has witnessed our forces in several engagements, what you thought of the Suez Canal expedition?"

Without a pause, I said, "Seemingly well planned, carefully organized, and unfortunate."

"Why do you say, 'unfortunate?'"

"Because the presence of your forces became known at a time when secrecy was vital. The British had time to gather forces and anticipate where you were going to strike. When the British discovered your forces in the desert, it altered your odds considerably."

"How did you feel about the decision to retreat from the Canal? Many of the Ottoman headquarters staff wanted to stay and fight it out. What was your opinion?"

Again, I spoke quickly in reply. "I heard that point of view, colonel, and it fits with what I know of Ottoman history. The Ottoman army is known for its tenacity in defending difficult positions. But because it is a part of military tradition does not make it right for this situation.

"So, do you favor that approach or not?"

"No," I answered, "The Ottomans put their trust in their German leaders, so it was not surprising that a retreat was undertaken. That is not my decision to dispute. I only report what happens. It was a reasonable decision, and I understand the logic of it."

"You were at Sarakamish, I am told. Is there a comparison?" He deftly changed the subject.

"There is no comparison. Sarkamish was an attempt to catch the Russians napping. It was badly planned and badly executed in really bad weather. The Ottomans were blessed when the Russians did not counterattack, as the entire front was left unguarded. No such possibility exists in this case, as Ottoman forces are located precisely where any British counterattack would occur."

Our conversation continued in this vein for half an hour when the colonel was satisfied that I was not his critic but understood his reasons for reacting to tactical situations as he had. We shook hands at the conclusion of the meeting, and I was returned to the project workstation. It was surprising that the colonel had taken the time to consult with me, but later discovered that he had hopes of becoming a military historian someday. I figured he was merely "practicing" for that later role in his life.

Amelia stayed with the photographer's office after the battle and moved into Anatolia with it. She liked her work as she oversaw the photo archives, and the members of her staff found her approach much like they had experienced in their training in Germany. She added features to that system that fit the Middle Eastern problems of filmmaking and preservation, which added to their abilities. Most of all, she said, she enjoyed being in a professional position where she was not 'questioned' about her motivations, or the quality of her work was not scrupulously examined. She said, as well, that despite her demanding work with the project archives, she was able to get some work done on the 'Armenian' problem.

She told me later that there were three occasions when the unit filmed sequences where "atrocities" against Armenians were undertaken. One was a round-up of young men who refused to report for duty in the armed forces. Two were forced marches to move Armenians from cities to make room for Turkic groups to replace them. All films were portrayed as patriotic efforts to "strengthen the state," "punish recalcitrant groups," and "remove dissidents." She brought copies of all three incidents back with her and added them to her files documenting Ottoman atrocities against minorities. She admitted that the films were hardly clear evidence of atrocities and that much rested on the interpretation of the events taking place.

She said the Ottoman soldiers with whom she served on the expedition sometimes showed empathy for the Armenians, but no one wanted to openly criticize the actions against them, seeing the Armenians as the cause of the animosity. Realizing this 'pro-Turkic' attitude, Amelia stayed quiet about her own feelings concerning the persecution of that minority.

She also undertook to contact Armenians going underground because of Ottoman action against them. She hit on a scheme that was to become a hallmark of her later efforts in Constantinople to make such contacts. She made discrete inquiries into the location of dissidents who fled to the cities and hid out in the 'outlaw jungles,' where dissidents lived outside the law and avoided police contact. Her efforts to make contact were often repulsed, but on two occasions, she did make contact and was rewarded with interviews from local dissident leaders. Those dissidents were trying to organize protest groups and underground movements to assist their fellow Armenians and put pressure on the society to become aware of the problem.

In Konya, she inadvertently met a woman at a 'war rally' who expressed pro-Armenian sentiments, and after a long conversation, the woman introduced her to two men who disbelieved her interest in the Armenians on the basis that she worked for an Ottoman military unit which was known for having 'Turkic' sympathies. Still, they passed her on to other Armenian sympathizers, and eventually, she convinced enough people that she was given access to two middle-aged women who reportedly had suffered severe reprisals from the Ottomans. One had been removed from her place of residence on three occasions so that the houses she lived in could be given to Turkic people. She had been denied ration cards, and her husband and teenage son had been killed in a gang killing that targeted Armenian males.

The second woman had been forced from her home in the middle of the night and then captured by a gang of thugs who repeatedly raped her. She had killed one of her abductors in her escape and was now wanted for murder by the police. During the interviews, Amelia found the two stories plausible and even heartrending, but on reflection, she felt that the issues involved were too general to be specifically tied to state sponsorship of anti-discrimination actions.

At Diyarbakir, Amelia met a man at a celebration who claimed he was a victim of police abuse. In the discussion that followed, he cited a long list of acquaintances who were Armenian and suffered the same type of abuse he had. She interviewed four of them and found their stories plausible but, like the women in the earlier case, did not have stories that pinpointed state-sponsored abuse.

Amelia often said later that when she returned to Constantinople, two of the contacts she made at the time proved helpful in making further contacts in the eastern cities.

As is often the case, the woman whom Amelia replaced in the photographic archives project did not want to return to her army duties but asked to remain home with her baby. The woman told authorities that Amelia was quite capable of holding the job and should be inducted into the army to do it. But it would have set a precedent that the army did not want, and so Amelia was released and given a train ticket back to Istanbul. She was blue for a week afterward as she reintegrated herself into the work of the *Tribune* office.

Enver Pasha did not give up on an idea that seemed productive to him. His first expedition had been a real success, especially from a public relations viewpoint. The second trip had been canceled because of the Suez Canal campaign but was hardly a failure, having fulfilled most of its objectives before it was canceled. After a month in Constantinople, Inver Pasha decided that the third expedition that had been planned at the beginning could be undertaken. The participants were limited to ten people, and no cameramen were included. It was to take us from European possessions across Anatolia down to Baghdad. It never left Europe but stopped on the rugged coastline of Thrace. Our visit to the coastal fortifications corresponded with the arrival of a British-French fleet that intended to 'force the Dardanelles.[6]'

We were at an artillery emplacement on the mountains above the coast, where the Ottoman navy had heavily mined the sea approaches. With glasses, one could occasionally see the mines, which had been placed directly into the shipping lanes. If merchant vessels were kept out by the British blockade, the Ottoman's own naval ships were stopped by the minefields as well. There were regular attempts by the British to destroy the minefield and to use battleships to neutralize the howitzers that the Ottoman forces in the

---

[6] The Dardanelles were straits into the Black Sea from the Mediterranean that passed through the heart of the Eastern part of the Ottoman Empire and through Istanbul in particular. The French and British wanted to capture the straits to have direct contact with the Russians, their ally in World War I. The northern routes to Russia were difficult to transverse during the winter months so great efforts were placed on 'forcing the Dandanelles.'

fortification used to cover the minefields. The day we were there the British and the French together made a daring attack which could well have succeeded, but for some reason did not.

The battle began with fishing trawlers entering the minefield area and attempting to remove the mines, but the personnel were only fishermen after all and were inept in managing such explosives. Several blew up, and others proved incapable of being removed, so the trawlers were in disarray as the line of four battleships closed in to bombard the forts above. But since the mines were still there, they had to lay offshore while the Ottoman howitzers did their deadly work. All four British battleships were sunk within hours of their arrival. The French force likewise tried its luck and lost a battleship to a mine. Several other capital ships were severely mauled, so the force withdrew. Enver Pasha could scarcely contain his joy as he watched the Ottoman artillery zero in on a particular ship and lash it with fire from two, and sometimes three, land batteries. I was surprised at the marksmanship and artillery capabilities of the Ottoman forces.

I was permitted to file my report from a military telegraph station near the artillery post, and Enver Pasha acted as my censor. He merely signed without reading my English version; he thought that the results of the battle were so convincingly clear about an Ottoman victory that I would hardly report anything differently. In this case, he was right. The message went out immediately.

Our group remained in the area the following day to see whether the British and French would attack again, but there was no naval action. In a discussion between Enver Pasha and two of his subordinates-- in which I was included for some unknown reason--the assessment was made that the British and French would try again and that major military action was likely to occur in that sector. With this assessment in mind, continuing the trip to the East was not regarded as an option. It was canceled, and we returned to Constantinople that night. Somehow, I knew that the war was close to home and, with great feelings of foreboding, I wondered whether I would survive it.

Chapter Six

The Gallipoli Nightmare

The battle of Gallipoli, fought on Ottoman soil just west of the Dardanelles Straits, was a test of human endurance on both sides. It began with an invasion of British-led troops, mostly from Great Britain, Australia, and New Zealand, on April 25, 1915, but eventually included Indian and French soldiers.[7] It ended with the withdrawal of Allied troops in the following December and January. The losses on both sides were calamitous: 230,000 Entente casualties and 300,000 Ottoman casualties. The Ottomans could claim that their territory was protected, but the Entente had to swallow a bitter setback in their drive to force the Ottomans out of the war and thereby weaken its ally, Germany.

The battle took place on an inhospitable coastline—rocky and desert-like-- that gave the advantage to the side that controlled the higher elevations, which the Ottomans did from beginning to end. The constant aim of the Allies was to reverse that situation by attacking at crucial points of terrain that would allow them to gain higher elevation. In every endeavor, they failed. They failed because of the stubborn defense of the Ottomans, who died rather than retreat

---

[7] It was an Entente operation only in name. Mostly it was a British operation with a British general in charge. It used Anzac forces, that is military units from Australia and New Zealand. Anzac and Sepoy troops from India were often referred to as Commonwealth forces. "Allies" was a term for the Entente powers in the United States and British areas used informally in those countries.

and suffered huge losses so as not to lose the advantage which was their key to outlasting the Entente powers.

Both sides were hemmed into narrow confines, where resupply was possible but difficult. The Ottomans had land it controlled immediately to the north and east of the battleground and had an easier time deploying men and bringing in supplies. The Commonwealth forces, on the other hand, had to move everything onto the thin beachheads they controlled, from distant Alexandria and Cyprus, via ship in every case. Hence, when pressure was put on the Ottomans, they called for reinforcements, which were close by, while the Commonwealth forces had to move their reinforcements hundreds of miles.

There was blistering heat much of the time and a pestilence of large flies that feasted on the unburied dead trapped in no-man's land. It rained at other times and flooded trenches, washing the debris of war and the dead into the areas inhabited by the fighters. In this respect, since the Commonwealth forces were on lower elevations, they got the worst of the flooding. Food and, especially water, were in short supply. Illnesses ran rampant through the armies on both sides and severely limited the ability to continue normal military routines much of the time. The health of the Commonwealth soldiers seems to have been more precarious than that of the Ottomans, although both sides suffered.

The battle involved trench warfare, but on an incline rather than flat land as in Europe. Commonwealth attempts to break out of the beachheads always had to contend with the slope, which gave the greatest advantage to the Ottomans. Both sides burrowed into the soil when it was possible, and the entire combat area was a mass of trenches and bunkers. If there was a battle in the Middle Eastern theater of operations that matched the drama, suffering, and sense of loss of places like Passchendaele in Europe, it was Gallipoli.

My journals indicate that there were approximately 240 days in the campaign, and of them, I was in forward areas about ninety of them, largely because my major sources of news and understanding of what was happening relied on Ottoman company-grade officers and non-coms. They came to know me and saw me as part of their surreal world, where any moment could be their last — and my last. On the line, I asked a few questions but listened to what was going on and what the concerns of my informants were. Were they in a dire situation? Were they expecting an attack? How badly eroded was their own strength, and when could replacements be expected? But sometimes one or another would relate experiences, express homesickness, or talk about the loss of comrades.

Without exception, officers, non-coms, and enlisted men accepted their fate and believed that it was totally in the hands of God whether they survived or not. They were Muslims, and God's power over life and death was part of the creed of that religion.

I always came with a few bars of chocolate, a newspaper or magazine, or some other popular item like a rubber ball or a container of matches. Once, I brought several packets of German marbles, which were a great novelty, although few enough among the soldiers knew how to play the game. My unpacking was always a moment of anticipation and joy for those near me.

Another twenty days of the 240 was spent at headquarters, where I spoke mostly with Ottoman officers because my German was not strong enough to converse very well with German officers, although, sometimes, I had good conversations with General van

Sanders, who always spoke French with me. The final ten days I devoted to the War Ministry officials, sometimes at Gallipoli or some other nearby site. Usually, on these, I was called to talk with the minister of war, Enver Pasha. So, about half of the time I was away from the war, about the same amount of time that a front-line soldier spends in the war, or in rest, or in reserve. In comparing my service with that of my colleagues from the *Herald,* who gave heavy coverage to the entire Gallipoli campaign, I find the *Herald* reporters were in combat less, but then they took turns there, but their time was not much short of mine.

My German colleague, Kurt Langer, by contrast, was at Gallipoli about a quarter of the time, and he spent most of it at headquarters, where he could speak German. At most, he sometimes visited Division headquarters but never went further forward. I suppose he was under orders from his newspaper, the Berliner *Tagesblatt,* not to do so. I always found it strange that he was reluctant to move to where the Ottoman troops were located since he spoke Ottoman Turkic very well and could have learned much from troops on the line. Also, he spent considerable time back in Constantinople and filed stories not necessarily connected with the battle. Amelia, who oversaw the office for most of the period, told me that Kurt contributed to the work of the office. Without him, she said, her own reporting duties would have been overwhelming.

Kurt and I saw one another seldom, although our meetings were always friendly when we did run across one another. On one occasion, he was with two German army colonels, and he not only spoke to me but introduced me to the German officers with him. He then allowed a short conversation to ensue between me and the officers about Ottoman behavior on the front lines. He did all the translation among us. I found that helpful, although there was no reason he should have necessarily undertaken that task.

On another occasion, Kurt and I were at a briefing held by Enver Pasha. We met one another as I was going in to talk with Enver, so I took Kurt with me. He had not been in to see Enver since leaving the great tour around the country before the Gallipoli campaign began. Enver waved him in when I asked whether Kurt could join in the discussion, and the two reconciled, although they were never close friends again. So I was helpful to him, even though I would not have had to do that.

I did not wear any uniform, although my coveralls, tunic, and cap were close enough to military garb that they passed for that. In any case, the enemy was not that discerning, so I was repeatedly shot at, shelled several times, wounded twice--but at no time really seriously,-- and captured twice. I did not carry a weapon, although there was a debate among some Ottoman officers as to whether I should or not. The argument was over my safety, not a desire for increased firepower when I was present.

On the two times I was captured, the Australians who captured me expressed surprise that they had netted a "Yank, and what the hell are you doing here?" Both times, I was turned over to their battalion headquarters, where I was asked for my journalist papers. After I presented them, I was no longer considered a prisoner, but they suggested I stay to talk with the battalion commander when he had time.

The first time, it was about half an hour. I was asked whether I wanted to stay with them, which the battalion commander thought I would want. He could not envision that the Ottoman side was anything but cruel and rapacious. But once I announced my choice, he did not try to convince me to stay on the Allied side. However, he was anxious to discover military information and asked some questions about the location of units. However, I shied away from such matters. Understanding that I was wary about such an approach, he abandoned that line of questions. Then, we had good conversations about surviving in warfare under the conditions that were dealt to us.

On the second 'capture,' I had a longer wait, as I was told that two newspaper correspondents were nearby and they had asked, via field telephone, whether I could wait until they could get to where I was. I waited for them for about forty-five minutes. I knew both by name but hardly remembered what they had written. Both worked for press pools, which meant that their releases went to multiple outlets in the English-speaking world. They wore nondescript clothing, much as I did, although they both had field vests like fishermen wear, where there are multiple pockets for various useful items, such as pencils, pen knives, and even small flashlights.

They were both talkative and competed with one another to ask questions of me. They could hardly wait for an answer before framing and asking a follow-up question. Yet they did listen to what was said and carried the main themes of the conversation over to their new questions. Both knew who I was from my book two years earlier; one reporter said it was like a bible for use in the Middle East. The other reporter said that he had seldom read anything as riveting as my description of the trek to Sarikamish and back in frigid weather.

They asked me why I had been captured since they were never that close to the front and wondered what had induced me to be that close myself. I explained my mode of gathering information, which they found exciting but unacceptable because of the profound risk of death, severe wounding, or capture. "Why does your firm allow you to do that?" one asked.

"Probably because they like what I send them and are willing to put up with it, so long as I am willing to do it," I responded.

We moved on to the role of a newspaper reporter in warfare. They both believed they were representatives of their populations at home. As such, they believed they had an obligation to be sure that the war was prosecuted with vigor, that leaders should be competent and able, and that goals should be clear and obtainable. They gave some examples in their own writing. Especially, they called for a review of the incompetence of the British officers in this current campaign and the failure of those military leaders to exercise good judgment. I was surprised at this use of the press for what I regarded as clear political objectives. So, I replied that I thought their definition of the role of a journalist was a 'tall order' and that my own experience suggested that more attainable goals might be accepted. "I am there to report what I see, experience, and discover, and report it within the framework of what my audience will accept and understand."

We discussed these two concepts for perhaps fifteen minutes, by which time the conversation had morphed into a discussion of how censorship affected us. The two British journalists were united in their disdain for censors. They confessed that they had frequent negative and, sometimes stormy encounters with those officials, who were usually army officers assigned that duty. The two reporters believed that the approach of the censors was to 'cover up' the mess that incompetent commanders made on the battlefield, especially the large number of casualties that the British and its allies suffered in most battles.

I responded that I did a great deal of 'self-censoring' to make it easier on the censors themselves so that they would be likely to overlook some crucial matters in return for toning down the negative sides of the battle, such as casualties. However, I noted that our audiences were different since I was not writing for a domestic audience of Ottomans but for a European population with several different views on who they favored in the overall war between the Entente Powers and the Central Powers.

We moved on and talked about access to important figures. They had about the same entre as I had with generals and ranking civilian figures, except that my relationship with Enver Pasha was much closer than they had with any government or civilian personage. One reporter asked whether it might be possible for them to enter our lines and meet with Enver Pasha since he was such a noted figure and more information about him was wanted on the British side. I quashed the request immediately but gave a technical reason for doing so rather than my real reason. The technical reason was the difficulty of arranging a meeting in this setting. They readily agreed that the moment was not propitious for such a meeting. My own private reason was that Enver was 'my' source and I did not want to share him with them. That was a selfish viewpoint, I know, but I was not exactly a 'buddy' of either of these two 'limeys.'

By this time, we had been talking for about an hour and a half, and I was weary of the conversation. We had covered our roles well enough and, to go further, would lead us into matters better left unsaid between men representing different sides of the battle line. I stood and said that it had been pleasant meeting them. I wished them both the best of luck. They accompanied me back towards the battle line itself. We shook hands, and I left them.

On both occasions, I was captured; there was not much fighting going on when I was ready to return, so it was a simple matter to take me to a point where the lines nearly converged and wave a white scarf. When a white cloth was waved in return, I walked across to the other side. In both instances, the Ottoman soldiers who received me knew who I was and greeted me warmly. Each time, a group of non-coms and men gathered around me and asked questions about what it was like on the Anzac side. They were disappointed with my answers, mostly because they did not perceive any traces of the high adventure that they expected. On both occasions, I wrote notes to Enver Pasha about what had transpired but received no response either time, just what I envisioned would happen.

I was wounded twice, once in the calf of my leg and the other time in my left bicep, but the shots merely tore up the skin and did not do internal damage. I bound the wounds with bandages and remained in the bunkers until I was on my way out later in the day. Then I stopped at a surgery and had antiseptic and fresh bandages applied. Both times, there was not much action, so the wait was not long. In each instance, the corpsmen who worked on me had been to school in Germany and looked after me with Teutonic efficiency. Both times, the corpsmen said that, as a non-combatant, I should be more careful. They were not really cautioning me but wishing me well.

I seldom ate on the line because food was scarce and had to be brought in under dangerous conditions. Sometimes, I had snacks along, which I might eat when the troops were enjoying a meal. I discovered some jerky made from elk that retained its flavor well enough, and, of course, I had biscuits with extra butter in them, which gave me a slight lift when I ate them. Near the end of the Gallipoli campaign, such biscuits were hard to find since they had been baked in Greece, which closed its borders to Ottoman trade. So I switched to a biscuit manufactured in Constantinople, which were all right but hardly equivalent to the Greek ones. I carried my own water, and the length of my visits usually depended on my supply. It would have been criminal of me to use any of the limited water supply that the units in the bunkers used. Usually, they rationed it, and anything I would have taken would have deprived others.

I slept wherever I happened to be at dusk and carried a thin blanket for that occasion. Sometimes, there might be some leaves and vegetation for a bed, and sometimes, field packs provided a good place to rest, but often, it was on the hard ground. It left me sore and stiff many days, and my nights away from the front were blessed events where I could stretch out and have the comfort of sleeping on soft beds with adequate blankets. If shelling occurred while I slept, I simply moved elsewhere since I was allowed to. The soldiers themselves could not do that, of course. Someone had to defend the place, and artillery fire often presaged an infantry attack on the spot of the bombardment.

Most of the time, I was not scared, simply because there was a routine I followed that kept me on the move most of the day. I spent a great deal of time avoiding dangerous situations. But, beyond that, attacks and counterattacks were predictable, and I stayed clear of such places so that I would not be in the way. As I said, I carried no weapon, so what use would I be in actual combat? But during the time of Commonwealth offensives, when shellfire was heavy, and the battle area was in chaos, I felt great dread, and I wanted to run away and never come back.

There were times when I could not avoid action, as there were sudden attacks when the enemy units worked their way surreptitiously into our lines, sometimes by tunneling. Firefights erupted spontaneously at such moments, and I was forced to remain where I was. On a few occasions, when there were prolonged periods of action, I helped to move the wounded to safe places and worked on them as a medic might, with tape, antiseptic, and surgical gauze. What medical knowledge I had came from Scout training years before. Only on one occasion did I help with the defense of a bunker. That occurred when we were under direct threat of annihilation, and I felt it prudent to aid the unit I was with by bringing up ammunition and distributing it to the members of the platoon I was with.

In the great summer offensive, when the British landed new troops and aimed them specifically at the crest of the small mountain chain that the Ottomans dominated, I was caught between the pincers of two converging enemy columns. The situation was so fraught with danger that I wet my pants from the panic I felt. I wedged myself in between some large rocks to protect myself and brought my panic under control. But it was difficult to do, as the enemy was only yards from our bunker at the time. Half of the number defending our position were casualties that day. All the officers were lost, and for a time, only a corporal was available to order the men to stay in their positions and repel the enemy. It came down to bayonet work, and the Anzac forces lost heart at that point. Afterward, I threw up, although I hadn't eaten for over a day, so there was not much to bring up. I was left in misery. As the enemy withdrew, several of the survivors on the Ottoman side joined me. They were as terrified as I was, but somehow, they had overcome their fear and kept fighting.

But some of the time, when there was a lull in the fighting, I got to know the enlisted men who occupied the same bunker I did. Often, in those situations, I would write letters for them as all of them were illiterate. The letters we wrote were short, expressed love, and wanted the relatives not to worry. It was like writing a formula, but I knew the parents would not mind and would be grateful for such simple missives. I encouraged each letter-sender to write his own scribbled name (in Turkic) at the end of the letter. This was a high point for many of them, and most of them practiced writing their signature several times under my direction before signing the letter itself. On one occasion, I took out twenty-two letters with me to Constantinople so I could send them from there, so they would have the Constantinople postmark and, also, because the letters would be delivered faster.

Religion and what many would call 'superstition' were strong among the men. There were two men, junior NCOs, who unofficially functioned as clerics (*imam*) that is, spiritual advisors. They conducted prayers, usually in the evening when it was convenient, and always on Friday. The enemy frequently used artillery as a disruption at noon on Friday, feeling that it upset the Ottomans or that it was a proper moment to announce their own importance. Such shelling did nothing to dampen the desire for prayer; it went on once the shelling stopped.

I frequently found soldiers, particularly after dark had fallen, reciting the 'remembrance (dhikr),' that is, 'repetition of God's exalted status' among individual soldiers or small groups. It is an expression used by Muslims when they feel panic or regard themselves in great danger. Often, they used a rosary to keep track of the number of repetitions. But other expressions were used as well, although I was not familiar with many of them. Many wore talismans from particular saints' shrines, which were intended to ward off harm from bullets, missiles, and the evil thoughts of the enemy.

It got me thinking. I told Amelia about it, and the Czech/German woman in our office volunteered to visit a living saint who lived on the outskirts of Constantinople. She told the saint she needed fifty talismans dedicated by him. He was reluctant at first to assist a heathen woman, but when she explained that it was for front-line Ottoman soldiers at Gallipoli, his attitude changed immediately, and he agreed to do them for no fee whatever. He had them specially wrapped so they would not be contaminated on their way to the front. I took them with me and gave half to each of the 'clerics,' who passed them out to the soldiers, who the clerics thought would profit from them the most. As the person delivering such a gift, my prestige rose appreciably, although no one thanked me at all. That is not a gift for which one receives thanks.

Occasionally, the Ottoman forces captured Anzac prisoners, and, of course, some of the Ottoman soldiers were captured by the other side as well. Like prisoners everywhere, Anzac soldiers were terrified that they would be beaten and killed, not understanding that the Ottoman Empire had signed the Red Cross documents on proper prisoner treatment. I am not sure the signings made much difference because I later heard of serious abuses of prisoners at the hands of Ottoman guards, mostly on marches and at labor camps. So, their fears were not groundless.

I remember talking with two Australian corporals who were surprised when I addressed them in English. They wanted to know what I was doing there. I gave them cigarettes, which they lit surreptitiously, afraid they would be confiscated. I assured them that would not happen, so they relaxed a little. After a while, they loosened up and told me that the living conditions in the Anzac bunkers were bad, that getting supplies in had to be done mostly at night, and that there was a lack of water, in particular. Officers and non-coms were charged with driving the soldiers hard, and there was always the golden promise of 'all you can eat and drink,' if you could break the Ottoman hold on the elevated parts of the peninsula.

A British lieutenant was scared badly after being captured and latched onto me like a savior, fearing he would never again hear a word in English. I tried to calm him, but it took time. He told me about the evacuation of the wounded on the Commonwealth side. Most of those wounded received immediate medical aid, but then had to wait until shipping was available. They were then taken out to Alexandria for further treatment and recuperation.

He had been out once when wounded, and, he said, he was sent to a minor city in the Alexandria estuary. The authorities responsible for him forgot about him for over two weeks. He said that did not bother him much because he knew he would be shipped back to Gallipoli, and any extra time away increased his chances of surviving the war. He had been back a month and was due for rotation back to Egypt, but then this happened. "Damn the luck!" he said.

Further questioning revealed that the evacuation of prisoners was an extremely difficult problem on the Allied side because of the exposure to fire from Ottoman snipers. He found that repugnant and a sign of the Ottoman bestiality but was loath to condemn the same action if conducted by an Englishman against an Ottoman. "Somehow, it's different," he said.

An officer prisoner, a major, was arrogant towards me, asking why I was such a traitor to the 'white world' that I had hooked up with the pagan Ottomans. I did not explain to him the role of a correspondent or contradict him about my perfidy but warned him that 'a little arrogance' goes a long way when one is a prisoner. For his own sake, I said, he ought to become quite a bit humbler, or he was likely to be mistreated "even as Anzac personnel would mistreat an Ottoman prisoner when he is 'full of himself.'" He merely repeated his disdain for me. I saw him the following day when it was obvious he had been savagely beaten, but I did not reproach him. One does not gloat when a prisoner has been abused, even if he probably earned the beating.

My last prisoner was a veteran sergeant from the French forces; he was amazed when I spoke French with him. He was from Algiers and had been in the French army for about fifteen years. He had once vacationed on this very coastline while hiking through the area. He lamented that the landscape had been so ruined, as he had enjoyed it so much during his own travels. He told me a little about the French situation, where the officers were so sure that they would not repeat the mistakes of the British in their prosecution of the war. But they were bogged down in the same sort of war that the British were, with the Ottomans still controlling the elevation, making military maneuvering virtually impossible.

I had plenty of time during the campaign to assess Ottoman strengths and weaknesses as well as German strengths and weaknesses. I came to regard both as superior in many respects and lacking in several features. Ottoman officers, especially middle-grade and senior ones, all of whom had been to the staff college, were well trained, knew what their responsibilities were, and were masters at managing their units. Junior officers were less well-trained but learned fast on the job. As in most armies, casualties in the junior officer group were the highest in the army, but those who survived were astoundingly good. NCOs with experience were quite good but were limited in their abilities to perform in combat, where they were not familiar with strange conditions that were thrust on them. Nonetheless, they were much like their German counterparts, and they did not have the German military tradition, which seemed to be passed on from generation to generation. Ottoman soldiers were particularly good when trained and, especially when they gained some experience, as occurred in the Gallipoli campaign. However, they were illiterate and had to be instructed orally in everything that needed to be done. Overall, the Ottoman army performed well in the field, especially when the command structure was close by, as it was at Gallipoli.

The German command, which fit over the entire Ottoman command structure, was especially good at planning and forecasting what the enemy was likely to do in given situations. The senior German commanders evaluated the Ottoman commanders and chose certain ones for tasks throughout the campaign. Mustapha Kemal was a favorite, but only after he had proven himself several times. Other senior Ottoman officers did well under this system as well.

The German command worked well with their Ottoman counterparts and treated them as equals, even if in private, they may have expressed reservations. One could not have chosen a better German commander for the job than General Liman von Sanders. Without his masterful leadership, the campaign might have been lost in the early days, but he led in the darkest days of the summer campaign when all seemed lost and forced the British to reconsider the campaign in the first place. I interviewed van Sanders several times, and he repeatedly expressed his high regard for the Ottoman effort.

I talked once with my colleague, Kurt Langer, about the matter, and he agreed with my assessments, although he was less charitable towards Ottoman non-coms and enlisted personnel.

Near the end of the campaign, I was just finishing a tour with the front-line units and was about to find a place to write up my latest report when I was informed by an aide that General Mustapha Kemal wished to see me. I dusted my uniform a little, straightened my belt, and adjusted my cap. I told the aide I was ready. He led me to a commander's bunker to the rear of the front, where Mustapha Kemal and an aide were waiting for me. "You wished to see me, general," I said.

"Yes," he answered, "I remember you from the second day of the battle at Hellas Point when we repelled the Anzac troops. That was a close moment when history hung in the balance. I was surprised at your bravery. You had no weapon but insisted that, as a correspondent, you had a right to witness the battle. You did that and kept out of the way of the regular troops. The carnage was so great that evening that I could not imagine that you survived, unarmed as you were."

"I remember as well," I answered, "How you took control of the battlefield and encouraged your battalion to not give any ground. They didn't, against great odds. It was a privilege to see such a moment in Ottoman military history. It ranks with some of the great successes of the past, such as Chaldiran and Kars.[8]"

---

[8] The battle of Chaldiran was a 16th Century victory of the Ottomans against the Safavid Empire of Persia. The battle of Kars was a18th Century victory of Nadir Shah of Persia over the Ottomans. The two battles were viewed as important historical events in the history of the Ottomans emblematic of the 'raider"spirit.

He seemed to like the comparison with memorable past battles, but he still switched subjects as if modest about his own achievements. "I understand," he said, "that you spend your time as a correspondent with the front-line units. That is unusual, of course. Did you know that you are considered a good luck talisman when you stay with a unit?" I shook my head, indicating 'no.' He continued, "It's true enough. I wonder why I never see you. Occasionally I see Mr Kurt Langer, who speaks very good Turkish. You speak better than he does. Why do you avoid me? Do you have something against me or my rank?"

"No, no," I answered. "Nothing negative like that. Generals are busy people and have much on their minds, so it is best not to annoy them. I always figure that if they want to see me, they will ask me to visit them, even as you have today. What do I know about strategy and even tactics? I was not trained in those areas of military science. I know some Ottoman history but nothing much more, so I would not do as an adviser. I suppose I could ask you how the war is going, but I can get good answers to that question from the men at the front lines. Does such an answer affront you, general?"

"No, of course not," he answered, "You are being realistic. But you probably have greater insight into the thinking of the front-line soldier than any of us in command. Perhaps you could drop by, say, once a fortnight and give me ten minutes of what the Ottoman private is thinking. For example, 'what is he thinking about this week?'"

I answered without hesitation. "He is concerned about winding down the campaign and how it will end. Some see the British simply leaving, while others forecast ruin and damnation being visited on them from the battleships."

"Not much different than the view from here," the general answered. "What is the majority view?"

"Last week, it was 'ruin and damnation' but 'Tommy' and his 'Anzac whipping boys' have been quiet lately, so the general view is that they are ready to slip away quietly and forget they were ever here."

He laughed at my use of 'Tommy' and 'whipping boys' and said, "I hope that mood prevails among the enemy. But tell me, what do they think will happen after this campaign is over?"

I smiled and said, "Can you imagine a son of Anatolia wondering about such a mystical exercise as that? He is much more fatalistic and will wait for God to decide such a weighty matter."

The aide laughed at this, and Mustapha Kemal smiled, saying, 'You really do know your fellows at the front, don't you? Thanks for stopping by today. It was refreshing and very, very honest. Do come again and impart more wisdom to me."

I turned and walked from the bunker. My car was there, so I went directly to it and laughed about the short, impromptu session with the great hero of the Gallipoli campaign.

Reporting on Crucial Encounters

I wrote several pieces that were never published because I knew they would not get the censor's stamp of approval. However, they were important enough to me that I recorded them anyway. I featured a collection of my reports after the war was over, and I knew that these unpublished pieces would find a fitting home in such a publication.

The first piece was written about the third day of the battle when I had time to write and could spare some time from the task of finding the means to survive. I was in battle during that entire time with no sleep and no letup in tension. The report covered the arrival of the Anzac forces, as they landed at Gabe Tepe before dawn and as they tried to cross the island to cut off the Ottoman forces guarding a strategic cape. The sea currents landed the Anzac forces two miles from their planned site, where they encountered two Ottoman rifle companies that were, happen-chance, at the landing site. The rifle companies had control of some beach fortifications, and they put out a withering fire, making it difficult to move around them and continue with the mission. Eventually, the Ottoman forces retreated, presumably when they were low on ammunition.

I obtained information from a reconnaissance officer I had been with at Sarikamish the previous winter, who shadowed the advance of the Anzacs and constantly reported back to the Ottoman commander at the interception area. The strategy was for Ottoman forces to remain at that point, to be able to move wherever and whenever a landing occurred. The reconnaissance officer said that the beach landing by the Anzacs was managed in an effective military fashion, although, if it had been more strongly opposed, the landing force would have suffered severe casualties. As it was, they suffered only light to intermediate losses. The presence of those two companies of Ottoman infantry delayed Anzac operations and put them well behind schedule.

Then, the hunt for a passage inland from the beach had to be found. The Anzacs had not sent in a reconnaissance unit to find such a passage beforehand, so the landing force itself had to do its own reconnoitering after it arrived. Considering the steep gullies, weathered terrain, and stubbled wasteland, it was a difficult task.

What might have taken a few hours to traverse with good intelligence beforehand turned into a difficult trek that lasted until late afternoon. The orderliness with which the force left the beach was easily broken up when units separated to track the scattered paths through the inhospitable landscape.

The Ottomans did not wait for the Anzac units to reach them but, instead, met them at a point where the Ottomans enjoyed better terrain than what the Anzacs were forced to accept. The Ottomans also had an opportunity to prepare their positions ahead of time with trenches and machine gun emplacements, which allowed the Ottomans the upper hand in immediate fighting at that line. The Anzac forces had to accept bad terrain and try to overcome the disadvantages by digging a trench line while under fire. The Ottoman machine guns were merciless in harassing the trench diggers and took heavy casualties, as well as spread widespread panic.

But Anzac officers pushed attacks on the Ottoman lines all afternoon to break the line or force a retreat. Neither happened. Late in the afternoon, Anzac forces pulled back and sought better terrain but had difficulty locating any. Finally, they dug in for the night, and the Ottomans, ready for a rest after the difficult work of the afternoon, allowed them some respite.

Overnight, the Anzac commander reorganized and, the following morning, threw his entire force into a 'do or die' attack, which the Ottomans met with a 'do or die' defense. Again, however, the Ottoman commanders selected good defensive sites, with machine gun emplacements and mass rifle fire, which slowed the Anzac advance and eventually brought it to a standstill.

Then, in the evening, the Anzac commander made one last gigantic effort, which nearly carried the day and had the Ottomans nearly beaten. However, Mustapha Kemal, then a battalion commander, rallied his troops and ordered his men to stay at their positions until reinforcements could be brought up. The reinforcements did arrive, but not before most of Mustapha Kemal's troops had been either killed or wounded. German and Ottoman assessments afterward, and probably Commonwealth assessments as well, isolated the late evening defense by Mustapha Kemal's battalion as the pivotal point that determined the campaign for the next eight months, giving the advantage to the Ottomans.

During this time, I spent most of my time in Ottoman trenches and in the area immediately behind them, observing the fighting close-up. I had to endure artillery barrages, counterattacks, and sudden raids at all times of the day and night. Sleep was taken in small amounts and was usually accomplished sitting in a slit trench or lying on the open ground in stubble grass. There was only one day that was different. That occurred when I spent the day with an Ottoman sniper.

The sniper was a corporal from Ankara who managed his Mauser rifle like it was an extension of his right arm. He made five 'kills' that day—two officers, one of them a major, and three NCOs. He was patient and selective, letting many, many men pass by his 'window' until he had the desired kind of enemy in his sights, and then he was deadly. He fired only eight shots that day. Twice, scout units were sent out to find us, but neither came anywhere close to our location.

My second article was written several days after the end of the mid-summer, or August, offensive by Commonwealth forces, which established a new beachhead at Sulva Bay with fresh troops. The plan was to seize the entire crest of the highlands for further Allied operations, designed to force a breakout to the east in the direction of Constantinople.

There was little secret that an invasion were coming. The small Ottoman air force, with an airbase on the Gallipoli Peninsula, had located the armada that was bringing in the troops. Anzac prisoners taken just before the offensive also gave indications of troop shifts to support the new invasion force. Accordingly, the German-Ottoman command brought in combat units drawn from the Russian front to meet the new threat. The Ottomans were well prepared to oppose such an invasion.

My sources were three company-grade officers—all captains at the time— who led companies into the battle and fought critical engagements. I supplemented their accounts with after-battle reports from the commanders of two reinforcement companies who were sent into battle on the final day. They were present when the attack reached a critical point, with a section of the crest in Allied hands. A staff major at Ottoman headquarters gave me access to the reports when Enver Pasha sent a message telling the officer I was to have such access. But the report I eventually wrote was so full of Ottoman losses that I understood that the censors would not give permission for its transmission, even though I discussed the terrible losses suffered by the Allied forces as well. It was a case of self-censorship.

The strategy of General Liman von Sanders, still the commander of the Fifth Ottoman Army at the time, was to keep forces not needed for current needs in a general reserve, where they could be shifted as needed. However, there is a lag time while the need is assessed and the units dispatched to manage the crisis. In this case, it proved fortuitous because van Sanders had the option of naming which Ottoman commander he could choose for each unit he sent into battle.

The strategy of the British commander was to open the battle with attempted breakouts at the two beachheads that already existed that had, heretofore, been contained by the Ottomans. In both cases, the Commonwealth soldiers—Anzacs, Indians, British, and French—burst forth and drove into Ottoman territory, aiming for the high ground. They were to link up with each other and with the new invasion force which would land at Sulva Bay. The two actions resulted in substantial Allied gains, and the front trenches of the Ottomans were breached, but the rupture was contained later in the day.

Again, Mustapha Kemal was dispatched with three Ottoman divisions and, over several days, drove the enemy's forces away from the ridge with a tremendous cost in lives on both sides. The Allies were exhausted by the effort so that when the Sulva Bay landing occurred, the Ottomans easily managed it. It had been designed to overwhelm Ottoman forces, who were supposed to be exhausted at that point, but the opposite had occurred. The three-pronged Allied offensive ground to a halt, with the Ottomans still clearly in command of the ridge.

The role played by Mustapha Kemal made him a hero, although he had already become one with his great defense in the opening days of the war. This time, as the commander of three divisions, he thoroughly put down the most serious threat the Entente had made in Gallipoli. He ruined any Entente hopes of winning in that theater of operations.

My final piece was done near the end of the campaign. I called it the 'balance sheet' or "Why the Ottomans Prevailed at Gallipoli."

Ottoman Strengths:

1. Fighting on its home soil.

2. Organizing a national effort, which included training a conscript army and organizing civilians to support the war. There were large reserves of potential military recruits.

3. The German alliance gave them modern weapons, key commanders, and sound military advice. German diplomacy opened the Balkans at a crucial juncture so that needed supplies could be brought to the Ottomans from Germany. German submarines, for a time, gave the Ottomans needed help in holding the British navy at bay, even sinking several of its capital ships.

4. Strong coastal defense system, consisting of powerful howitzers in fortress settings, with a capability to prepare and maintain naval minefields. Those defenses proved almost invulnerable to British naval attacks.

5. The dedication and endurance of the Ottoman fighting men, who came from all parts of the empire and from among all its disparate people.

Ottoman Weaknesses

1. While the industrial base was good, it was not sufficiently developed to provide all the armaments and war materials necessary for a prolonged and demanding war. It relied very heavily on

German industrial strength, and it was dependent on a long supply line that was politically interrupted at several crucial moments.

2. Had to fight a two-front war against the Russians in the north and Great Britain in the south.

3. Operating in an empire that was vast in size without a fully developed communication and transportation system. There were huge gaps between Constantinople and some of the outlying provinces in the east and far south. Great Britain took advantage of this to begin an invasion of the southeastern provinces, during which time Basra was taken and Baghdad threatened.

Entente Strengths:

1. Worldwide empires with large populations, from which to draw needed manpower reserves for fighting and for labor battalions.

2. A first-class navy with a worldwide network of ships at sea to support Entente presence wherever it was needed.

Allied Weaknesses:

1. Fighting on foreign soil with little knowledge of the conditions facing its army.

2. Long supply and communication lines that stretched thousands of miles to home countries. There was great difficulty in establishing intermediate and forward positioning depots to keep the forces supplied and operating.

3. The Gallipoli Theater was a diversion with the single purpose of driving the Ottomans from the war, while the European theater

clearly was the more important theater that could demand vital resources when its political leaders insisted.

Overall, the British had better long-term prospects for ultimate victory. However, the cost of the campaign in troops committed and the time needed to accomplish victory spelled defeat for the the Commonwealth forces, largely because the European priority drew troops and resources away. It was the Ottoman persistence and heavy sacrifice that prevailed in the Gallipoli campaign.

Somewhere along about the middle of the campaign, I received two letters that did not get opened and read by me for several more weeks because of the time I was at the front. The first was from Aunt Bea.

Dear Marty,

I don't know how to tell you this, but Janet Everett has decided to get married. Who can say whether this is true or not? It may simply be a ploy to bring you home and force you to accept her. You know how dramatic she can be sometimes. Your mother and father do not want you to marry, as they say, she is too erratic and that being with her would be no real life for you. I must agree with them. But you may see it differently, and if you do, please forgive your old Aunt Bea for sticking her nose in where it is not wanted.

Your sister has a new boyfriend. This one is a Baptist, which does not please your father very much, but your mother is fine with it. In any case, the boy seems nice and does not do the looney things that the Watchtower beau did.

Keep safe, and I hope you are not involved in the terrible Gallipoli offensive, which seems to be a meat grinder. But I know you have more sense to get yourself into something like that.

Love, your Aunt Bea.

The second letter was from Janet Everett herself.

Dear Marty,

You haven't been writing very much, so I know you must be chasing after that Amelia woman again. You are distracted, or otherwise, you would pay more attention to me. It must be her.

Why won't you grow up and face your responsibilities instead of running around the world trying to be a newsman? Well, I have grown tired of waiting, and so I am going to marry Gary Abernethy, who we both knew when we were younger, and he was even on the cross-country team with you. I have gone out with him now for several months, and he has grown on me. I have always been so wrapped up in you that I never knew that he always adored me. It was a real revelation and made me feel like I was wanted. Not just someone who is always available when you call. He asked me last week if I would marry him, and I said 'yes.' I am now wearing the diamond ring he gave me for the engagement. We plan to be married before Christmas.

I want you to know about this beforehand so that you can decide whether to rectify the matter, although you would have to be awfully persuasive for me to change my mind.

Love, your former girlfriend, Janet.

Good for both, I thought. I am sure they will be happy, and they will remind me of their happiness for the rest of their lives, whether true or not. I remembered Gary had once said in the locker room after a cross-country run that he thought Janet had exceedingly small breasts, while he himself preferred something a lot more substantial. But then he wasn't thinking of the bank balance that was going to come with Janet when she married. I had long expected this to happen, and now that it had, I was tremendously relieved. I resolved not to write back because she would certainly see that as further interest on my part in her, and I wanted to shut that possibility out for good. I realized that I was now free to become even closer to Amelia without fear of outside entanglements. Events sometimes have a way of straightening themselves out.

Other things happened during this span of time. At the office, Jon Bylice left to head the press unit at Vienna, which he had always wanted and which was given to him because of his unfortunate personal conflict with Kurt Langer. That happened just before the August offensive. In fact, I was just leaving the 'forbidden area,' which marked the battle area, and was about to get in the car that had been sent to get me for the trip back to Constantinople for my three-day rest. The driver handed me a message, which stated: "Call me before you return to Constantinople, Boris."

I backtracked to the press office, which I knew had an outside line that I could use. It was available, so I rang Boris, got an office assistant, and was connected to Boris immediately. "Thanks for calling, Marty. A big load has just been lifted off your office. You won't have Kurt and Jon fighting anymore, as Jon has been reassigned to Vienna. He is en route even as we speak."

"Well, I' m not surprised," I said, "Kurt ought to be easier to live with now. Who is taking over? Are you bringing in someone from elsewhere?"

"It's either you, Kurt, Amelia, or Cynthia," said Boris. "I haven't anyone else with the language skills to manage the job there. I don't really want either you or Kurt to leave the field reporters' positions because you both have substantial readerships. Practically, that leaves the two women."

"I agree about my own participation. I was hired as a reporter and like what I am doing now, and I certainly would not want to change that role over to manager of the office. Have you talked with Kurt?"

"Only generally, a few days ago, before this situation came up. He was talking about a southern tour to see Germans in action in the southeast, so I doubt if he would be interested." Boris paused and then continued. "He has always spoken of the position in negative terms, so I doubt if he would want it. But I will talk with him."

I said, "Well, if he will take the position, I have no objections, and he would be my first choice. Between the two women, I would choose Amelia because she has been a reporter for some time now and her writing has improved considerably. She knows the drill very well and brings her photographic experience with her, which is a real plus. The two women have been running the office for the last couple of months in any case, so the situation would not be much different."

"Agreed," said Boris. "Amelia has grown in ways I can hardly recognize, and she has given the office some reporting that extends beyond you and Kurt. Her own reporting and that of the stringers have given us a good copy. I was down on her when she let that nincompoop German officer into her bed, but he has been transferred to the Baghdad front, so he's out of the picture. I like Cynthia, but she lacks the leadership traits that Amelia has."

Later, when I got back to the hotel, Amelia was already there with a bottle of champagne. She said, "We had a party at work earlier when Boris called Cynthia and me and told us that I had been made office manager and Cynthia was assistant office manager. He gave raises to all the office staff. I thought you would want to celebrate with me tonight."

"Hey," I answered enthusiastically. "I'm all for that. I called Boris at Gallipoli, and he told me about it. I am delighted. It seems you are out of Boris's doghouse."

"Kurt left for Baghdad this afternoon," she said, "so all the grouches are gone. You are not one, thank God! I think the office will function a lot better now. Or, at least, it will be a more pleasant place in which to work."

In the evening, we ordered room service, ate well, drank champagne, reminisced, and then we went to bed together, again with our skivvies on. I will admit, however, I had an erection, and not only did Amelia not object and say something about it, but she even held it through my underwear as if it was something to be treasured. It was apparent to me that our relationship was going to have to be reevaluated sooner rather than later.

As if in celebration, George and Amelia sent out a seven-part series on the 'Home Front in the Ottoman Empire,' in which they described the integration of millions of women into the labor force, how it was done, and the results to date. The first number told about the Navy Patriotic League, which had raised money from the public for the purchase of two battleships that had been completed shortly before the war began. The British government had confiscated them and held them as ransom for Ottoman assurances of neutrality in the war. When war was declared, the ships had been integrated into the British navy with English names.

In many respects, the German gift of the two cruisers had been seen as a sort of compensation for those seizures. The new work of the Navy League concentrated on raising awareness and support for the families of servicemen who had been inducted, leaving the families without a breadwinner in many cases.

The second number in the series talked about the Red Crescent Society, which tried to support families who were uprooted. Mostly, these were peasant families who moved to factory jobs in the city, where many facilities were either lacking or the families did not know about. The Society also looked after people in dire straits, much like the Red Cross was doing in Europe, where assistance was given during disasters and hard times. The third number told about the National Defense League, which, like the Navy League, worked with families of servicemen.

Further numbers talked about the induction of women into the workforce throughout society, taking the place of men who were in the service, and how they managed to keep their families together while performing their new duties. Still, later, numbers in the series expanded on these themes and concluded that the adjustments made by societies in Europe, especially the role of women in the new arrangements, were common in the Ottoman Empire as well.

Boris sent a letter of congratulations to the office for its work in working on the series and for its great success. Since it came right after the reorganization of the office, Amelia took it as a sign of her own growing success in the operation. It most certainly was an achievement.

Aftermath of a 'Failed' Campaign

The final month of the Gallipoli campaign was cold and even snowy, with temperatures well below freezing. The Commonwealth forces left in a surreptitious hurry, trying to get out as fast as possible and to keep the enemy from knowing just how rapidly they were departing. Then, one morning, everyone from the Commonwealth side was gone, and the armada that had been there supporting operations began disappearing as well. Soon, nothing but the ships of the British naval blockade of the Dardanelles was left. Ottoman coastal artillery kept a careful watch on the ships of that blockade.

I invited Amelia to come over from Constantinople to see the site where the battle had been fought. She got there in time for a tour organized by von Sanders' headquarters to see the mounds of supplies the Allied forces had left. When van Sanders discovered that Amelia was alone, he asked if she would accompany him. While he did not say so, it seemed apparent that he wanted to meet and talk with the woman who had caused such a ruckus in the German community of Constantinople when she had her affair with Werner, his one-time staff assistant.

 The general was relaxed that day and had little on his mind about the future, so he kept up a lively conversation with her in German throughout the entire two hours that the tour took. Amelia said afterward that von Sanders was the perfect German gentleman, soliciting her opinion on matters and pretending that those opinions mattered when she knew he didn't care one way or the other on the subject. "He was just like Werner in that respect," she said.

All the British artillery and other heavy weapons had been taken away, but there were stacks of disabled pistols and rifles, where some salvage might be possible. More importantly, there were some ammunition supplies that could be transferred to the Ottoman navy, which still had a considerable number of British guns from pre-war years. There was a large amount of medical supplies that were being taken away by the Ottoman army's medical corps, as such supplies were low in the Ottoman reserves. Food was hardly salvageable, as the Ottoman troops had gotten to it before the last Allies left, as their own rations were very meager at that point in time. So, the soldiers ate well for a few days.

There was discussion in the entourage about why the Allies even left. I gleaned enough from the conversation with two Ottoman officers who understood German that, in fact, there was a buildup on the Allied side in France and Belgium for a large offensive there. Troops had been taken from Gallipoli precisely for that purpose. It was also freely admitted in the group that Ottoman resources had been stretched to the limit during the siege and that another offensive on the magnitude of the August offensive might well have carried the day. But it was also believed by von Sanders' staff that the Allied leaders at Gallipoli lacked the will to attempt such a major effort until way into the next year. It was not worth staying to find out.

The entire entourage had refreshments after the tour, and General von Sanders stayed to enjoy 'Kaffee und Kuchen,' when he kept Amelia by his side. Midway through the refreshment period, an aide came to me and said that the general invited me to his table. I found the general, two of his aides, and Amelia talking animatedly in German. When I arrived, the general said, good-naturedly, in French, "Well, messieurs et mademoiselle, we must now switch over to our schoolboy French. Monsieur Mintz has arrived."

I said, "Bon jour, mon generale, monsieurs, et mon cherie Émilié. It is so thoughtful of you, general, to invite me to your table." I sat down at the only vacant chair without being asked to sit. It was an informal session, after all.

The higher ranking of the aides, a lieutenant colonel, asked me, "Mr. Mintz, the story circulated that you told Mustapha Kemal that his soldiers held that only God could decide where we could go next after winning at Gallipoli. The context seems important. How was it phrased at the time?"

I answered, "when the general asked what thinking is like on the Ottoman front lines about where they would go next, I answered, 'Can you imagine a son of Anatolia answering such a mystical question? He would wait for God to decide such a weighty matter.'" Fortunately, I rendered the original Turkic into good French.

"Now that makes better sense than what we heard," said General von Sanders. He continued with his thought, "But we could substitute 'Enver Pasha' for 'God' and then it would make even more sense." Everyone laughed.

We all talked about the matter for a few minutes, and it was agreed that the Ottoman high command had little choice than to send reinforcement to all the other fronts where the enemy had made gains or might make gains. "Baghdad will be first, I suspect," said the senior aide, "with the northern front also getting its share of manpower."

"Don't forget the Suez Canal beckons as well," said the general. At headquarters, it was known that one of their own members, Colonel Kress Kressenstein, headed a task force in the Sinai area for just that purpose.

Then, when that subject was put to rest, the general turned to me and said, "I want to apologize for taking away your charming colleague today. It only occurred to me at the end of the tour that you yourself wanted to show her some of the sites that are personal to you. Do forgive me if I interfered with that effort."

I replied, "No, I assure you, that was not the case. I am pleased that you gave her your attention today. She works hard in our office on the war stories that Herr Langer and I produce, so she deserves some special attention at times like these. I owe you my gratitude for your kindness in allowing her to accompany you."

"Marty is right," interjected Amelia, "It was a real treat for me, and I enjoyed talking with you ever so much." The general rose, and we all knew the tour was at an end, and we were free to go about our own affairs.

In the car on the way back to the city, Amelia said at one point, "The day reminded me of Werner, of course. Speaking German with his fellow officers could be expected to dredge up memories of that sort. However, surprisingly, I was not nostalgic about it, as I expected I might be. I'm over him, or, at least, getting over him."

"Do you stay in touch with him," I asked.

"No, of course not," she answered, "Neither does he write. I think he made a real commitment to reconcile with his wife this time and intends to honor that commitment. In any case, I am not going to sit around and mope about it, or I'll become the old maid my mother constantly warns me about." She was silent, and I did not want to break the spell. Then she finally said, "Which brings us around to the matter of your erections over the past several trips from the front. We said we would do something about the matter, and I think the time has come for us to do. Supposing we ask Boris for some time off to recharge our batteries in Greece or even Italy."

"That's not a bad idea at all," I answered. "He's not apt to refuse with the Gallipoli campaign just over, and there is a lull that has descended because of it."

We never got a chance to ask Boris the question because the 'sky fell in.'

Chapter Seven

The Armenians

Interrogations

When we arrived at our offices after the trip back from Gallipoli, there were several official cars with drivers parked outside. Inside the office, work was at a standstill, and police were foraging their way methodically through all the files, bookshelves, and other repositories, apparently looking for evidence. The office staff were all gathered in the typists' alcove, and no work was being done. They were chattering like sparrows in their native Slavic language, which probably meant that they were excited, not afraid. That cheered me up some. Cynthia was bravely talking to the official who appeared to oversee the investigation squad. She seemed concerned but certainly not browbeaten. On seeing Amelia, Cynthia said, "Here she is now!"

The official turned and confronted both Amelia and me. "You are Amelia Caruthers and Martin Mintz?"

We both said we were. He responded, "Then you will be taken away for questioning in a case involving state security. You are not under arrest at present but must come with us. Do you understand!"

"Certainly!" we both said.

He took us to the front of the building and put me in an automobile with a driver and a police officer, and the same was done with Amelia. We drove off in different directions, so I realized that we were obviously being interrogated separately but probably for the same infraction of the law. I had no idea what it could be, and I doubted whether Amelia would know either. But she told me later that she knew almost immediately it had to do with the office's reporting on Armenian discontent and public reaction to it.

I was taken to Enver Pasha's office, where one of Enver's assistants met me. I did not remember his name and had seen him previously only when he sometimes sat in on my meetings with Enver. We had said "hello" to one another several times but little else.

This time, he said, "Mr. Mintz, we generally see one another under more pleasant circumstances, but this time, there is a problem that needs investigation, and we need your assistance in unraveling it. I hope you will cooperate with me so that we can get this meeting over with as quickly as possible."

I responded, "I have no idea what this is all about, but I have nothing to hide. I will be as cooperative as possible and give you the information you ask for to the best of my ability."

"The Minister of War has told me that you would give that answer, and it pleases me greatly that you will be cooperative," he answered.

He pushed a copy of the latest *Tribune* (Bucharest edition) across to me. The headline read, "Official proclaims Ottoman strikes against Armenians." I quickly scanned the front-page article, which said that there had been a series of incidents throughout the Ottoman Empire in recent months in which Armenians had been accosted and some killed. A few of the incidents were summarized, and some of the incidents went back several months in time. That section was written under the byline of Amelia Caruthers. Following that beginning, a second paragraph, which was identified as having been taken from the *Greek Gazette* (Rhodes), stated that a document obtained by a reporter from reliable sources instructed local vigilante groups to carry out an extermination campaign against the Armenian residents in a particular area. The document was purportedly signed by Mehmet Talaat Pasha, Chairman of the Government Council and leading CUP official. Then came further information about action against the Armenians, supposedly supplied by Amelia.

This was the first time I had seen any evidence that the government itself was involved in anti-Armenian activities, although I had heard statements by Enver Pasha and others that they blamed the Armenians for many of the problems that the Ottomans experienced, particularly during the Balkan Wars and border incidents with Russia. None of those statements directed anyone to act, even though, at times, it was sometimes strongly hinted that action might be taken.

I pushed the newspaper back without comment.

"Your newspaper is making a defamatory accusation against a leader of this nation," the aide said, "and your editor makes it plainly and brazenly."

I realized I had to be careful and not excite this interrogator, but keep it on a civil basis, if possible, even a friendly level. So I attempted to back him off his assertion that Amelia was at fault. "Well, my good friend, this is indeed serious business. I do not want to make light of it at all. But let us look at what Miss Caruthers really reported. She noted a series of incidents, reported widely in the past, plus one at present, where Armenians have been involved in disturbances and that they got the worst end of it. Later, she repeated and summarized some of these statements. All that is generally found in the press, and, if I am not mistaken, the censor approved her copy. You have a copy of that approved statement, don't you?

The aide did have the censored copy and presented it. We looked at it together and found that it corresponded to what Amelia reported under her byline.

"Now," I said, "It appears that the statement about His Honor Mehmet Talaat Pasha was made by someone from the newspaper in Rhodes. Miss Caruthers is a very meticulous person, and it is doubtful that she would have had that added without approval by the censors. It probably was added by the editor in Bucharest, don't you think?"

"But you have a Greek reporter working for you," came the reply. "He has written articles in the past about so-called abuses to the Greeks, problems with the Assyrians, and supposed humiliations of the Armenians. We regard him as an agent of 'run-away' Christianity. Surely, he is the culprit here. You must see that?" I was satisfied that I was keeping this interrogation at a conversational level but unhappy that a fellow journalist from our office was being charged with sedition. But there was little I could do about it.

"Well, that's very possible," I said, "but the only thing on that one is that Michael works for the *Smyrna Registry,* and he would have to go through the same censor approval process if he sent a copy of such a report to Rhodes. Our office is strict on the matter. All our reports go through such a process, without exception, as the Minister of War can attest." I could tell from the facial expression of the aide that he believed that Michael had deliberately avoided the censor.

On my part, I believed that Michael had not really avoided the censor; he had simply left Ottoman territory to report the story in Greece and that he was not about to return. Moreover, I knew as well that the editors in Bucharest were at a point where they could no longer publish Armenian atrocity stories without assigning fault for them, and, in Michael's report, they had a clear source. Of course, it left Amelia holding the bag.

If I thought I was playing a clever game, I had to admit that the aide was playing one as well. Without further comment about Michael, he shoved another newspaper across the table to me. This one was the latest edition of the *Istanbul Herald*, the newspaper that had provided my cameramen and with whom I had shared stories many times. The *Herald's* lead article used much the same material as the *Tribune* copy but went deeper and clearly assigned the blame to the government. It hinted that Mehmet Talaat Pasha might himself be involved. In addition to the document used by Michael, it had two other documents that 'allegedly' confirmed the involvement of state officials. All the bylines were those of local Constantinople reporters.

I took my time reading the article that was indicated to me and even reread it to be sure of its contents. After all, it was written in Turkish, and I am not always sure of clause antecedents, which can lead a person to wrong conclusions. But I felt I had mastered it well enough. I returned the paper to the aide, who had been waiting patiently.

He said, "This newspaper has the complete story and is nearly identical in information to what the *Tribune* carried. Surely, they come from the same source. Don't you agree?"

"Perhaps," I answered, "It certainly shows that several newspaper reporters are going after a story and using the same sources."

He paid almost no attention to my answer and immediately came back with, "You are known to be close to the editor of the *Herald*. You have given him information on many stories, such as your trip with the navy to raid the Russian ports. Moreover, you use the *Herald* cameraman and, in fact, many times use the same photos as the *Herald* does for your articles. Surely you don't deny that?"

"Not at all," I said quickly. "The editor of the *Herald* and I occasionally consult with one another about certain potential stories, and I have given information, on occasion, when I have found it convenient to do so. But I have never given a story to the *Herald* that would embarrass the government, nor that I was going to have to submit through the censor for my own publication. I did not do it this time, either. If you check, you will find that it is true. I have no reason to publish stories that the government does not want to be published. Both Amelia Caruthers and I have thought hard about certain submissions and changed their contents at times to get our articles through the censors. We do want to be in conformity with government sensitivities about such matters."

He did not give up on this assertion of collusion between me and the editor of the *Herald*. "But how do we really know about this latest submission? You could have fed the editor the story."

"Not really," I said, "I have been at the front for several months now, sending news from there, and have filed no stories on other matters. Nor have I used any of their cameramen for some time. I was at Gallipoli almost the entire last week and have not left there until today after a battlefield tour with General Liman von Sanders. There are few phones at the front, and the only one I ever use is at the portal to the battlefield where the information office is located. One must sign to use the phone and pay for the call. You will not find a call credited to me in the past ten days. That should tell you I have had no contact with the *Herald*."

"But you do not rule out that another member of the *Tribune* staff might have coordinated with the *Herald's* editors," he charged.

"True enough," I said. At that point, I was unsure that something like that might have happened, but I was not about to admit it. I was not much worried about Michael; he had left the country and was safe. The *Herald's* editor had his own lawyers and was likely to get a slap on the wrist with a week's or month's suspension, so he was safe enough. I was most worried about Amelia, who was a foreign national and could end up in prison for violating censorship regulations. But I knew that to try to defend her too strongly would be an indication of guilt, so I kept quiet about her. But the next remark of the aide indicated that it was, indeed, Amelia that was the chief suspect.

"In looking back over the time your colleague, Amelia Caruthers, has been here, she has shown great interest in groups that are at the heart of unrest in our country," the aide said.

I said nothing. He proceeded with his thought. "She once went to Smyrna to report on unrest caused when Greeks were dislodged from their occupation of residential homes. The government had assigned those homes to Turkic peoples who had been exiled from Greece. It is the policy of our government to exchange such people, and the government's action was in total accord with the agreement. Yet your colleague reported that the actions were outside the law and suggested that they were probably immoral, warning the government it was mistreating its own citizens."

I said nothing. The aide continued. "On another occasion, Armenians in Alexandretta were voicing great criticism of the government, and they were also in contact with the ships of the British fleet, giving them information on conditions in the area. The government moved in to secure the area from possible invasion and to shut off the unauthorized flow of information. Your colleague wrote a series of articles, based on the reports of local newsmen, assailing the removal of potential collaborators to new homes in the Adana area and their replacement with reliable Turkish speakers. She claimed the actions smacked of 'draconian' attempts to stifle the voices of people who disagreed with the government. She completely ignored the very real concerns connected to the contacts with the British fleet. Her articles were one-sided and blamed the Ottoman authorities for all incidents that emerged from the relocation efforts.

Again, I said nothing. The aide chose another case. "The reporter Michael reported on a case where Armenians south of Erzurum expelled the Ottoman police and legitimate officials from their county, saying that the area now belonged to an 'independent Armenia.' He, of course, sided with the Armenians, as he always has. That is to be expected, and I certainly hope, for his sake, he has left Ottoman territory, for he will certainly be charged with sedition if he is found in our territory.

"But, back to your female colleague. She could not leave the matter alone. She herself went to the area and filed two reports in which she followed up on the incident, reporting that the Ottoman response was swift and harsh. She certainly quoted Ottoman law enforcement officials about the need to put down threats to public safety, but at the end, she deftly inserted a sentence saying that some non-Armenian neighbors had said that "with more understanding and negotiation," it might have been possible to resolve the situation without such harshness."

I still said nothing. He looked at me and said, "You say nothing about these reports. Surely you have a reaction?"

I moved in my chair, cleared my throat, and said, "I don't know what to say. You have picked out several reports that she has filed over the past year and say they reveal a pattern of 'disrespect' for the Ottoman government. At the same time, you ignore the many, many reports on a great array of subjects, where she shows great admiration for the Ottoman cause, such as her fine series on the action of the government in mobilizing the population for the war effort. Or her earlier articles on city life in Anatolia, where she praised the efforts of CUP women in raising the consciousness of modern life throughout the nation. My colleague, Amelia, is a discerning reporter and praises, when she finds praise merited, and she criticizes when officials fall short of their just responsibilities."

Our roles were suddenly reversed. He said nothing, waiting for me to say more. I obliged him but told myself I would not go much further. I said, "The government could have stopped any of these reports from being filed merely by having the censor say the text was unacceptable. You cannot reasonably say that any of us in the office–and this includes my colleague Amelia–violate the censor's signature. If the government has had difficulty with Amelia, it had the means to stop her submissions at the time they were submitted. Why weren't they?"

The aide decided this remark needed a response. "Individually, the reports may be able to pass the censor because it is questionable but not objectionable. It is the sum of such reports, the great repetition of a questionable theme, that is the objection. Your colleague has been playing a dangerous game, and her actions have caught up with her."

The aide left me at that point, and I was then alone in a small conference room. After two hours of waiting, food from the street stalls was brought to me, which was tasty and certainly very welcome. I was tired, so I laid down on the conference table and slept for an hour. At that time, a functionary came in and roused me, saying that Enver Pasha wanted to see me. I stood up, straightened my clothing, and went to Enver's office. He was alone, and the window showed it was past sunset. "It's been a busy day," he said, "so it was inevitable that you had to wait. But you are accustomed to that, sitting in a bunker waiting for a raid to begin, are you not?"

I nodded and stood before his desk, where he was seated. He indicated with a wave of his hand that I should sit in the visitor's chair. "I have just come from a meeting of the council of ministers where the case of you and your colleagues was discussed. We had your statement, those of the editor of the *Herald,* and those of your colleague Amelia Caruthers.

"The editor of the *Herald* said he was merely following leads and published the news as it came to his attention. If he inadvertently stepped over the line, he apologized. He said his contacts with you were professional, that you had occasionally shared information, and that he had 'rented' a cameraman to you several times. All shared information was about the Russian front action.

"Amelia Caruthers admitted a bias for those groups in society that seem to be the victims of more well-off groups and officials. She cited the reports on the Armenians and Greeks as examples and saw the cases where the Ottoman nation could well improve itself with kinder treatment. She was unapologetic about that viewpoint. She also stated she was not against the Ottoman state but did want it to be more careful about its treatment of minorities, even as it had in its great past.

"You, of course, tried to explain everything away with reinterpretations of what reportedly happened, perhaps trying to sow doubts in the minds of those who must deal with the case. It is your usual way of remaking reality that those of us who know you are so familiar with."

The last remark was not expected because I do not see myself as clever, disingenuous, or false, and Enver had implied, with his remarks, that I was all those things. But I knew that when confronted with adversity, the worst thing is to say much at all, lest one be further misunderstood. Enver expected my silence and, when it had reached fully twenty seconds or thereabouts, said, "Now comes the 'silent treatment' when you don't fully know how to respond and your instincts tell you to wait and see what your accuser has further to say."

I merely nodded. He said, "Well, the Council of Ministers took immediate and unequivocal action. The license of the *Tribune* is immediately revoked, its office closed, and its office personnel dismissed. The parts of the office that support the *Tagesblatt* can relocate to Damascus, as that is where its next work will be located. No fault is found with *Tagesblatt*. The journalist papers for Michael Agropoulos are revoked, and if he is apprehended, he will face charges of sedition. The journalist papers for Amelia Caruthers have been revoked, and she is to leave the country within twenty-four hours. The journalist papers for Martin Mintz are left unchanged, but he is to depart for Baghdad within twenty-four hours, where he is to report on the siege of Kut and render reports to the Minister of War until that siege ends when his case is reviewed. He may not depart from Ottoman territory."

I looked at him rather puzzled. I asked, "Why do you want me in Baghdad?"

"Because I can't get any really good information from the Ottoman officers on the site. You were not really part of the 'sedition' ring, and I know from your earlier reporting that you can be relied on to deliver a straight message about what is happening. You enabled your colleague and need to be punished for that, but I am delaying any punishment until I am finished using you. Are you refusing it?"

"Not at all," I said. "I understand, probably better than you think I do, what's at play in all of this. Amelia is coming out far better than could be expected, and if I must pay the cost for that, I'll do it gladly."

I thought he was finished with me, but he was not. He said, "You have heard me say repeatedly that I hold the Armenians responsible for much of the mess that the Ottoman Empire is in today. They have undermined the societal consensus of the empire that has existed for hundreds of years, and they have allowed their own whims and identity to lead them to a path of opposition to the rest of us. I am unsympathetic to their plight when officials move against them for their demonstrations, which call for British conquest over us, with their cooperation with the British fleet, with their cooperation with the Russians, and so on and so forth. I will not call for their expulsion or extermination, but neither will I prevent either from happening. I know that it will happen one way or the other. I suspect they are going the way of the Greeks and the Bulgars, who want their own identity at the expense of ours.

"I expect that there is more adversity coming to the Armenians, and I will not stop it, even if I am able. They have made it a choice between us and them, even siding with our enemies to win at all costs. If that is the case, we will win at all costs."

There was silence, and finally, he said, "Enough. Maybe you have time to see your 'girlfriend' before she heads out to Bucharest. As for us, I doubt if we will ever see each other again. The results of the war are likely to forestall any such reunion, which would be strained in any case. Be sure to catch your train."

An office clerk entered at that moment, handed me an envelope, and said, "Effendi, here are your rail tickets, introductory letter to the officials at Baghdad, and some expense money." I took them without comment, stood, nodded to Enver Pasha, and left the office.

When I arrived back at my hotel room, Amelia was there. We embraced and stood holding one another for perhaps a minute. Then she said. "I don't have much time. My train to Bucharest leaves at midnight and its nine o'clock now. I have got most of my packing done. Are you scheduled to leave with me?"

"I'm afraid not, love," I said. "I'm ordered to go to Kut, near Baghdad, to get Enver Pasha one more report. Then, my case will be reviewed. I have no idea what that means. My train leaves at eight a.m."

Amelia replied, "I'm not surprised they won't let us leave together. The Ottomans do not want to do me any favors. They see me as the center of a plot to support the Armenians against the government. Did they tell you that?"

"Yes, they did," I responded. "I had a long chat with my interrogator about that, but his mind was already made up. I expected a prison sentence for you, but I guess that might have triggered an international incident, and it was easier just to expel you."

"But why keep you," she responded. "It doesn't make a lot of sense to give you one more assignment. What does that accomplish?"

"Because he needs information badly about the front in Baghdad, and I'm the best way to get the unvarnished truth. But he knows that I will not stay now that the office is closed and you are sent away. But he also knows I will not upset your departure with my own protest. He is right about that. This is the best way out. I will endure the discomfort of a trip to Baghdad and, perhaps, the ordeal of the front lines again to fulfill my agreement with him.'

It was only at the railway station that Amelia raised our own relationship. "Marty," she said, "Now isn't a great time to talk about 'us,' but I want you to know that I was serious when I suggested a trip to Greece or Italy to reshape our relationship. I meant it then, and I still want to do it, even if we must put it off until later."

"I have not forgotten either," I responded. "When I exit from the Persian Gulf, as I fully expect to do, my first goal will be to find you to determine whether we have a personal future together."

Having pledged ourselves to one another, we let the subject go, and I helped Amelia get settled on the train. Then we kissed goodbye, and afterward, I waved to her as the train pulled out for Bucharest. I felt totally alone and more than a little defeated. To think that only the preceding morning, I was happy and was looking forward to an enjoyable trip to Greece or Italy with all the delights I could have wished for. It is strange how life does not run in smooth grooves but veers off continually into uncharted territory.

Carnage in the East

My own trip was uneventful until we reached Urfa in the Southeastern section of Anatolia, where the railway line ceased to exist. The section down to the Tigris-Euphrates river valley was still under construction, and it was necessary to use alternate transportation. There, a collection of conveyances was available for use by passengers. A large section of the conveyances had already been rented or leased by officials, army officials, and businessmen. Enver Pasha's staff apparently had been unaware of the situation or else decided I needed to make my own way.

I found a family of two women and a young man in the same predicament that I was in. The two women wore the veil (*hijab*), which presented some moral restrictions for them, but their choices were not many, and they regarded me as a probable good traveling companion. We rented a chaise with two spare horses and two drivers. The trip was scheduled to take eight or nine days. Included was overnighting and a meal a day at private homes along the way. We put a cardboard shield between the men and the women to afford the women the privacy that could be expected in a Muslim society.

Mostly, we had a good time and, except for the boredom of traveling in areas where the scenery does not change much, time passed quickly enough. We covered about thirty kilometers a day over a road that was well-used, although the traffic was light in many places. Overnighting was hardly luxurious, but plain, simple homes with wooden or stone floors and homemade mattresses that varied in softness and comfort. The food was local but very edible, always with some type of bread and local wild meat, usually rabbit.

On the road, there was not much conversation, but in the evening, the four of us passed an hour before rest in conversation. They were Arabs who had been born and raised in Constantinople and occasionally visited their ancestral home in Irbil, a small city north of Mosul. Hence, they had attitudes that were in keeping with 'big city folks,' who saw the Ottoman Empire as a noble enterprise bringing civilization to wide parts of the Middle East. They were supportive of the Ottoman government, and they recognized that Ottoman citizens spanned many cultural communities.

The three of them were entranced at having a foreigner–an American at that–traveling with them and asked lots of questions about New York City, which was their chief point of interest in America. They wanted to know about the skyscrapers, the Hudson palisades, and Bedloe Island with the immigrant boats. They talked as well about Harlem and its music, Chinatown and its uniqueness, and Yorktown and its German food. I told them absolutely nothing about being a newspaper reporter or about the battle at Gallipoli. That would have dominated the conversation, and I liked the discussion about New York City, which they saw as a magical place, not the everyday city that I always experienced when I visited it. Nor did they want to hear about the conditions of the garment district, the sweatshops, or the foundries on the New Jersey side of the river.

Two days out from our starting point, we passed through a construction zone, where land was being cleared for further construction of the railway. There were numerous people–men, women, and children–undertaking the work, which was strange, as usually only men worked at such jobs elsewhere. I did not mention it to the other members of our traveling party, but during a rest break, I asked the lead driver about the matter.

He said, "I don't like to talk about such things, Effendi, as they are delicate matters concerning the government. However, you are a learned man and will understand such things better than me, so I will tell you what I know. Three months ago, there were problems with the Armenians who were located at Diyarbakir, and they were sent south to Syria. The transportation officials were not too gentle.

It caused a reaction, particularly from the railroad administration and other construction employers, because Armenians constitute the largest group of employees in the region. The relocation was intended to provide jobs for Muslim workers, primarily Turks, but there were not enough to take the place of those Armenians forced to leave. As usually happens in such cases, entire groups of Armenians were 'overlooked' in the deportation scheme to preserve workers with needed skills for the local work force."

"But why are women and children working?" I asked.

"Because there are not enough workers otherwise, Effendi," he answered with a shrug. "The Armenians do not want outsiders imported into the area to take those jobs, lest it affect them, so they put their entire families to work."

"Are they mistreated?" I asked.

"I think not, Effendi," he answered, "So far as I know, they get pay and rations as has always been the case. There are rumors, however, that the CUP government in Constantinople is not happy with these 'exceptions.' 'Inspectors' may be sent out to review the matter and make new plans for the removal of the Armenians. CUP has made it abundantly clear that the Armenians cannot be trusted, largely because of the attitude of many of their number favoring the Russians, whom many see as their patron."

"I had not heard about the Diyarbakir case; can you tell me more about it?" I asked.

"Please, Effendi, I have told you enough and worry that repercussions would occur if I was to tell you more. Please do not insist on anything further."

"Of course not, driver, of course not," I responded. "You have been kind in satisfying my curiosity."

I certainly wanted to know more, but decided not to push someone to reveal matters if they did not want to, so I turned and went back to the chaise to get ready for the next stage of our journey. But that evening, after eating at the home that provided us with accommodations, I went outside to use the outhouse. On the way back, I ran across the two drivers and two of the workmen of the household, who all greeted me cheerily. The driver said, "I related the conversation you and I had earlier, and these two fine fellows say they have heard of other instances where Armenians are working under somewhat different circumstances."

"Yes," said one of the workmen, "On the railroad construction crew just north of here, there is a shortage of workers, which affects employment even when all other places have enough workers. There, they have hired Armenians in particular, but without women and children. They take those with criminal records or who have escaped from deportation groups and use them poorly. They often are beaten, and some have been killed as punishment for various infractions. There is little they can do to remedy their situation, so they put up with intolerable conditions."

For the next hour, I heard anecdote after anecdote about the Armenians. Some stories found the Armenians guilty of undertaking actions that called their loyalty to the state into question. Most stories told about cases where the government had decided to undertake action against the Armenians for a variety of reasons. The second driver said, "There seemed to be a feeling that the many, many jobs created by the new railroad and other projects benefit the Armenians more than the Turks, and the government is trying to turn that around so that Turks benefit more. Deportation is seen as the best method of doing that. But the authorities are not particular about how that is done. Rape, overcrowding in sheep cars, lack of food and water, illness, and bad treatment is the result."

"Do all the people hereabouts feel as you four apparently do," I said.

"Yes," came the answer from the first driver. "Many of us have some Armenian blood, so we sympathize, but further east, the plight of the Armenians is barely discussed. and when it is, the feeling is that the Armenians are the cause of their own disgrace." I left the conversation a short time later and felt depressed. Amelia had warned me about the callous reactions of the CUP government against its Armenian minority, but I had always hoped she was simply exaggerating. After this conversation, I felt what she warned me about was almost certainly true.

We were nearing the halfway point in our travels when we ran across a man's body lying alongside the road. Our driver did not stop, but I could see that the dead man had been shot through the head and that much of the back of his skull was missing. It looked like an execution. Apparently, no one else noticed it, or they took the body to be an animal that had been killed in the area and found its way to the road. Two hours later, we encountered two more bodies, this time both older women, whose throats had been cut. They were on their backs, eyes open wide as if staring at the sky above. This time, everyone noticed, but the driver kept the carriage moving. I stood up and spoke to the driver, telling him about the bodies, and asked whether he intended to stop. "No, Effendi, not on your life! This is the work of the vigilantes that operate hereabouts, shuttling unwanted malcontents out of the area into Syria. The bodies you see are those who have perished along the way. There are always a great many of them. We never stop, lest we arouse the vigilantes against us."

"Do you report this kind of action to the gendarmes?" I asked.

"Certainly not, Effendi!" he countered. "Often, they act in concert with one another, so it is best to pretend none of this happens." I sat back down and explained to the others what the driver had said. There was considerable indignation about the matter, as the three believed that this breakdown in law and order should not go unreported. The women wanted to find a police outpost to report the incident. They were still arguing about the pros and cons of such action when we came upon the group itself.

There were five guards and about twenty people. Several of the people were tying the captives into lines of about five and six people, all of them women and children. One group was being led away by a man. Two men were passing money to guards. I knew what was happening immediately. The group was now devoid of men who had been executed earlier. The old women were gone as well, executed when they could no longer keep up. What was left were younger women and an assortment of children. Local farmers were buying them for labor used in the fields, among the flocks, and in the household.

Our driver did not slow down but did not speed up either. He passed by the scene as if it were not there. My fellow passengers did not understand what was happening until I explained it to them. All three were outraged and said, "Such things do not go on in the Ottoman world. Surely, the padishah will not countenance this!" They wanted to find a police outpost to report this incident. The drivers would not do that, even though the young man in our group ordered that it be done. The drivers said it would put us all in danger, and we might not live until morning if anyone protested at all.

That evening, I tried to talk with the drivers about what had happened. The older one said it was sad, but to protest was to bring calamity to the person rendering a protest. He walked away. The younger one said he had a friend who had reported such an incident and had been told to forget what he saw or his house was apt to be burned. He, too, walked away from me.

The people who provided us with shelter that night were of still another mind. When one of the women mentioned the selling of women and men to local farmers, the host said, "Who do you think hunted the hare you ate tonight and prepared the vegetables you liked so well? The household group that prepared your food came from a vigilante group last year, and they have been good workers. They are not members of the family yet if they ever will be, but they see this farm as their home, and they work without complaint. It is better that they are here as servants than dead on the road to Syria."

The following day on the road, my three traveling companions spoke some about the vigilantes but agreed that raising the issue locally with the police was probably a bad idea. They decided to wait until they were in Irbil when the rest of their family could be consulted and a plan of action undertaken. They thought that the local CUP (Committee of Union and Progress) representative would know how to deal with such delicate issues. I agreed that their view was probably the best one to be followed.

From that moment, the incident was closed, and I never heard any member of the group mention the matter again until we parted at the railhead north of Mosul. I knew from the demeanor of all three that not only would they not raise the issue with the CUP representatives, but they would not raise it with anyone because they did not know how to deal with the issue in their own minds. They were not brave enough to consider the reality of the situation and to force the matter into the public.

We were about two days from our destination when the next crisis occurred. It was one that I did not expect at all, and it presented me with a real quandary on how to deal with it diplomatically yet firmly. It began in the early afternoon after a thunderstorm had passed when we had to take shelter for a time beneath some large trees. The roads were temporarily flooded, and the horses were having trouble moving with any sureness. We decided to make a rest stop and even had some tea that one of the drivers prepared for us, along with some small cakes that the two women travelers produced from their belongings. I was seated on the stump of a tree away from the rest of the company to give the women plenty of space to move around.

I was not thinking of very much at all, except that the journey's end was not too far distant.

The young man came towards me, and I immediately noticed that there was something different about him this time. Usually, he was relaxed and carefree. This time, he was serious and looked determined to carry out some chores he apparently found troubling. I noted his demeanor and body language and prepared myself for the unexpected. A couple of ideas ran through my mind as to the likely issue that the young man would raise. The first was the Armenians and what should be done about the incidents the family had witnessed, but I thought that unlikely as nothing had been said about them in days. The second was that I had inadvertently bumped into the younger woman going to the outhouse the night before, and, as it was dark, the bump resulted in a full-body meeting where our chests and thighs met. I had felt the impact of her soft breasts and even the fullness of her inner thighs, which gave me an erection afterward. It had been exciting. But I had excused myself and moved on. She had said nothing.

I was instantly sure that the second incident was going to be the subject of the upcoming discussion. I pictured myself being upbraided for my violation of the private space (*aurat*) of the younger woman, and the brother was going to give me at least a reprimand, more likely a tongue-lashing. That was his role as her guardian on this trip. I rose to meet him and prepared for the onslaught. The young man said, "Effendi, while we wait, could I speak to you on a delicate matter."

I responded without hesitation. "Most certainly. I am at your service."

He said, "Our family has listened with great attention to your conversations in which you have described some of your past life. You have not said so, but it is apparent that you are well-to-do, know important people, and are someone who will count in the affairs of our empire. We know the expense of this trip alone and realize that you are probably wealthy."

I had an inkling as to where this conversation was going but was unsure. But I knew one of the daughters was involved. I did not want to presume what would come next, but as the young man had paused, I felt compelled to say something. "You may be exaggerating my wealth, my friend, but you are right in that I am not poor by any means." It dulled the impression of 'great wealth' but acknowledged what they had seen of me was true.

He continued. "You have mentioned your family: father, mother, an aunt, and a sister, but the mention of a wife has never crossed your lips. Is that correct, or have we missed something?" I knew now that this was the start of a marriage negotiation, and the only item left at all vague was which sister would be offered. It was usually the older one, but she had talked about a male cousin in Irbil she was anxious to meet again, which indicated she was about to be married. It had to be the younger sister, and it explained the 'accidental meeting' last night, which had been planned by the two sisters.

"You are right, young man. I have a family that I hold very dear, as every good son does."

The next statement indicated that the family was more observant of what I said than I had realized. "You have also mentioned a young woman from a neighboring city that interests you and with whom you have had considerable contact. It is unclear whether she is your betrothed or not. Can you clarify for us, please?"

Well, here it was. The issue was at hand, and I realized I had to have my wits about me to bring my rejection of the sister to a good conclusion without harming the goodwill that we had built up during the trip. I answered, "She is my betrothed, as you so rightly have ascertained. She is the light of my life and the joy of my being. I look forward to marrying her when this trip is past when I return to Constantinople, where she awaits with great longing and will rejoice at my return." Well, I thought to myself, that is a rather idealized version of what Amelia and I feel towards one another at the present time, or at least when we parted.

"But, Effendi," he continued, "She is an American and will undoubtedly live in America. You have no wife to share your life and care for you in Ottoman lands."

So far, there had been no hint about which daughter would be offered, and I did not want the discussion to get to that point. We were now on Amelia, and I thought it best if the family dealt with that factor for a time, so I said, "Wives must be compatible in a household. My present fiancé insists on being the first wife, and I am so enraptured by her beauty, grace, and abilities that I am inclined to surrender that right to her. So all I could offer another woman would be life as a second wife so that at any time the two wives are in the same household, there would be the status of each to be considered."

I could see the young man's face fall. This was a mitigating circumstance that would have to be considered by the family beyond the three of them. I decided to push the idea further and said, "I like your family, what I have met of it. The three of you are good conversationalists and very considerate traveling partners. You also seem like a good and sensible person with great compassion for others. I like that very much. But I know that your own family, that is, your parents, brothers and sisters, and on and on, will want to weigh in on this important matter and have their voices heard. We are only two days from your home, so let me suggest that this matter be considered by the wider family before proceeding further."

The young man's head fell to his chest, and he said in a voice that was barely audible, "You are right, Effendi, the matter needs the attention of our larger family, particularly on the matter of 'second wife.'

To give them something more to ponder, I said. "I have some pictures of my betrothed that I would like to have you look at so that you can understand the feelings of love I have for this handsome and talented woman."

We walked back to the carriages, and I asked one of the drivers to get out my valise, which was near the top of the baggage carrier. I had seven pictures of Amelia there. I chose two—one seated in an elegant pose and the other with her behind her camera. I gave them to the young man and said, "Here she is. Isn't she lovely? Share the pictures with your sisters." The drivers indicated that we were about to travel again, and the young man climbed into the chaise with the two women. I said I was tired and would try to sleep on the luggage rack. The family needed an opportunity to talk.

On the morning of the last day of travel with the horses and carriages, just before departure, the young man came to me again. He said, "Your wife-to-be is most handsome, dresses modestly, and well. You have not told us that she knows photography, which is a skill that many women wish they had. You are indeed a fortunate man to have arranged such an advantageous marriage. We rejoice in your coming nuptials." He passed the pictures back to me.

I took the pictures but said nothing. He continued, "We will talk with our family in Irbil about the matter, particularly about the position of second wife, but I believe they will not be sympathetic to such circumstances."

"I understand," I said. "I, too, share their feelings and would not like to see any member of your family placed in such a disadvantageous position; that is the reason I have not raised the issue of alliance earlier in the trip. Please forgive me for any misunderstandings I may have caused, particularly with your very dear sisters, with whom I share good memories of our joyous trip across the great East. It is something I shall not forget easily.

The Baghdad Front

At Irbil, the chaise dropped me at the railhead and then proceeded to take the family to their home in that city. We did not indulge in sentimental goodbyes, as we had done before our departure that morning. Not so surprisingly, there was no talk about the plight of the Armenians or about any further contact between us, shutting out the possibilities of pursuing the matter of a marriage alliance. Rather, I merely saluted them with a wave of my hand, and they waved back. The drivers, who had been rewarded earlier, were more demonstrative and whistled loudly on my departure.

It was good to be on a train again, and despite the somewhat rough ride, it was far more comfortable than the chaise. I disembarked at

Mosul, wondering what I would do here in a section of the Ottoman Empire I had never visited. I did not even know where I would stay. However, on the platform stood Werner Aussenfeld, Amelia's former sweetheart, and he recognized me immediately. He smiled when I crossed to where he was standing, "*Guten Tag*," he said and then lapsed into Turkish. "Are they sending you over here so soon after Gallipoli? They didn't even give you a sufficient rest."

"It's a story I must tell you sometime, but probably not today," I said. "I suppose this is the northern outpost of your arena of action."

"Yes," he said, "I am expecting a German army inspector from Berlin, but knowing the exact schedule is hard to predict with that unfinished stretch just north of here. How long was that connecting trip? Do you remember?"

"Twelve days," I answered, "We used a horse-drawn chaise, although there were some automobiles that made the trip in half the time, but unfortunately, we couldn't obtain one."

We chatted for a few minutes, and he gave me the name of his hotel and suggested I try to get a room there. He also suggested that we have dinner together as well, an invitation I accepted. He then moved on to his regular duties, which were preparing an advanced training area for reinforcements coming across from Gallipoli. They were expected to arrive in the next several weeks. "When we get enough of them ready, we can begin our campaign to retake Basra," he said as he moved off.

I decided to stay several days before moving on to Baghdad, as I thought that Mosul, as a staging area, might tell me a lot about future Ottoman plans. Moreover, I had Werner explain what was going on, as well as tell me what was happening further south in the combat area. I believed that I would learn more from him than from being with military men in the capital, who often did not have the full picture and sometimes had a skewed understanding of what was happening.

The hotel had a room, a nice one with a view, and was not expensive at all. The host was impressed with my Turkish and said he had only once before met an American. He was all smiles and graciousness. I asked whether he could put through a telephone call to Bucharest. He said he had never placed a call to that city, but he was willing to try. Half an hour later, he had Boris on the line.

Boris said, "I'm delighted to hear from you and hope everything is going all right. Where are you?" When I told him, he said, "I guess I need to get out a map to find that one. Never mind, I will find it. I want you to know that I was tempted to file a protest with the Ottoman government about kidnapping our journalists, but Amelia said not to do it as you had worked out a deal with Enver Pasha. Still, I will not feel relieved until you are beyond the reach of that government. How long do you think it will take you to wrap up this assignment?"

"No more than two or three weeks," I said. "I am not spending a lot of time on this report, nor will I hurry it, but I especially will avoid any side issues that might bog me down. It's going well so far. I doubt whether I will be able to file any reports until I'm finished, but I have some good stories that I will send on as soon as I am able."

"Don't worry about that. Just get out of there as quickly as you can. I worry the Ottomans will imprison you." Boris sounded concerned.

"I will! I will!" I repeated in response.

"How will you get out? Do you have to retrace your steps to Constantinople? he asked.

"No, I thought I would cross the lines near Basra and surrender to the British authorities. Undoubtedly, they will send me to Cairo," I said.

"Good thinking," came the response. "Be careful crossing those lines. I'm sure it can be dangerous."

I said, "give my love to Amelia, goodbye," and rang off.

I felt good about the call, and it relaxed me considerably. I had an opportunity to take an afternoon map, which was welcome after the strange beds I had slept in the previous week and a half. But I woke, not fully rested, and it took over an hour before I felt awake enough to meet Werner.

Werner was very expansive that night and seemed to enjoy meeting someone he knew from earlier. We spent most of our time talking about Gallipoli, and about the great August offensive, which he had missed, and about how the campaign had ended. "I should have stayed where I was," he said, "but the general pointed out that I would assuredly get my own command, a battalion, and who can resist that?" He had reluctantly accepted the transfer. That was as far as he got with that line of thought, and then he was back to the events of the West. He did not mention Amelia, and I did not tell him about the end of our office in Constantinople, so he assumed I was simply on assignment in the East.

The second night, we met again, and he told me about his time in the East. "The commander here, Cevdet Pasha, understands that he is alone confronting the English from India and that he is at the end of long supply and communication lines, so he is left to his own devices on how to handle most matters. Given those conditions, it is not surprising that he runs the campaign here like an autocrat, taking little advice from anyone, least of all from the German advisers who have been sent to assist him. Consequently, his campaign falters, his coordination of forces seldom works, and the English outguess him much of the time."

He told me as well about the genesis of the fighting in the east. Particularly, he told me that the Allied force was operated out of Dehli in India under the aegis of the English viceroy there. The British army was a mixed force of Muslims and Hindus, commanded by English officers, mostly from families that had been in India for some time. The force had first attacked Basra and had quickly taken that city but had not been able to mount a strong offensive up the Euphrates to take Baghdad. Mostly poor weather with lots of flooding hindered the Allied advance. Also, it had been difficult to bring enough forces into the region, the same problem the Ottomans were having in countering the Anglo-Indian attack.

The advance had stalled at a bend in the Euphrates near Kut, which the Anglo-Indians had bypassed on their way up the Euphrates. Then, Ottoman counterattacks had changed the momentum, and the Anglo-Indian force had retreated to Kut. Surrounding the city, Cevdet Pasha trapped several hundred Anglo-Indian officers and men inside. The Ottomans had prevented several attempts of the Anglo-Indian force outside from breaking through the blockade. Then, the two sides entered negotiations. That is where the matter rested at that moment.

Werner said, "Obviously. New Ottoman forces might break the impasse, as Cevdet Pasha only had a force of 5,000 troops. But then again, the British have about the same number, but they are bringing in more troops from India and even Europe."

Werner was hopeful that, with Gallipoli out of the way, the German commander, Liman von Sanders, would bring his influence to bear on the way the campaign was run in the East and insist on German leadership of it. That would give Werner a more meaningful role, probably as a field commander. He was sure that such moves would make it possible to drive the enemy back down the Euphrates and remove them from Basra, the end goal of the Ottoman campaign.

After we had discussed the campaign so thoroughly, I felt I was getting a grip on it. We talked idly for a few minutes, and then Werner told me he was leaving early the following morning. At that point, he finally broke his silence about Amelia, saying that he was now reconciled with his wife and had no intention of ever going back to Amelia, whether Amelia wanted to or not. With the family he had, such a move was unthinkable.

I did not respond, and for some reason, perhaps the alcohol we drank took hold; he made an astounding statement. He said, "You know, don't you, that you are the one Amelia really loves. She talked all the time about you and your abilities. She talked about how you were always there to talk with her in dark moments and how you could cheer her up when things went badly. I sometimes wondered why she even wanted to be with me. I felt I was always competing with you."

"Unbelievable!" I said. "I wonder why she has not told me about this."

"It's true," he responded. "All that is necessary is to tell her you are interested, and she will be at your side immediately. Martin, I would be much relieved if I knew you did indeed work out some long-term arrangement with her, preferably marriage. I would know then that she would be well taken care of."

I was puzzled by this confession and did not know how to respond. I wondered if he was simply trying to ferret out information about the relationship between Amelia and me for his own reasons. On the other hand, his remarks might be accurate about how he felt and that he did want Amelia and me to be together. I decided that since I did not really know, it would be better to leave him in doubt about my relationship with Amelia. I said, "Amelia and I have been colleagues for a long time, and there is certainly a bond between us, but only time can tell whether it will develop into something more substantial. Sometimes, I think it will, but most times, I doubt it. But Werner, do not worry about Amelia; she is a capable woman who can certainly take care of herself." We shook hands, said goodnight, and each went his separate way.

The following morning I thought I would be on my own, but at breakfast there was Kurt Langer, who had come in late the previous evening. He was pleased to see me but not as much as Werner had been. Kurt had been down the river to Kut covering the siege, but after three weeks of waiting for developments, he had decided to take a break. He said that Mosul was a better place to get away from the war than Baghdad, which was, after all, the main staging area for Cevdet Pasha's forces.

He described the living conditions in tent cities as living in a swamp, with pestilence, fungal diseases, and other medical problems rampant. "About half of the troops are unable to meet roll call on any given day," he said.

"So, it's the weather conditions that are at fault?" I asked.

"In part, but the history of this campaign is marked with terrible leadership on both sides and an inability of those in charge to deploy troops, move over bad terrain, and surprise the enemy. Neither side seems to have any idea how to fight in such conditions. Martin, don't go there if you don't have to."

I tried to sympathize with him, so I said, "I had no idea things were so wretched and that the campaign was going so badly. One only hears general comments, and I think most of them are incomplete and often misleading."

It was as though he was not listening. He said, "I must tell you about the other factor that is so interesting. The Anglo-Indian force utilizes Sepoy troops, that is, soldiers raised from both Hindu and Muslim societies of northern India. There is a faction in the Muslim contingent that has been infected with the ideas of Muslim solidarity across the lines of war. That is, they believe that the Ottomans are not the enemy but rather brothers in religion. There have been periodic disaffections from the Muslim sepoys over to the Ottomans. It is not often that it happens, perhaps one or two a month, but it occurs just enough to put the British commanders on edge and wonder about the loyalty of their own forces."

I had heard nothing about this earlier, so I immediately wanted to get further information. "Do they stay committed to Muslim solidarity after they defect or not," I asked.

He answered, "It's hard to say because the group of defectors is not large enough, but I sense that any assertion of belief is probably artificial and that there is not enough commonality that it will last over the long run."

Kurt had little idea about what happened in Constantinople with the expulsion of the *Tribune*. He only knew that his home office was now located in Damascus, which he thought was a good idea because he was sure the front would shift in that direction, and he would work from there. I did not enlighten him except to say that I was the only correspondent left of the *Tribune* team. He accepted that statement and showed little interest in other people and what became of them. I thought surely he would remember Amelia, with whom he had close working relationships when they were covering the internal politics of the Ottoman Empire. But he did not mention her.

Kurt was more interested in getting back to the West again, as the Eastern theater of operations was not as attractive to him as what he had known while at Constantinople. He thought that going to Damascus, or even Jerusalem, would be more to his liking. We talked about that for a while, but our conversation kept stalling, and so we called it quits long before we might have when we were back in Constantinople. We did not see one another again, largely because I left soon after, but I did leave him a message at the registration desk wishing him "good luck" in the coming days.

The phone call with Boris made me realize that the longer I stayed in Ottoman territory, the more vulnerable I would be. I remembered one of Enver Pasha's final remarks when he said he expected me to report on conditions on the Baghdad front and, afterward, would decide how to deal with me. That sounded like a threat of possible imprisonment or further duty in onerous places. I decided to get out as soon as possible, even while giving him a report to fulfill any sense of obligation for letting Amelia leave without punishment. So, after breakfast, I checked out of the hotel and took the train to Baghdad.

The good hotels in the central city were all taken, of course, but in a nearby 'suburb,' I found a residential hotel that boarded guests. It was only because I spoke Turkish and Arabic and assured the host that I could eat the food that would be served that he allowed me to stay. I had to prepay for a week's lodging. The room was sparse but comfortable. There was a shared bathroom and toilet at the end of the hall, and two meals–a light breakfast and a hearty dinner– were served every day.

The host told me that all the other guests were technical people working in the area, such as a telephone-line installer, a delivery van driver and mechanic, an overseer in a warehouse, and an organizer of public trips to pilgrimage sites. "Effendi," said the host, "They are usually polite, but they take advantage of others when they get the chance. I give you fair warning that they may see you as effete and try to exclude you from the meat platter."

"Thank you for the warning," I said. "I shall be on my guard." I excused myself and went into the city, using a trolley, which I was surprised to see still running. While prices had gone up in the city in general because of the war, trolley car rates had stayed low.

At the Ottoman army headquarters, I presented my letter of introduction to the 'Officer of the Day,' who went away and left me standing in the anteroom. There was no place to sit, so eventually, after half an hour, I moved outside and sat on the steps, which were broad enough that I was not in anyone's way. After another half an hour, an enlisted man came and got me, and took me back to where the 'officer of the day' had sat earlier. He was still there, but standing, while sitting in his chair, was a colonel who spoke to me in Turkish. He asked who I was. As I responded, I could see his face relax and concluded that he did not know ahead of time how much Turkish I knew. He then asked what newspaper I worked for, and I said, "The *Tribune,* which is published in Bucharest." He nodded. All that information had been contained in the letter, but he was like many officials who believe that their job is not properly undertaken unless everything is revealed to them in the open, even if they have written access to the same information.

He looked at the letter of introduction and then at me and said, "If the Minister of War is willing to let you report from here, why are you here bothering us?"

In my most carefully worded response, I said, "That is kind of you to acknowledge that the Minister of War vouches for me. But I think the minister expects me to report to you so that you are fully aware that he has given that permission. The commander of the region, Cevdet Pasha, is clearly in charge here, and I think it best if he either certifies the letter or turns it down."

The colonel was surprised at this answer and said, "I don't think the general would ever countermand the wishes of the Minister of War, but I can see that you cannot assume that. You did right by bringing the letter to the general's attention." He handed the letter back to me. Then he said, "If you wait here a few minutes, the general will see you personally. It is not every day that the Minister of War calls the general's attention to a reporter, so the reporter must be someone the general should certainly know."

We went into an adjoining office where the general sat behind a rather small desk with his aide standing alongside him at parade rest. The general remained sitting and did not invite me to take the visitor's chair. We had met previously in Constantinople nearly a year earlier at a party given by Enver Pasha, but he apparently did not remember me. He asked, in Arabic, "How did you arrive in Baghdad? That is, what route did you take?"

I answered him in clear Arabic, and he then said, "Did you have difficulty in the big gap in the railroad line?" I said it was mostly boring but had its moments of interest."

The general then switched to Turkish and asked, "How is it that you know the Minister of War well enough that he writes a letter of introduction for you?"

"I was of use to him in the very beginning of the war when the two German cruisers were chased into the Dardanelles," I answered.

"Ah, yes," he said. "It seems like a million years ago." He switched again to Arabic and asked, "Were you at Gallipoli?"

"Yes, I was, general," I answered in Arabic. "I was up in the trenches and bunkers for over 120 days." The general raised his eyebrows and said, still in Arabic, "Wounded?"

"Twice," I responded.

The general turned to his aide and said in Turkish. "Major, set up two or three appointments with knowledgeable staff members so that our correspondent friend will know exactly what is going on. We do not scrimp on information with people who come with such high recommendations and have shown their fortitude in the present war." He turned to me and said, "It has been a pleasure talking to such a well-qualified newsman; we don't often see people of your caliber. Please wait in the anteroom, and you will be given the appointments I mentioned to my aide."

It took nearly an hour before the aide came to me, saluted smartly, and said, "Effendi, there are two appointments, one following the other, with the director of planning and with the director of operations. They start at nine a.m. tomorrow." He left, and I went home, again using the trolley. Pickpockets tried twice, unsuccessfully, to separate me from my wallet.

The evening meal was about to start when I arrived at my hotel, so I went to the table and competed with the other guests who used the hotel for their meals. The food was plain but good, and I ate all I wanted, which pleased my fellows as they ate the part of my share that I left on the serving platter.

That evening, I went to the host and told him that reporters often had to go places secretly and needed careful helpers to accomplish such goals. He said that he knew of such people but that they would be expensive to hire and, of course, his own silence would need to be bought. He asked where I wanted to go, and I said, 'The British lines below Kut.'

"Are you leaving us, Effendi?" the host asked.

"Probably not, just making contact there for one of my stories." The host nodded and said he would make some inquiries.

The following day, I went to my interviews and spent not just two hours but some six hours talking with a host of officials, each of whom was anxious to tell me of his own tasks in bringing the siege of Kut to a close and ultimately closing in on Basra. I was impressed with the knowledge of the general's staff and concluded that it must be the weather and terrain that were the spoilers in Cevdet Pasha's operation. We ended the interviews back in the general's office, who asked to see me again. He said, "A German Army inspector is visiting the Kut siege operations tomorrow, and I thought you might like to accompany him. The briefing will be in German, but there will be a German-Turkish translator, so you will not miss anything." I thanked the general for his thoughtfulness.

As I left the general's office, I noticed a small group of Arabs with two Europeans (*ferangi*), which I took to be English, waiting to go into the general's office. I nodded to them as they passed me, going in to see the general. I wanted to ask who they were but felt I might be rebuffed, but the general's aide, who was with me, said, "That is a team of negotiators from the British side seeking to obtain terms for the release of those besieged at Kut. There is considerable debate in our army and in the British army about the honor involved in such an arrangement, although such deals were often made in previous eras. The two Englishmen are troublemakers, trying to convince Arab tribes to side with the British."

"Then why is the general meeting with them?" I asked.

"It's the adage of keeping your friends close and your enemies closer. The general believes they tell him more than they intend to. But then the British probably think the same thing about the general."

Back at my boarding hotel, I got into a scuffle over a piece of meat one of my dinner mates decided belonged to him rather than me. I quickly grabbed his hand and bent his fingers back so that he doubled over and fell off his stool in pain. I kicked him aside and grabbed the piece of meat he had filched from me. He sat up again on his stool, gave me considerable room, and was no trouble for me for the rest of the meal. I could tell that there was grudging respect for me from the others as well.

The host came to my room later and told me in subdued tones that the trip would take two nights to get me to the British lines and probably only a day to get back. "Which night do you want to start?" I said the next night would do, and it was agreed that the trip would begin at midnight of the next day. I paid an advance fee, with the remainder due when we were at the British lines. I only hoped that I could really trust the group not to betray me.

As it was, the next day, I met the German staff officer who was doing the 'inspecting,' and he was a marvel indeed. First, he spoke good English, so I did not have to rely on a translation through Turkish. Moreover, the staff officer knew who I was and felt that, through my articles, I was a military specialist and that he could use me as a sounding board. So, as we proceeded through the day, he made numerous observations and asked me to confirm or question his analysis. Usually, I felt he was right, but on a few items, I raised a red flag, causing him to reassess. But I never contradicted him, lest he take offense.

The German officer evaluated terrain, manpower, and equipment. He found the terrain to be abominable but noted that the enemy chose that, not the Ottomans. He found the men to be relatively well-trained but too few. He marveled at the state of the equipment, which had to endure extremely wet weather yet was well cared for. He concluded that the weather was the major drawback in the operation and, in his notes, urged patience until it got better.

We finished the task two hours ahead of time, and we were back in Baghdad in the late afternoon. Both the German officer and I used the railroad time as an opportunity to write reports. I had most of my final report for Enver Pasha nearly finished before we undertook the trip and wrote the findings of the visit when we returned. I was able to get my report to Enver Pasha off to him before I headed back to the boarding hotel. I made the report appear as though there was another report that might be filed a day or two later, lest Enver Pasha decide the report was finished and that he could have me arrested at that time.

Leaving the Ottoman Empire

At the hotel, I ate with no problems from the other boarders, and then changed into traveling clothes and laid down to rest. Near midnight, the host came to wake me and took me to the stable area, where there were six horses and two other riders. I said goodbye to the host, said I would be back, and asked him not to give away my room. Then we set forth, made a huge swing around Baghdad, and found a back road that paralleled the main road down towards Kut and Basra. We passed Kut and then found a peasant's hut with a hay loft, where we slept through the day. After a small meal, we left at dusk.

A little past midnight, a full day after I left my suburban motel, my guide said that there was a British checkpoint on the road and asked whether I wanted to turn myself in there. I said I did, gave him the money due him, plus a magnificent tip, and wished him well. "Go in peace, Effendi," he replied.

There was some surprise when I came to the checkpoint, and the British sergeant on duty saw that a strange white man had suddenly appeared. He came out, pulled me behind the barrier, and pointed a gun at me. "What's up, mate?" he demanded.

"I'm an American journalist crossing over from Ottoman territory where I was assigned. I've had it living among the heathen and want to come home to a Christian land where I can speak a language that makes some sense."

The sergeant smiled and said, "I don't blame you none, sir. But I cannot make any decisions. That is an officer's job, and the officer-of-the-day is at the far end of his circuit and will not be back until near morning. He gave me a blanket and shoved me into the rear of a personnel carrier, saying, "Grab yourself some sleep while you wait." I fell asleep immediately.

The officer of the day was there when I awoke at daybreak. He was suspicious. I showed him my press papers, and he said, "I didn't know there were any correspondents out this way, particularly among the Ottomans."

I assured him I was not the only one, but I could tell he did not believe me. He then said, "Well, you're not armed and don't seem threatening, so I can't see why you shouldn't be sent back to Basra. Headquarters can determine what to do with you. Hang around here, have some breakfast, and you'll be on the next truck heading in that direction." Breakfast was canned, stewed tomatoes with diced toast. It was served lukewarm, which was not really to my liking, but then I remembered all the cream of wheat and mush I had eaten in the last year, and the canned tomatoes began to taste a lot better.

That afternoon, an official from the public relations staff met me as the truck pulled into the yard at a Basra headquarters building and said, "Martin Mintz, I've read some of your articles. Damn, how did you end up here? I thought you were at Constantinople?"

"Wars take people to strange places," I said. We went into his office, where we had an interview. He sent several reports off to my newspaper, including the two on the Armenian incidents (taking copies of everything for himself), and he allowed me to make a call to Amelia, whose number I had from Boris. She was flabbergasted to hear from me, cried when I told her I was on the British side of the front, and kept saying, "I was so worried, I was so worried."

After the call was over, I asked what was next. "Well," said the officer, "You're in luck. A ship bringing reinforcements just came in from Europe, and it will load up with the wounded to be taken back to Port Said. I'm sure you can have space on it. Till then, enjoy the officers' club.

Meetings with Gertrude Bell

But two days later, I was in a café within walking distance of the British army post when a woman came to my table and said, "Martin Mintz, I believe?" She was in her late forties, stylishly dressed in Western clothing, with a large hat. I wondered immediately whether the hat was to shield her from the sun or to be in style. Probably both, I concluded. I knew instantly who she was.

I stood and said, "Miss Bell. I am honored. Please have a seat." She sat, and I said, "On my first press expedition, your book on Syria[9] was the first one I read to prepare myself for the daunting reporting

---

[9] (G. Bell, *The Desert and the Sown*, 1907)

adventure I was about to endure. It helped me immensely." She smiled in response.

She agreed to have some coffee and some pastries while we talked. When the order was complete, she said, "I was surprised when I was told that you had miraculously appeared in Basra, as I thought you were firmly ensconced in Constantinople. The debriefing report says you left Ottoman territory because the Minister of War told you to give one last report on Ottoman dispositions in Kut and then wait for punishment on charges of sedition. What an odd thing!"

"On the surface of it, certainly, but it was inevitable, I think. My colleague, Amelia Caruthers, has always paid too much attention to minority problems and finally was implicated in a report that tied Armenian discrimination to Talaat Pasha, or at least to his support for the pogroms. The government lifted the license of our newspaper and exiled Amelia. Since the Minister of War was at a loss on what was happening on the Baghdad front, he decided he needed a report from me on that subject, so he allowed Amelia to go free in exchange for my willingness to do the report. I gave him the report and then left Ottoman authority immediately, lest he decided he wanted to punish me further or find other work for me to do."

"I was not aware of all of this until I read the debriefing report," Gertrude Bell said. The coffee and pastries had arrived, and she was enjoying both. "Incidentally, I put a 'stop' on the article detailing your interview with the German Inspector General. He discussed matters we do not want known in public or the enemy to know that we now know it as well. That was really a coup on your part. It is amazing that he was so forthright with you."

I smiled and said, "Well, it was serendipity, really. Cevdet Pasha arranged that I accompany the Inspector General, largely because people thought I was a close friend of Enver Pasha and wanted us both out of the way, lest we find out things they would sooner not have known. When the Inspector General arrived, I wondered how I was going to communicate with him, as I knew he did not know Arabic or Turkish. My German is very weak, but I hoped he might know French well enough for a conversation. The key German officers in Constantinople often use that language when I speak with them. As it turned out, the Inspector General was proud of his knowledge of English and wanted to show me how much he knew. He was also suspicious of the Arab commanders at Baghdad on the Kut perimeter, so he used me as a sounding board for his observations. I obliged him as much as I could, as he could not be quieted, nor did I want him to be, of course."

"Well, you nearly sucked him dry, I think." She finished her coffee and poured a second cup from the coffee canister. "Did you put everything into the report, or do your notes have more?"

"It's all in my report, even the material that I kept in my head that was not included in the notes themselves.

"What about your travels across the Anatolian frontier, where you observed nasty actions against the Armenians? Do you have more on that subject or not?" she asked.

"Quite a bit more, that I was saving for Amelia, who has her own collection of incidents, which incidentally she did manage to take with her when she was expelled from Constantinople. I was surprised no one went with her to the station to examine what she took. I suppose it was done so quickly that the security services were not contacted soon enough."

"Do you think Amelia would allow me access to your materials while you are here? I would return the originals to you before you leave."

"I suspect you are going to get those notes one way or the other, Miss Bell," I said. "So I may as well save us all trouble by letting you see them immediately. They are my notes, not Amelia's, so I have authority over them. You certainly may see them. I know you are with the Arab Bureau in Cairo and probably have been seconded to some intelligence agency here in Basra if you are interrogating me on my arrival."

"I've heard that you are very perceptive," she answered. "It makes it less awkward if you know who I am and what I am doing here. So, I will confirm that your suppositions are correct. " She was silent for a moment and then said, "How in the world did you get from Kut to Basra? There are enough checkpoints and obstacles that it difficult to imagine you doing that without the help of someone very prominent."

"Not at all," I said. "I simply stayed at a suburban hotel and made contact, through the owner, with some adventurous souls who knew the territory and took me to the proper checkpoint. We went cross-country on horses, avoiding towns and cities, stayed overnight in a peasant's hayloft, and came to the checkpoint the following night. I paid well for the subterfuge, and everyone involved was satisfied with the arrangement. I doubt if anyone in authority on that side of the border will figure it out, if, indeed, anyone even wants to look.

No one really wanted me there, and certainly Cevdut Pasha will probably forget I even arrived; he is so absorbed in the siege at Kut."

"Perhaps you could give me the name of the hotel and its location?" she said.

"Certainly," I responded.

Our meeting lasted an hour the first day, and then I saw her two more times for about an hour each time. Mostly, we covered information about the conditions near Kut. She said that her office had interviewed several people about Kut but that none of them were trained observers. As a newspaperman, I had especially good powers of observation, and what I had to report was of high interest.

On the fourth meeting, we took a short trip on camels to a village to the west of the Euphrates River, where she talked with a woman who reported how many of the enemy were coming through their area on their way to the battlefields around Kut. When we got back, I asked whether there was something she wanted from me that would involve a camel ride.

"Well, I wanted to see whether you could ride a camel, as you indicated in some of your writings. I really did not need any more proof as soon as you arrived with desert robes, complete with a veil. However, I did want to ask you an important question sometime, and it seems like this is the proper time to raise it." She did not say anything more.

I finally broke the silence by saying, "How long are you going to keep me in suspense?"

"I judge you already know the question," she said.

"Probably," I answered. "My answer is 'no.' I will not go back on a clandestine mission for you. If America were involved in this war and US officials asked me to do it, I would, in a heartbeat. But this is not my war, at least, not yet. None of my relatives would understand it, and I put great faith in their advice on such matters."

"Really," she said, "They had no objection to your cooperating with German officers." Americans are not fond of the Germans; at least reports say that."

"Well, some don't like it, I will admit," I said, "But I have never willingly cooperated, but at Sevastopol, I did go on a raid aboard a German cruiser that was then in the employ of the Ottoman navy, but it was inadvertent, not planned."

She ignored the caveat and asked, "But what about Amelia? You have not mentioned her, and I know that the two of you are close. Some say you even sleep together at times. Don't you think she would want you to gather information on the minority peoples, especially the Armenians? She seems particularly attracted to them and identifies with their plight. Don't you think she would want you to go in and report on them more fully?"

"You are right about Amelia and me," I answered. We are close and probably will marry somewhere along the way, but that will not be anytime soon. If you asked her to go in to report on the Armenians, she would certainly consider it. Most likely, she would accept the challenge. But I can't imagine that she would ask me to do it."

Not getting her way with that tact, Gertrude pulled the final arrow from her quiver, but I knew what it was and was ready for it. "And, if I told you that unless you agreed to go into Ottoman territory on the mission I have in mind, your chances of being a reporter in the British zone would not be approved?"

"I would still say 'no' because I do not want to go on that mission. Such a threat would be unbecoming to you, so I hope you don't ask it."

"I won't then," she said. The conversation was not pleasant for either one of us, I suspect. We parted without a farewell, even though I suspected that Gertrude's interrogations of me were at an end. I was right, and there were no more requests to meet with her.'

When I did learn, sometime later, that my ship would be leaving for Egypt, I called the number she had given me earlier to contact her. She herself answered, and I identified myself. She said, "Well, Martin, You and I are finished with our business, so we have no reason to converse anymore. I do thank you for your most splendid cooperation, and I assure you there will be no impediments in your way if you decide to do reporting from areas held by the British."

"Thank you for that," I said. "Actually, I was calling for quite another purpose."

"O, I see," she answered, "What would that be?"

"I leave in two days' time for Port Said, so I would like very much to have a social dinner with you. I would very much like you to consider me a scholarly colleague so you could hear the summary of my dissertation, which is before my graduate committee now. And, certainly, I would like to hear of your scholarly concerns from you personally rather than through books and articles."

"You have taken me completely off-guard, Martin. I get so dominated by my work that I often forget the important things. You are right. You and I should certainly meet for dinner, perhaps at the civil servants' club, which has good food and is not as packed as the officers' club. Say, tomorrow at eight. I can meet you there. Oh, May I ask what the title of your dissertation is?

"I answered, "Indicators of social change in the Middle East."

"Interesting topic," she said, "And which institution are you working at for your Ph.D."

"Winston-Meritt University"

"Very good," she concluded. "Ta, ta, till tomorrow evening."

The evening went well. Several of Gertrude's friends dropped by her table to talk for a few minutes, which interrupted the conversation from time to time. Nevertheless, each time, the thread of the conversation was picked up again, and by the end of the evening, it came to a natural close.

The dissertation was handled early. Gertrude said she liked the topics and generally agreed with them, except for the Zionist movement, of which she knew little but felt it was probably a good addition to the rest of the selections. On the other hand, she found the Committee for Union and Progress too autocratic for long-lasting success. She thought the Arab reformers at Al-Azhar were on the right track but too opinionated. She wondered whether the British and the Americans would bring anything new and modern to Persia. Finally, she worried that Sudan would last after a new governor was named.

She herself talked about mountain climbing in the Alps and then about riding camels into the southern realms of the Arabian Peninsula. I then told about the first trip across the Middle East and what we had found. She said she been contacted two years earlier by Emile for just such an expedition, but it had been canceled by the editors at the *Tribune* as not likely enough to produce a good copy. When she was contacted a year later, she was already busy with events in Damascus and told Emile she was no longer interested.

"If I had known what the expedition turned into, I might have been more interested," she said, "But then, I calculate that it was you and Amelia who made the expedition what it became. It would have turned out entirely different if I had been the lead correspondent."

We ended the meeting on that note. Gertrude said, "Now that I have met one half of the *Tribune* team, I need only to contact the other half."

"Who knows, there is still ample opportunity," I said.

We said goodnight in the club's reception area and went our separate ways. It had been a fine, social evening.

Chapter Eight

The Tour

Capture in Aden

It took two and a half weeks to load the ship with the wounded who were to be taken to recuperation facilities in Aden and Alexandria. I used the time cleaning my notebook of half-written pieces and found eight that were worthy of publication with a little work. I sent them to Bucharest but did not immediately receive any word about them other than a brief acknowledgment to say that they were accepted.

Two days before our scheduled departure, I was in a temporary officer's quarters when I received a telegram from Bucharest. I thought it referred to the articles, but I was mistaken. It read:

> Marty stop consultations with Emile lead to a new assignment for you stop strong rumors of an Ottoman buildup in Aden near British facilities stop you are to leave your troopship there and undertake reporting duties for duration of the threat or military action stop probably three weeks at most stop new subject stop Amelia working as editor on Austrian military events stop she says hello and love stop regards stop Boris.

It never surprises me when new assignments come my way. Correspondents have to be ready to respond quickly as the news occurs without warning. Still, the sudden assignment to the Aden-Yemen area was unexpected. I thought I was destined for the

263

Egyptian-Palestine theater. Of course, this short-term assignment did not preclude the latter, but it was unexpected, nonetheless. I immediately sent a reply, which read:

> Boris stop arrangement complete for leaving ship in Aden stop request that appropriate Tribune office make press arrangement with Aden officials stop to which office do I send my reports stop love to Amelia stop regards stop Marty.

I found the information officer for the British headquarters unit in Basra and persuaded him to let me look at the file on Aden. In 1913, near the beginning of the great swing through the Middle East that the *Tribune* arranged, I visited Aden and Yemen. I wanted to know what had transpired since then to go to work immediately on landing.

The file revealed that the political situation had changed somewhat, although the present situation bore some similarities with the earlier period. In Aden, there was a confederation of seven tribes that had an agreement with the British Government of India for the operation of a coaling station and to give political and military support when necessary. Before the war, military support was a formality; in 1915, that support was a necessity. Aden's northern neighbor, Yemen, was under the control of Sultan Yahya, who had to share control of his region with an Ottoman governor. At the outset of the war, the governor had been instructed by Ottoman authorities in Constantinople to take control of Aden, to control shipping in the Red Sea, part of Great Britain's 'lifeline,' to the Far East.

But Yemen was an Ottoman outpost, isolated by the very arid Arabian Peninsula and British control of the sea routes around that Peninsula. By marching along the coast and using some clandestine shipping, the Ottomans managed to garrison and supply Sa'na, the capital. They brought enough troops that they could undertake action against the Anglo-Indian troops that the British used to man their defense force in Aden. The situation was more than a little confused, however, by the status of the Imam of Yemen, who believed he was an independent ruler, only nominally allied with the Ottomans. He wanted good relations with the British in Aden. The Ottoman governor, sent out by the government in Constantinople, saw himself as the absolute ruler of Yemen and undertook military action against the British whenever he felt strong enough to do so. When I arrived earlier, this was the general political situation.

A major spate of fighting had occurred in this area the preceding year when the Ottomans had sent a force into the territory nominally controlled by the British at a place called Lahij. Lahij was the major center for a small sultanate that had a ruler allied with the British. Afraid that the Ottomans wanted to bring Lahij under their control, the British sent a troop of 250 Anglo-Indian troops to prevent any attack on that outpost. A British force had marched through a tropical day to reach Lahij by dusk. After only a short time, the Ottoman forces entered from the other direction, not realizing the British force was there.

There followed a melee in which the local sultan was accidentally killed, a number of Ottoman officers were captured by the British, and chaos reigned throughout the night. The Anglo-Indian force withdrew with its prisoners but without its machine guns and ammunition. The Ottomans followed them to Aden, where they occupied the ground immediately across from the harbor. In that position, they could bombard the city with artillery and destroy the water treatment plant if they wished.

The Ottomans needed time to bring up their artillery, and this lapse of time allowed British troops to be brought from other areas nearby. They drove the Ottoman forces back to Lahij, but the British drive stopped there. The British commander did not want to overextend his forces, knowing he had no reserves in Aden. He simply fortified the areas to the immediate north of Aden so that the Ottomans would have difficulty returning. Neither side had threatened the other since that time.

A slight buildup of Ottoman forces this year and the movement of some artillery led some observers to believe the Ottomans were preparing for a new offensive. Other observers held that the Ottomans were simply strengthening their own defensive positions. The file ended at this point, prompting me to conclude that the prospects for full-blown warfare between the two sides were highly unlikely. Undoubtedly, I was being dispatched only because I was in the area and could check out the story with minimal effort and expense. I go where I am sent, so I accepted the judgment of my employer without question or doubts. But I was also prepared for a quick exit if nothing materialized.

The *Tribune* office in Paris had sent my correspondent's credentials ahead of time so that when I arrived in Aden, there was no delay in becoming registered with the Aden authorities. The formalities were handled by an Arab officer in the Immigration Service who had been there on my earlier trip. He did not remember me, and I would have been hard-pressed to say anything much about him either, although I did recognize his face when I met him. He said that there were two Indian journalists, one from the *Bombay Semanchar* and one from the *New Dehli Times*. There was only one Western journalist, Robie Gunderson, from the *Toronto Globe*. I recognized the last name from the names of the journalists I knew had been at the *Tribune* the year before. I met all three on the very first day, and I found all three 'difficult' and 'standoffish.'

Finding a place to stay presented a problem as the hotels were full, mostly with British officers and civilian bureaucrats, and, in any event, there were not many hotels. Staying with private citizens was an option, but there were few enough rentals available, and most were sub-standard in any case. I remembered a retired German professor living at the edge of the city with his Arab wife and sent a radiogram when I was still on the ship, asking whether I could stay with them. He answered immediately and said he would be delighted, as authorities were constantly putting pressure on him to rent some of his rooms. He would rather rent to me than others since he had some inkling as to who I was.

I wondered about the loyalties of the professor since he was German but came to the conclusion that, since he was operating freely, the British authorities must not regard him as much of a threat. It seemed to me that he identified mostly with the Arab tribes of the region where he had innumerable contacts and where his studies had given him invaluable information and insights about the Arabs and their culture.

The wife had children from a previous marriage, who roamed the small estate of several acres, riled what wildlife there was, and were rambunctious and unruly. Their mother was indulgent to a fault, and the professor paid absolutely no attention whatsoever to the pandemonium the three children made, although once a day, for about an hour, he forced them to sit in his study and recite the Qur'an with good diction, and then to translate into English what they had read. He said that was going to be the extent of their educations until they reached the age when they could go to some school they themselves would select for a formal education.

The Arab wife was a collector of Arab artifacts, and each year, she tried to get to a new site where ancient Arabs had once lived. She had discovered three significant sites and was hoping in time to interest some archeologists to come and do a 'dig' to learn more and relate it to other sites. On my earlier trip, she had shown me her boxes of relics, but only once. She was shy around men from outside.

My room was airy, the food was very good, and the few evenings when I was at the house with the professor were delightful, as his knowledge of Arab tribes, their customs, and their aspirations were everything a reporter wants in a source. Well, perhaps he was a little too involved, and much of his knowledge was esoteric and even arcane. While interesting, much of it was not of much practical use to me or, for that matter, to many other scholars.

So far as reporting went, I visited several of the officials, all British, in the Indian (colonial) Service who reported to New Delhi rather than to London. Consequently, they had a different slant on war than I had expected. For instance, they were less concerned about the war in Europe than they were about the war with Ottomans in Yemen, at Basra, and at Kut, in particular. After all, that is where Anglo-Indian forces were fighting, and the immediate interests of the Delhi government lay. I did not keep up so well with the European front, except in a general sense, but I knew that it was only a matter of time before the need for manpower would draw Anglo-Indian troops to the battlefields there and, at that point, the officials in Yemen would see the war entirely different. It was a matter of direct involvement.

After the interviews, about six of them, all of us reporters were anxious to move to the front lines and discover what, if anything, was transpiring of a military nature. The two Indian reporters and I went forward to the Lahij line, which was not well demarcated; we nearly lost our way twice. We located several Anglo-Indian outposts, where we got information about what was happening on the front lines. Mostly there was patrol action, which was heavier than earlier but not in any way more sustained. Nor were the Ottoman patrols more heavily armed than before. In four trips forward over the period of two weeks, we three journalists encountered no hostile forces, which probably made us a little careless.

Then, an inconvenient thing happened. We three journalists went forward to examine the front line again and found that one of the forward posts we often visited had been relocated. We searched for it, and worst luck, we ran smack-dab into an Ottoman patrol. Being journalists, we calculated that, as non-combatants, we would have our papers checked and then be released. We believed we would be home by dinner time. Not so.

The patrol leader had no idea what to do with us and was at a loss as to who we really were. He took us to headquarters some miles behind the fortified line, where a junior officer understood that we were non-combatants and correspondents, but he did not know how we should be handled. He thought we would be exchanged in Geneva, Switzerland, sometime in the next year. He sent a camel and rider to get instructions from his headquarters.

We were not mistreated but kept in a storage building and given some food that looked like rations for enlisted men. There were pallets of straw to sleep on, but blankets were not provided, as it was hot in any case, and air moved only slowly in the closed storage buildings. We sweated profusely in the afternoons. Strangely, we three did not talk much with one another about anything; we remained strangers, except the two Indians talked Hindi briefly with one another, but never for very long.

Finally, on the fourth day, we were taken from the storage building to a modern office, where we were ushered into the presence of a lieutenant colonel. He had our passports and journalist papers and passed them back to us. He said, in Turkish "You are non-combatants who are free to go, but as journalists, I have a favor to ask. The commanding general is here locally on an inspection trip, and I think it would be splendid if you would interview him for your newspapers. How about it?"

The Indian journalists did not understand Turkic, but I knew they had Arabic skills, so I translated. We all agreed with the colonel that interviewing the general would be something we would like to do. So, the meeting was set up for the following morning. We were given better food that night and allowed to sleep in officers' quarters, where it was still hot, but at least the air moved better than in our previous quarters.

The interview did not take place until three p.m. the following day because the general was late in arriving. But he was affable and liked the idea of a press interview where he expounded on all sorts of things, including his hobby, which was stamp collecting, and his interest in astronomy. He told about being a cadet and receiving training in Germany and how he had fought at Gallipoli prior to this assignment. He had a wife and two children and thought all of them were about the best family in the world. At the end, he wished us well and had us delivered to the spot where we had been taken captive and released.

On our passage into the buildings where we were held, during the time we were there, and during the time we came out of the Ottoman-held area, I did not notice any unusual military activity that would lead me to believe that an Ottoman offensive was being prepared. Quite the opposite, the long delay we experienced getting ranking officers forward to see us led me to conclude that the Ottomans were content with their defensive posture and were not anxious to have it upset. I said as much in my reporting, and apparently, so did the other reporters.

Two days after returning, I was told at the public relations office that the two Indian reporters were leaving that day and that the following day, the Canadian was leaving as well. I went to their respective ships to say 'bon voyage,' but none of the three was anything more than cordial, and I suspect they would not have missed my visit if I hadn't made the effort. It was such a different experience than I had with other reporters throughout my travels, where there is usually goodwill and acknowledgment that all reporters belong to a common club where civility and even friendship are involved.

Visiting Sharif Hussein again

It was only two days later that I received a cable telling me to take passage on a ship going to Jiddah and then to take overland transportation to Sharif Hussein's palace. There, a news conference was being held announcing his plans for becoming the next 'king' of the Arabs. I had interviewed him two years earlier when he had said that he intended to eventually bring all Arabs under his rulership. He had said then that both diplomatic and military means

271

would be employed to accomplish this. I packed, settled my bill with the German family, and finally left for the steamer. The last time I had left Aden was with a camel caravan pushing into Yemen. This time it was a ship headed for Jiddah in the same direction. Life is circular, I concluded.

At Mecca, I found the venue and sat in a shade-enveloped bower with about two hundred tribal leaders, notables, and a small smattering of reporters. I listened for two hours while Hussein told the history of his family, intertwined with the history of Islam. His theme was that the two stories were congruous and that both were working for the same goal in this age: the renaissance of Islamic culture and Arab political ascendancy.

In the speech by Hussein, one sentence would be high and lofty, the next crass and self-serving. He mentioned time after time his lineage to the prophet, which he claimed gave him the absolute right to claim the title of King of the Arabs. I hardly knew what theme to strike in my article on him, particularly whether to reward him with the label of 'destined hero' or 'out-of-touch windbag.'

As I was about to leave the conclave and find a place to write my article, Prince Faisal, Hussein's son, came to my side and said, "I have searched everywhere for you. You obviously came in when I wasn't looking. Come, you must meet my father before you go. I understand you have been in Yemen. My God, what a trip that is. You must be exhausted!"

He must have thought I came overland rather than by ship, but I decided it was not worth explaining. I barely said anything in response but let myself be led to a nearby tent that was furnished with opulent divans, rugs, and other furnishings. The sharif and a few of his entourage were relaxing after the rigors of the royal speech. Nearly everyone unobtrusively left when Faisal ushered me into the tent.

"Father," Faisal said, "Here is Martin Mintz, the reporter for the *Tribune* who wrote that glorious article a few years ago that captured so well the spirit of your mission." I bowed deeply and muttered "As-salaam alaikum," and the sharif muttered the response and waved me to a nearby divan to sit.

"Yes, yes," the king responded, "You did indeed write a glorious article before. But tell me how you feel about the speech I delivered today. Was it as meaningful? Was it as spirited?"

I said, "Your majesty, I was struck with the credentials you delivered in asserting your right to a reclaimed title of 'King of the Arabs.' It was clear and creditable, I think to any Arab of the region."

"Ah, your Arabic is so rich," answered the king, "That you can use such fitting terms to describe my goals."

"Your majesty," I essayed again, "I have traveled extensively since being in Mecca nearly three years ago and have witnessed much. Would you permit me to share an observation?"

"Certainly," he said.

"It is this, Your Highness, that in all the lands of the Middle East, the primary loyalty is to the caliph of Islam, which, as you know, rests with the Ottoman padishah. Even you have acknowledged that claim. How do you intend to gain that title so that the crown of the king of the Arabs reflects that responsibility and honor, as it properly should? A king of the Arabs without an Islamic attribute would be incomplete, I think." Actually, I had asked him this question before, but I knew he would not remember."

"Yes, yes, exactly," enthused the monarch. "You have put your thumb on it entirely."

Prince Faisal interjected, "Not to worry, Marty, I think the present caliph will lose his claim to that title in the coming years as his empire continues to diminish and fail. It can then be picked up easily and assigned to the king of the Arabs."

"I see," I answered, "You are astute, sire. Fortunately, you have able sons who will be ever on guard about this and other matters so that you do not falter. Undoubtedly, they will take advantage of the affairs of this world so that golden opportunities such as the availability of the title of 'padishah' will be gathered at the proper moment." I believed I was 'gilding the lily' perhaps too much, but would-be royalty loves it, after all.

Still, I wanted to make one more point before giving way to total platitudes about the greatness of the monarch. I said, "Your majesty, if you permit me one more observation taken from my travels. Last year, I had the opportunity to talk with pilgrims to the great shrine at Mecca; there were perhaps fifty of these beloved souls who had just completed their circumlocution of the Ka'abah. They talked first about the great spiritual journey they had undertaken during their days on the lesser pilgrimage, and then, as all people will, their conversation wandered off to other matters. In particular, they talked about the tribal feuds of the Arab Peninsula, and, without exception, there was a consensus that there should be unity above all else. But when the discussion moved to the matter of who should be the 'uniter' of the tribes and towns, there was division among the people, with some favoring this candidate or that candidate, and still other candidates."

"The two most popular were You, Your Majesty, and Ibn Sa'ud. When comparisons were made, many cited your illustrious lineage and organization of the nearby tribes on your behalf. But others were impressed with Ibn Sa'ud, who had the religious might of the Wahhabi sect behind him, and his great harem of wives he married for political advantage. Perhaps, Your Majesty, you or your sons might enlighten me as to your strategy to negate these very powerful weapons in the Ibn Sa'ud arsenal." I realized I was being audacious and maybe foolhardy to raise such sensitive points, but I am a reporter, after all, and I take chances to get a story.

There was a short pause as the father looked at his sons, and they looked back. Prince Faisal was the first to respond. He said, "The Wahhabi are fanatics, Marty, and you should know it. They are pious certainly, but it is a false piety. We have religious scholars here, Marty, who are far more learned than the Wahhabis, who are more in tune with the essence of modernity among Arabs than that small band of troublemakers in Riyadh. As for the harem, the women will grow old and unappealing, and so, too, will the family alliances. They will disappear into the dust of history." The matter was quickly closed, perhaps as too sensitive for the monarch to acknowledge in a press interview.

I, wisely, I think, abstained from the obvious follow-on questions regarding Ibn Saud's competition with Hussein. Rather, we talked about generalities for the next fifteen minutes, and then I excused myself and bowed myself out of the 'king's' presence. Prince Faisal accompanied me and saw me to my conveyance, which would take me to my hotel. "Your visit was fortuitous, Marty. My father is sometimes despondent over prospects. You told him a little of what he wants to hear and a little of what he needs to hear. It is a message I think he will heed." We shook hands; I got in the car and departed.

The following morning, there was a radiogram that said:

> Marty stop private interview with Hussein a masterpiece stop proceed to Port Said stop board Reine Antoinette to French Riviera stop then to Basel stop arrangements made for you to meet with Zionist organization officials stop Shimon Erfan among them stop Amelia to meet you at Hotel Adler stop call me at Port Said regards Emile

The fastest way to Port Said was with a tramp steamer run out of Nairobi, which had a load of timber for the shipyard in Port Said that had stopped for engine trouble, but it was repaired and ready to go. I did not really like traveling on such ships since they can be terribly unclean, and the food is often badly cooked. All that was true on this ship. Most unappealing was the toilet, which followed the pattern of the old sailing ships, where a seat was rigged that hung over the side of the ship and allowed the waste to simply fall into the water. One was terribly exposed, but worst of all, it was difficult to get on and off the seat.

I had two days at Port Said, so Emile took a train over to see me, although I said I would be happy to come to the office in Alexandria. When he arrived, he raved over the interview with Hussein, saying that no one had ever caught the 'pie-in-the-sky' outlook of Hussein as my interview had. "Incidentally, Marty, you better stay away from British headquarters for a few days as the propaganda people think you are messing with their tool for fomenting an Arab revolt against the Ottomans."

"Undoubtedly," I answered, "But I doubt whether either the Sharif or the British will be much concerned, and they will go ahead with what they are scheming because it suits them to do it. I just don't think it will work in the final analysis."

We then moved on to what I was supposed to do in Basel. "Contact Shimon Erfan, whom we have already contacted. He said he remembered you and would give you updates on what the Zionists are busy doing these days. He says he will be delighted to see you again." Emile gave me a number to call when I got there.

Then we moved over to my future and, incidentally, that of Amelia as well. "You have been in out-of-the-way places, Marty, so you are not aware of the stir that the expulsion of *Tribune* from Constantinople caused, particularly as it related to Amelia's exposé of the Armenian brutalities. After your escape through Basra, Boris kept the pot boiling by publishing the story of the conditions that you had to fulfill in order to get Amelia out, which got good coverage in the U.S. and Western Europe."

He continued, "Moreover, you are the only correspondent from the West who has gone through the war in Ottoman territory, and you are now in demand, as is Amelia for her courage in tracking down the atrocities and her superb camera work. You both can probably make deals with any number of publishers, but, of course, we all at the *Tribune* want you to stay with us. Boris wants you both, and so do I. Even Paris has made noises about assignments from there. Paris is going to ask you to visit the home offices after your stay in Basel, so you have some time to think through what you want to do for the next few years."

I needed to process what he told me, so I did not immediately respond. Emil took the opportunity to continue his monologue. "You will remember I hired you, and I would remind you that I took a chance on you when I doubt anyone else would have. But I fully recognize that you developed largely on your own from a modest reporter to someone quite special in the correspondent's world. We had some severe differences on the first tour, which I blamed on your youth and temperament when you were trying to figure out what to do. I was far too dogmatic in asserting my own control to handle you right. For that, I am greatly sorry. I only want you to know that if you would choose to come back to my area of responsibility, I would be delighted to have both you and Amelia. Moreover, you would be your own boss, with some overall direction from me, but with great latitude in completing your assignments. That's my pitch; I will leave it there."

Wow! Apologies, do not come every day of the week. Nor do job offers. I was nearly floored but knew that any real thinking on these matters had to wait until I got to Switzerland and saw Amelia. Undoubtedly, she would have much to say about these matters. I wanted to hear all of it. I missed the woman terribly.

Visiting Switzerland

Zurich is a city of business and reflects the no-nonsense style of the Swiss, but not Swiss elegance, which is more on display in Geneva. Basel is a third choice, and a somewhat rural one at that. Amelia's train arrived within fifteen minutes of mine, so we met in the great hall of the station, each with our luggage. She had on a cocky hat with a feather protruding from it and a black fur coat. I had pulled out a dark overcoat I wore in the winter months of Constantinople with a brimmed hat. We looked like most other people in the concourse. We kissed, almost chastely, when we met but held the kiss for long, enjoyable seconds. Then we both laughed and looked one another in the eyes. "God, it's good to see you again," I said.

"Don't you know it," she responded. We gathered our things and moved to the taxi stand for a trip to the Hotel Adler. Our conversation on the way there was pretty mundane, mostly about the trips each of us had made in the past few days but nothing about duties or work at all. Most of all, it seemed to me that we were happy to be with one another again after the absence of two months. At the hotel, the receptionist staff was as polite as one would expect a Swiss staff to be.

There was a moment of awkwardness about our passports not exactly matching our reservations. The Paris office had made the reservation for a suite in the name of Mr. and Mrs. Martin Mintz. Amelia's passport did not have the crucial "Mintz" as the surname. But the head clerk merely stated, when it was brought to his attention by the clerk who was attending to our registration "I see. Yes, obviously, Mrs. Mintz is traveling under her professional name." Amelia nodded her concurrence.

There was one other matter, a rather pleasant surprise, in fact. The head clerk delivered that news to us himself. "Your company has signed you up for a two-day mountain climbing excursion for the final two days of your stay after your regular business is complete. You will use our mountain chalet for two nights, of course, before returning here for your final night. We will take care of the transportation of all your luggage. Mountain gear is also provided as a part of the tour. I am sure you will enjoy the experience. A description is provided in the brochure, found with your other registration materials." Neither one of us knew what to say, so we merely shrugged and waited until we were alone to talk about it.

Our suite was posh, with a sitting room, a large bathroom, and a bedroom. When the bell boy had left, we both took off our coats, threw ourselves on the bed, and smooched each other for a few minutes. Then we laid back and talked about all sorts of things that had happened since we last saw one another. But we were both famished, so we changed clothes and went to the dining room to eat, where we had a marvelous meal based on veal cutlets and hash-browned potatoes, but with an Italian-sounding name. Leave it to the Swiss to be international.

Our last conversation of the evening was about commitment in Constantinople, when we had promised ourselves that we would move our relationship over to one of lovers rather than as close colleagues. We agreed that our thinking on the matter had not changed but, if anything, had grown stronger as a result of the separation that had taken us apart. Amelia said she thought it best if we did that at the mountain chalet or on our last evening in Basel. "we'll be passionate by that time," she said, echoing my own sentiments. I, too, felt our relationship would simmer in the meantime and might peak by the end of the stay. That decision should put real zip into our initial lovemaking.

It was evening, so I called Shimon, who said he would meet me for breakfast and was looking forward introducing me to his Zionist colleagues.

Of course, we slipped into bed together as we usually did, in our skivvies again. We talked to each other to sleep with our usual recitation of the banal and nonsense, but it was relaxing and comforting to be able to do that again. Again, she held my erection like it was a treasure.

At breakfast, the waiter brought Shimon his boiled eggs without even asking. "Still at the cracked eggs thing, are you?" I said. "I thought you liked the natural cereal?"

He smiled and said, "I never said I liked the cereal, only that it probably did not violate the rules regarding dietary obligations."

"I stand corrected," I said, with exaggerated humbleness.

We talked about many things as we worked our way to the purpose of the visit, and finally, he said, "Since our meeting in Constantinople, things have gone much better for us. It has been an upward curve, particularly with the British, who see things much more to our advantage. I don't wish to get into the substance here in the hotel, as we might be overheard, and the subject becomes a part of the rumor mill here in the city."

When we left the restaurant and went through the reception hall of the hotel, there was a woman and three children, about ages six, seven, and eight, sitting politely, apparently waiting for us. "Ah, you made it after all," said Shimon. He introduced us, "Marty, my good friend. I have the great pleasure of introducing my wife, Judith, and my children, Ruth, Aaron, and Yael. They all stood and shook hands."

Judith said, "Marty, Shimon told me that the trip to Constantinople two years ago would have been a complete failure if he hadn't met you. He thinks highly of you."

"I share similar fond memories of him and am delighted that I can see him again. I am also pleased to meet all of you and understand who stands behind Shimon. Judith, are you in town to go shopping?"

"No, it's a school day, and we are on our way. We must hurry, or we will be late." Then to the children, she said, "Kinder, schnell, wir haben eilig!" They were suddenly gone. "What a well-behaved family, I said."

"This morning, they are, but wait until tonight when they are released from school after being pent up all day. Then they are like a hurricane, and Judith encourages them in their chaos."

"But you don't encourage such behavior?"

"Absolutely not," he said with a broad grin. "I am always a model of propriety."

Over the two days I spent at Zionist headquarters, I met about ten people who were all fervent believers in their ideology of creating a new Jewish state in Palestine, whatever the cost. I heard nary a doubt about the outcome, and all discussions had that unstated goal constantly in mind. I talked mostly with small groups of people, sometimes with Shimon present, but mostly not. The conversations varied from agricultural settlements to the creation of working governments, to societal structure, to holy places, to whatever. There was always the assumption that the Jewish movement would move mountains when called to do something and that the success lay in the determination to 'do,' Once things were in motion, the outcome was ordained. 'Such confidence,' I said to myself more than once.

Shimon's statement in the hotel that great things seemed to be in store rose soon after I met with two leaders in a small group setting. "We cannot announce it, nor can we confirm it, but we are nearly certain that the British government is going to, sometime in the next six months, make a statement that will lead to the open immigration of Jews into Palestine."

When I heard the statement, I said, "That assumes that the planned British offensive in Palestine and Syria will take place."

"Yes, of course, British officials assure us that the offensive will take place soon and that it will be successful."

"Not to throw cold water on your assumptions," I said, "But the British have had a hard time in the Middle East. The cauldron of the Western Front in France and Belgium continually sucks dry any manpower reserves the British scraped together in the Middle East. Gallipoli failed, in some part, for that reason, and the Mesopotamian offensive is mired down for lack of soldiers, even though most of them come from India."

But my argument was tossed aside as irrelevant. As one official put it, "The British assure us they have the manpower. After all, India is teeming with potential soldiery who only needs to be organized and trained."

When we got over to the subject of open immigration, I pointed out that the natural resources of Palestine would have to be mightily expanded to handle an increased population. In particular, water sources were tight. The counterargument from a committee member was that Jewish brainpower was vast and could be mobilized to overcome these deficiencies with little problem. I was laughed at, if politely, for worrying unduly.

However, it was in the future of the present Arab inhabitants of Palestine that the good humor of the group broke down a little. I noted that simply saying the Arabs don't treasure the land and make it produce enough was not a sufficient argument for removing them. The argument always came back to "this is our promised land, not theirs," and "The Arab lands are so vast that they can be accommodated elsewhere easily." Tempers grew short in this debate, and I finally said, "In any case, even open immigration will not change the population ratio for at least fifty years, so it can be debated later. I am satisfied in knowing your position and don't need to discuss it further." There was a relief, but I don't think I was forgiven for not accepting their version of the truth.

We moved on to government and listened to a primer on democracy. After hearing it, I said, "At present, most of our European governments are remnants of empires and have merely adorned themselves with democratic and republican symbols and institutions. I suppose that's possible for a Jewish state as well. But have you noticed that strong men continually arise in France, in Germany, in Russia to challenge those institutions or to 'give their nations guidance?' How will the Jewish State operate to prevent this from happening in its territory?"

There were a multitude of answers to this question. Mostly, they boiled down to the faith and goodwill of the Jewish people themselves. I said, "My God, people, you all sound like Americans. Almost none of you come from there. What an interesting application." They laughed.

Mid-way in the second afternoon, Amelia joined us and had a slide presentation, centering largely on her trip two years earlier to the Kibbutz we had visited. I was surprised by how well she remembered names, and nearly everyone was identified. Her pictures of the fields, animal pens, and gardens were especially enjoyed. The Basel office seldom saw the real products of the cooperatives, mostly hearing about their problems and the difficulties of keeping them going. The audience asked a lot of questions, and a session that was to be an hour stretched out to an hour and a half. I realized, not for the first time that my colleague was more than knowledgeable in handling the questions of the group. Her answers were rife with insights and analysis.

When we left after the presentation, nearly everyone in the offices came to say goodbye. Their good wishes came across as very sincere. Amelia's slide show was liked especially well. Shimon said to me that, overall, the visit was highly productive for the staff, which tended to be too sure of itself. He said that I had challenged it in ways that no one else had recently. I responded, "Well, get ready, friend. When the British announce their plans for open immigration, there were going to be lots of people who won't like it one iota." He agreed and shook his head. "Don't be a stranger," I said at the door as we climbed into our taxi. We shook hands, and then we left.

The following morning, Amelia and I were up at dawn and departed for a two-day mountain climbing trip, all at the expense of the *Tribune*. There were eight of us, three women and five men, and the climbs were pitched at the intermediate level so that we were challenged at times and scared only once or twice. Actually, it probably was about the equivalent of the trek to Sarikamish, only not as long. We got to know our fellow climbers reasonably well, mostly because during breaks, we talked a lot and made fun of one another.

We stayed overnight in a chalet at the foot of a mountain we were to climb the following day. We ate as a group, and everyone drank heavily in the social hour that followed. Consequently, we all were a little worse for wear the following morning. It was only at noon that we began to function properly.

We arrived back in downtown Basel at about eight in the evening after a tough climb, in which we used carabiners, rappel devices, belay devices, and various ropes and harnesses to handle the difficult parts of the climb and descent. The experience was more than most of us had expected. Rather than tiring us, the ordeal released enough adrenaline that we were raucous on the way back to the city in our touring cars. We wished each other cheery goodbyes as we were deposited at different hotels.

Awaiting us was a telegram from the *Tribune* office in Paris. It read:

Martin and Amelia stop proceed the day after tomorrow by afternoon train to Paris for a two-day orientation at home offices, stop reservations at Hotel Montmartre, stop article on Zionists top drawer stop C. E.

We took the telegram and read it in the room, and then Amelia threw it on the desk in the sitting room. She said, "Never mind that stuff. It can wait. I still have a buzz from the descent, so let's not waste it. If you still have your erection problem, I think we should handle it right now!"

"Let's do it!" I said. "It has become a chronic condition, I think." We peeled off our clothing and were coupled before Amelia's butt hit the bedspread. I knew the world would never be the same after that, and it wasn't.

Consultations in Paris

The train to Paris was increasingly crowded as the French capital came near. Many passengers were soldiers, but there were anxious relatives as well. There was a jumble of people in the central rail station, but eventually, we found a young woman with my name scrawled on a child's chalkboard that she held in front of her. She did not look over sixteen but later discovered that she was nineteen. She wore a frown, perhaps thinking she had missed us, but her face lit up in a radiant smile when I identified myself. She spoke French with a Briton accent. She said, "I thought either I had missed you or the train did not come in as planned."

It was noisy enough that I couldn't clearly understand her, so I merely nodded. We left the station and got in a small car with the name 'Tribune' on it. It took us some time to get to the hotel, which was small and almost hidden among the other, more garish houses on the block. We checked in and then went to our room with our luggage while she waited in the lobby. When we returned, we found her in an animated conversation with a doorman. Afterwards, she explained that the doorman was from the same town in Brittany as she was from. They had recognized one another and passed the time of day for a few minutes.

At the office, the workday was just winding down, but the head secretary agreed to stay a few minutes to get our schedule set for the following day. We were to visit several of the publishers and editors in the morning, then go to lunch at the French foreign ministry, located at the Quai de Orsay. In the afternoon, we were to address the Middle East staff of the ministry on "Life at the Front during the Battle at Gallipoli" and "Reporting on the Armenian Relocations." These lectures would be repeated the following afternoon to the reporting and editorial staffs of several Paris newspapers. On both days, the addresses would be followed by a question-answer session by members of the audience. There would be a reception in our honor on the second day, but no dinner as ration stamps for such events was difficult to come by, so they were avoided.

The visits to the publishers and editors were easy. We knew several of them, so it was nice to renew acquaintances. The new people were mostly in awe of us, probably because of our long service in reporting from a very difficult area of the globe. It all went by in a blur. Since we had some difficulties in our previous visit to headquarters, I was surprised that everyone was so amiable. But I understood that some people were no longer there and those that were had probably become our friends or good colleagues in the meantime. Zoe Toussaint, who had vowed not to ever talk to me again, was true to her word and always managed to avoid meeting me throughout the sessions we had at headquarters.

There were six officials from the French foreign ministry at lunch. They were all business for the hour and a half the session lasted. They informed us that the British and French were interested in creating long-term stability in the Middle East when the Ottoman Empire finally collapsed, which, they assumed, would be sometime before the war was over. "The collapse is inevitable, and even a person who admires their fighting skills like you do, Mr. Mintz, must admit that will happen." I reluctantly agreed with him.

The chair of the meeting said, "When that occurs, the Ottoman Empire will be split up, we think, but we are not entirely sure of that.

Here, and in White Hall, there is a growing feeling that the Turkic element of the population has enough popular support and military manpower to maintain itself. It is likely to create a Turkic nation of its own, probably encompassing most of Anatolia, but hardly larger. That leaves the Italians out of the spoils since they have claimed Anatolia as theirs. The Arabs to the south will be on their own, and despite British aims of creating an Arabic uprising against the Turks, it is highly unlikely that a unified and energetic Arabic state will have any staying power."

At this point, another speaker took up the presentation. "However, it is the Arab lands that concern us. When the war ends, the British and French will, together, announce an agreement to divide the Arabic provinces into zones of influence. Lebanon and Syria will go to the French, while Palestine and Mesopotamia will go to the British. Obviously, we would prefer to simply make those states colonies like our possessions in Africa and Asia, but world opinion may preclude that arrangement. Accordingly, we may promise to make independent nations of the zones and give them some political autonomy but retain economic control."

I listened because I had heard some of this planning before, but never in such clarity and by an official of the French government. I did not know Amelia's reaction to any of this. I could not imagine that she liked it very much since she is an American who believes all peoples should rule themselves, and this included Arabs, Armenians, and Turks. There was silence in the room when he finished, and the other officials looked at us, apparently expecting a response. So finally, I said, "Why are you telling us this? Aren't you afraid we will blab this in our next news articles?"

"No," said the spokesman with a slight smile. "You're smarter than that because you know you would be regarded as crackpots with wild ideas about the Middle East. You like to be taken seriously when you write. So, whether you want to or not, the gist of this arrangement with the British will begin to appear in one form or another in thought pieces that will be written in London and Paris. When the full announcement happens, you will be free to explain it fully even as it was explained to you today. You will be ahead in the game, and so will we. We have decided to do this with five other opinion makers. You are the only newsmen."

I asked a question, and so did Amelia. Mine was, "What if the Arabs decide they don't really want to be ruled by the French and the British? Haven't you then simply changed one war for another? The Arabs are formidable and relentless. Maybe that is the kind of war you will inherit."

"Perhaps," came the answer, "but we French are accustomed to fighting malcontents in all of our colonies, and we always manage to put them in their place so that what we want to be done is done, whether the malcontents are happy or not. That is the chief reason we have the Foreign Legion, which does that sort of work for us. But you are talking about the frontiers. We are talking about areas of the Middle East that are more settled and urban, where civilizations breed willingness to sacrifice for comfort and success rather than raw freedom. The citizens of Sidon and Damascus, long accustomed to our priests and nuns educating their youth, will go along with us, I am sure."

Amelia's question was, "What if the rest of the world does not like your extension of empire?"

"Well, we'll be the victors, so who will oppose us? The United States? The US is not even in the war and, besides, always sides with Europe. If there is a loud outcry, we will compromise, even as I said. The Americans, in particular, like compromise and think it a way through all sorts of tribulations, whether such compromise solves a problem or not."

We stopped there, as it was time to go to the presentation, which was well attended by over a hundred people. Our presentations took an hour and ten minutes. Afterward, the question-answer session lasted for another hour and a half. Several questioners said that they came to the presentation believing we were pro-Ottoman, but after hearing us, they changed their minds. Some observed that we found good things and bad things to say about both sides. Of special interest to the audience were my conversations with Entente prisoners. They liked the human touch that those episodes produced.

Afterward, a civil servant with the French Medal of Honor came to me and said that the French soldier I had talked to was his nephew, who had been imprisoned for six months and was only recently paroled. "He said that you gave him the courage to see the imprisonment through, even though you said it would be an ordeal. I want to thank you for that."

The afternoon session the next day went differently than it did the day before because the audience was markedly different. Before, it had been an official French audience; today, it was a gathering of newspapermen whose perspectives and requirements took a different direction. These newsmen saw the efforts to get information out of common soldiers as very challenging, and some observed that the devices I used to become friends with the soldiers were interesting and informative. Most had never seen information gathered in this way, and they wondered whether they could try it sometimes. In answer to a specific question on that subject, I advised against trying it ordinarily, as the time and place for it to work had to exist before it could be used. "I didn't invent it and apply it; it emerged from the situation itself, and I took advantage of it."

Much the same was said about Amelia's questioning of the survivors of the Armenian pogroms, who revealed so much of themselves in the conversations Amelia had with them. In the same way as I had, Amelia said the information was gathered using a technique that emerged from the situation itself and probably could not be transferred automatically to other situations.

The reception was something of a smash, at least from my perspective. Probably seventy-five people attended, and many of them stayed beyond the hour when the doors were closed. I had two young men who wanted to become my assistant and wondered how they could apply for such a position. A young woman asked Amelia how to get started in newspaper work, as there was no clear path for a woman to follow. She saw Amelia as a pioneer and wondered whether she herself had the smarts to follow one as successful as Amelia.

Then it was all over, and we went to our hotel for a final night in the City of Lights, which was dark lest the German balloonists detected a target for their bombs. We didn't go out that night but stayed in instead. After all, we had finally uncovered the great delights that go with sexual activity, and we spent the evening in wonderful expansion of that knowledge.

The following morning, we went to the *Tribune* offices to determine our fate. We talked about the next assignment off and on. We had considered all sorts of possibilities about what we should do. Actually, we had whittled the problem considerably in our time together. We did know that we wanted to stay with the *Tribune*. Pay and benefits were good, and, most of all, we were familiar with the system and personnel.

Then we decided that the Russian front, either in Germany or Austria, would be too cold in the winter. Both of us did not want to revisit our experience in Sarakamish. But both of us liked Boris as a boss and felt leery of Emile despite his apology to me. But language ability pointed us towards the Middle East, and even Amelia said that her Arabic was good enough to operate there. She said my ability with Arabic should not be wasted. So, on the way to the meeting, we decided to opt for the Middle East and Emile Bowdoin.

That did not leave us much to do at the headquarters. We were with the head of personnel for only half an hour, where we signed papers and got some pay and tickets for the railway to move us to the Riviera to catch a boat to Alexandria. It was all anticlimactic.

On the boat to Alexandria, both of us began to prepare ourselves psychologically for the upcoming campaigns that we knew we were going to endure. By the time we arrived in Alexandria, we were both ready.

To be continued in Volume III of *A Reporter's War*.

Glossary

Aurat Coverage of parts of the body for modesty

Berlin to Baghdad Railroad Major railroad being built with German assistance

Caliph Islamic ruler of the first rank

Censors Officials who pass on suitability of reports from the battlefield and other sensitive areas

CUP Committee of Union and Progress Ruling elite of the Ottoman Empire during World War I

Effendi Sir

Harem Place for women in a Muslim household

Hijab A shawl that covers a woman's hair, neck, and breasts

Hijaz Railroad Major Rail line from Constantinople to Madinah

Padishah Ottoman title for emperor

Pasha Noble

Sepoy Indian soldier (without regard to religious community)

Wahhabi Religious group of Arabia that held (and holds) stern views about Islamic behavior, who are often regarded as pietistic by many other Muslims.

Historical Note

Istanbul is Constantinople, the capital city of the Ottoman Empire. In these volumes it is Constantinople because the Ottomans wanted that title to emphasize that their empire owed something to its predecessor empire, the Byzantines (330-1453). This was part of the effort to promote Ottoman identity rather than the more narrow identities reflecting solidarity with ethnic, racial and religious communities.

In the same way the empire is Ottoman, named for the dynasty, descended from Osman (reigned 1299 to 1323/24). Its greatest expansion was during the reign of Sulayman (the Magnificent) (reigned 1520-1566). The last ruler of consequence was Abdul Hamid II (reigned 1876-1909). The popular title of the ruler was *padishah* (emperor) although, officially he was the Sultan-Caliph, a combination of two ranking titles of Islamic derivation. Historically the Ottomans have been called >Turks= which was the major ethnic group in the empire and the leading supporters of the dynasty. Arabs were strong supporters until World War I when they were broken off through revolts and dismemberment of the empire. ATurks@ is only used in this set of novels when someone refers to the ethnic group, not to be regime. Of course the Turks (with the Kurds) were the largest of the surviving groups at the end of World War I, when all other groups were stripped away for new nations in the region. The rump group took the name Turkey.

In this book eight historical personages have been incorporated into the characters of the novel where they speak and act within the context of their real life roles. They are Enver Pasha, Ottoman leader; Admiral Wilhelm Anton Souchon of Germany; General Liman van Sanders of Germany, Cedet Pasha, Ottoman leader; Mustapha Kemal, Ottoman officer, Gertude Stein, British author

295

and intelligence agent; and Sharif Hussein bin Ali of Mecca, an Arab leader.

There are innumerable histories of the Ottomans, a few good and a great many bad ones. Two of the best is found in Hodgson=s *Venture of Islam*, 3v. (Chicago, 1961) and *Cambridge History of Islam* 4v. (London, 1970). For the period of World War I three more recent volumes were used. Eugene Rogan, *The Fall of the Ottomans* (New York, 2015), Michael Provence, *The Last Ottoman Generation* (London, 2017), and Kristian Coates Ulrichsen, *The First World War in the Middle East* (London, 2014)